FIRST LOVE AND OTHER SORROWS

FIRST LOVE
AND OTHER
SORROWS

Stories

Harold Brodkey

An Owl Book
Henry Holt and Company
New York

Henry Holt and Company, Inc.
Publishers since 1866
115 West 18th Street
New York, New York 10011
Henry Holt® is a registered trademark
of Henry Holt and Company, Inc.

For information about the original publication
of the stories, see
Bibliographical Note, page 320.

Library of Congress Cataloging-in-Publication Data
Brodkey, Harold.
First love and other sorrows: stories / Harold Brodkey.—1st
Owl book ed.
p.   cm.
"An Owl book."
Contents: the state of grace—First love and other sorrows—The
quarrel—Sentimental education—Laurie dressing—Laura—Trio
for three gentle voices—Piping down the valleys wild—The dark
woman of the sonnets—Gloria mundi—The sound of Moorish
laughter—A well-regulated impulse.
ISBN 0-8050-6010-3 (alk. paper)
1. United States—Social life and customs—20th century—Fiction.
I. Title.
PS3552.R6224F5   1998   98-21213
813'.54—dc21   CIP

First Owl Book Edition 1998

Printed in the United States of America
All first editions are printed on acid-free paper. ∞

1   3   5   7   9   10   8   6   4   2

To William Maxwell

Contents

THE STATE
OF GRACE

THERE is a certain shade of red brick—a dark, almost melodious red, sombre and riddled with blue—that is my childhood in St. Louis. Not the real childhood, but the false one that extends from the dawning of consciousness until the day that one leaves home for college. That one shade of red brick and green foliage is St. Louis in the summer (the winter is just a gray sky and a crowded school bus and the wet footprints on the brown linoleum floor at school), and that brick and a pale sky is spring. It's also loneliness and the queer, self-pitying wonder that children whose families are having catastrophes feel.

I can remember that brick best on the back of our apartment house; it was on all the apartment houses on that block, and also on the apartment house where Edward lived—Edward was a small boy I took care of on the evenings when his parents went out. As I came up the street from school, past the boulevard and its ugliness (the vista of shoe-repair shops, dime stores, hairdressers', pet shops, the Tivoli Theatre, and the closed Piggly Wiggly, about to be converted into a Kroger's),

past the place where I could see the Masonic
Temple, built in the shape of some Egyptian relic,
and the two huge concrete pedestals flanking the
boulevard (what they supported I can't remember,
but on both of them, in brown paint, was a large
heart and the information that someone named
Erica loved someone named Peter), past the post
office, built in W.P.A. days of yellow brick and
chrome, I hurried toward the moment when at
last, on the other side, past the driveway of the
garage of the Castlereagh Apartments, I would be
at the place where the trees began, the apartment
houses of dark-red brick, and the empty stillness.

In the middle of that stillness and red brick
was my neighborhood, the terribly familiar place
where I was more comfortably an exile than anywhere else. There were two locust trees that were
beautiful to me—I think because they were small
and I could encompass them (not only with my
mind and heart but with my hands as well). Then
came an apartment house of red brick (but not
quite the true shade) where a boy I knew lived,
and two amazingly handsome brothers, who were
also strong and kind, but much older than I and
totally uninterested in me. Then came an alley of
black macadam and another vista, which I found
shameful but drearily comfortable, of garages and
ashpits and telephone poles and the backs of apartment houses—including ours—on one side, the

backs of houses on the other. I knew many people in the apartments but none in the houses, and this was the ultimate proof, of course, to me of how miserably degraded I was and how far sunken beneath the surface of the sea. I was on the bottom, looking up through the waters, through the shifting bands of light—through, oh, innumerably more complexities than I could stand—at a sailboat driven by the wind, some boy who had a family and a home like other people.

I was thirteen, and six feet tall, and I weighed a hundred and twenty-five pounds. Though I fretted wildly about my looks (my ears stuck out and my hair was like wire), I also knew I was attractive; girls had smiled at me, but none whom I might love and certainly none of the seven or eight goddesses in the junior high school I attended. Starting in about second grade, I always had the highest grades—higher than anybody who had ever attended the schools I went to—and I terrified my classmates. What terrified them was that so far as they could see, it never took any effort; it was like legerdemain. I was never teased, I was never tormented; I was merely isolated. But I was known as "the walking encyclopedia," and the only way I could deal with this was to withdraw. Looking back, I'm almost certain I could have had friends if I'd made the right overtures, and that it was not my situation but my forbidding pride that kept them off; I'm not sure. I had very few clothes, and all that I had had been passed to me from an elder cousin. I never was able to wear what the other boys wore.

Our apartment was on the third floor. I usually walked up the back stairs, which were mounted outside the building in a steel framework. I preferred the back stairs—it was a form of rubbing at a hurt to make sure it was still there—because they were steep and ugly and had garbage cans on the landings and wash hanging out, while the front door opened off a court where rosebushes grew, and the front stairs were made of some faintly yellow local marble that was cool and pleasant to the touch and to the eye. When I came to our back door, I would open the screen and call out to see if my mother was home. If she was not home, it usually meant that she was visiting my father, who had been dying in the hospital for four years and would linger two more before he would come to terms with death. As far as I know, that was the only sign of character he ever showed in his entire life, and I suppose it was considerable, but I hoped, and even sometimes prayed, that he would die— not only because I wouldn't have to visit the hospital again, where the white-walled rooms were filled with odors and sick old men (and a tangible fear that made me feel a falling away inside, like the plunge into the unconscious when the anesthetic is given), but because my mother might marry again and make us all rich and happy once more. She was still lovely then, still alight with the curious incandescence of physical beauty, and there was a man who had loved her for twenty years and who loved her yet and wanted to marry her. I wished so hard my father would die, but he just wouldn't. If my mother was home, I braced myself for unpleasantness, because she didn't like me to sit and read; she hated me to read. She wanted to drive me outdoors, where I would become an athlete and be like other boys and be popular. It filled her with rage when I ignored her advice and opened a book; once, she rushed up to me, her face suffused with anger, took the book (I think it was "Pride and Prejudice"), and hurled it out the third-story window. At the time, I sat and tried to sneer, thinking she was half mad, with her exaggerated rage, and so foolish not to realize that I could be none of the things she thought I ought to be. But now I think—perhaps wistfully—that she was merely desperate, driven to extremes in her anxiety to save me. She felt— she knew, in fact—that there was going to come a moment when, like an acrobat, I would have to climb on her shoulders and on the shoulders of all the things she had done for me, and leap out into a life she couldn't imagine (and which I am leading now), and if she wanted to send me out wrapped in platitudes, in an athletic body, with a respect for money, it was because she thought that was the warmest covering.

But when I was thirteen, I only wondered how anyone so lovely could be so impossible. She somehow managed it so that I hated her far more than I loved her, even though in the moments before sleep I would think of her face, letting my memory begin with the curving gentleness of her eyelids and circle through all the subtle interplay of shadows and hollows and bones, and the half-remembered warmth of her chest, and it would seem to me that this vision of her, always standing in half light (as probably I had seen her once when I was younger, and sick, perhaps, though I don't really remember), was only as beautiful to me as the pattern in an immeasurably ancient and faded Persian rug. In the vision, as in the rug, I could trace the lines in and out and experience some unnamed pleasure, but it had almost no meaning, numbed as I was by the problems of being her son.

Being Jewish also disturbed me, because it meant I could never be one of the golden people —the blond athletes, with their easy charm. If my family had been well off, I might have felt otherwise, but I doubt it.

My mother had a cousin whom I called Aunt Rachel, and we used to go and see her three or four times a year. I hated it. She lived in what was called the Ghetto, which was a section of old houses in downtown St. Louis with tiny front porches and two doors, one to the upstairs and one to the downstairs. Most people lived in them only until they could move to something better; no one had ever liked living there. And because of that, the neighborhood had the quality of being blurred; the grass was never neat, the window frames were never painted, no one cared about or loved the place. It was where the immigrants lived when they arrived by train from New York and before they could move uptown to the apartments near Delmar Boulevard, and eventually to the suburbs —to Clayton, Laclede, and Ladue. Aunt Rachel lived downstairs. Her living room was very small and had dark-yellow wallpaper, which she never changed. She never cleaned it, either, because once I made a mark on it, to see if she would, and she didn't. The furniture was alive and frightening; it was like that part of the nightmare where it gets so bad that you decide to wake up. I always had to sit on it. It bulged in great curves of horsehair and mohair, and it was dark purple and maroon and dark green, and the room had no light in it anywhere. Somewhere on the other side of the old, threadbare satin draperies that had been bought out of an old house was fresh air and sunshine, but you'd never know it. It was as much like a peasant's hut as Aunt Rachel could manage, buying furniture in cut-rate furniture stores. And always there were the smells—the smell of onion soup and garlic and beets. It was the only place where I was ever rude to my mother in public. It was always full of people whom I hardly ever knew, but who knew me, and I had to perform. My mother would say, "Tell the people what your last report card was," or "Recite them the poem that Miss Huntington liked so well." That was when the feeling of unreality was strongest. Looking back now, I think that what frightened me was their fierce urgency; I was to be rich and famous and make all their tribulations worth while. But I didn't want that responsibility. Anyway, if I were going to be what they wanted me to be, and if I had to be what I was, then it was too much to expect me to take them as they were. I had to go beyond them and despise them, but first I had to be with them—and it wasn't fair.

It was as if my eyelids had been propped open, and I had to see these things I didn't want to see. I felt as if I had taken part in something shameful, and therefore I wasn't a nice person. It was like my first sexual experiences: What if anyone knew? What if everyone found out? . . . How in hell could I ever be gallant and carefree?

I had read too many books by Englishmen and New Englanders to want to know anything but graceful things and erudite things and the look of white frame houses on green lawns. I could always console myself by thinking my brains would make me famous (brains were good for something, weren't they?), but then my children would have good childhoods—not me. I was irrevocably deprived, and it was the irrevocableness that hurt, that finally drove me away from any sensible adjustment with life to the position that dreams had to come true or there was no point in living at all. If dreams came true, then I would have my childhood in one form or another, someday.

If my mother was home when I came in from school, she might say that Mrs. Leinberg had called and wanted me to baby-sit, and I would be plunged into yet another of the dilemmas of those years. I had to baby-sit to earn money to buy my lunch at school, and there were times, considering the dilemma I faced at the Leinbergs', when I preferred not eating, or eating very little, to babysitting. But there wasn't any choice; Mother would have accepted for me, and made Mrs. Leinberg promise not to stay out too late and deprive me of my sleep. She would have a sandwich ready for me to eat, so that I could rush over in time to let Mr. and Mrs. Leinberg go out to dinner. Anyway, I would eat my sandwich reading a book, to get my own back, and then I would set out. As I walked down the back stairs on my way to the Leinbergs', usually swinging on the railings by my arms to build up my muscles, I would think forlornly of what it was to be me, and wish things were otherwise, and I did not understand myself or my loneliness or the cruel deprivation the vista down the alley meant.

There was a short cut across the back yards to the apartment house where the Leinbergs lived, but I always walked by my two locust trees and spent a few moments loving them; so far as I knew, I loved nothing else.

Then I turned right and crossed the street and walked past an apartment house that had been built at right angles to the street, facing a strange declivity that had once been an excavation for still another apartment house, which had never been built, because of the depression. On the other side of the declivity was a block of three apartment houses, and the third was the Leinbergs'. Every apartment in it had at least eight rooms, and the back staircase was enclosed, and the building had its own garages. All this made it special and expensive, and a landmark in the neighborhood.

Mr. Leinberg was a drug manufacturer and very successful. I thought he was a smart man, but I don't remember him at all well (I never looked at men closely in those days but always averted my head in shyness and embarrassment; they might guess how fiercely I wanted to belong to them) and I could have been wrong. Certainly the atmosphere then, during the war years—it was 1943—was that everyone was getting rich; everyone who could work, that is. At any rate, he was getting rich, and it was only a matter of time before the Leinbergs moved from that apartment house to Laclede or Ladue and had a forty-thousand-dollar house with an acre or so of grounds.

Mrs. Leinberg was very pretty; she was dark, like my mother, but not as beautiful. For one thing, she was too small; she was barely five feet tall, and I towered over her. For another, she was not at all regal. But her lipstick was never on her teeth, and her dresses were usually new, and her eyes were kind. (My mother's eyes were incomprehensible; they were dark stages where dimly seen mob scenes were staged and all one ever sensed was tumult and drama, and no matter how long one waited, the lights never went up and the scene never was explained.) Mrs. Leinberg would invite me to help myself in the icebox, and then she would write down the telephone number of the place where she was going to be. "Keep Edward in the back of the apartment, where he won't disturb the baby," she would tell me. "If the baby does wake up, pick her up right away. That's very important. I didn't pick Edward up, and I'll always regret it." She said that every time, even though

I could see Edward lurking in the back hallway, waiting for his parents to leave so he could run out and jump on me and our world could come alive again. He would listen, his small face—he was seven—quite blank with hurt and the effort to pierce the hurt with understanding.

Mrs. Leinberg would say, "Call me if she wakes up." And then, placatingly, to her husband, "I'll just come home to put her back to sleep, and then I'll go right back to the party—" Then, to me, "But she almost always sleeps, so don't worry about it."

"Come on, Greta. He knows what to do," Mr. Leinberg would say impatiently.

I always heard contempt in his voice—contempt for his wife, for Edward, and for me. I would be standing by the icebox looking down on the two little married people. Edward's father had a jealous and petulant mouth. "Come on, Greta," it would say impatiently, "We'll be back by eleven," it would say to me.

"Edward goes to bed at nine," Mrs. Leinberg would say, her voice high and birdlike, but tremulous with confusion and vagueness. Then she would be swept out the front door, so much prettily dressed matchwood, in her husband's wake. When the door closed, Edward would come hurtling down the hall and tackle my knees if I was staring after his parents, or, if I was facing him, leap onto my chest and into my arms.

"What shall we play tonight?"

He would ask that and I would have to think. He trembled with excitement, because I could make up games wonderful to him—like his daydreams, in fact. Because he was a child, he trusted me almost totally, and I could do anything with him. I had that power with children until I was in college and began at last to be like other people.

In Edward's bedroom was a large closet; it had a rack for clothes, a washstand, a built-in table, and fifteen or twenty shelves. The table and shelves were crowded with toys and games and sports equipment. I owned a Monopoly board I had inherited from my older sister, an old baseball glove (which was so cheap I never dared use it in front of my classmates, who had real gloves signed by real players), and a collection of postcards. The first time I saw that closet, I practically exploded with pleasure; I took down each of the games and toys and played with them, one after another, with Edward. Edward loved the fact that we never played a game to its conclusion but would leap from game to game after only a few moves, until the leaping became the real game and the atmosphere of laughter the real sport.

It was comfortable for me in the back room, alone in the apartment with Edward, because at last I was chief; and not only that, I was not being seen. There was no one there who could see through me, or think of what I should be or how

I should behave; and I have always been terrified of what people thought of me, as if what they thought was a hulking creature that would confront me if I should turn a wrong corner.

There were no corners. Edward and I would take his toy pistols and stalk each other around the bed. Other times, we were on the bed, the front gun turret of a battleship sailing to battle the Japanese fleet in the Indian Ocean. Edward would close his eyes and roll with pleasure when I went "Boom! Boom! BOOOOM!"

"It's sinking! It's sinking, isn't it?"

"No, stupid. We only hit its funnel. We have to shoot again. Boom, Boom—"

Edward's fingers would press his eyelids in a spasm of ecstasy; his delirious, taut, little boy's body would fall backward on the soft pillows and bounce, and his back would curve; the excited breathy laughter would pour out like so many leaves spilling into spring, so many lilacs thrusting into bloom.

Under the bed, in a foxhole (Edward had a Cub Scout hat and I had his plastic soldier helmet), we turned back the yellow hordes from Guadalcanal. Edward dearly loved to be wounded. "I'm hit!" he'd shriek. "I'm hit!" He'd press his hand against his stomach and writhe on the wooden floor. "They shot me in the guts—"

I didn't approve of his getting wounded so

soon, because then the scene was over; both his and my sense of verisimilitude didn't allow someone to be wounded and then get up. I remember how pleased he was when I invented the idea that after he got wounded, he could be someone else; so, when we crawled under the bed, we would decide to be eight or twelve or twenty Marines, ten each to get wounded, killed, or maimed as we saw fit, provided enough survived so that when we crawled out from under the bed we could charge the Japanese position under the dining-room table and leave it strewn with corpses.

Edward was particularly good at the detective game, which was a lot more involved and difficult. In that, we would walk into the kitchen, and I would tell him that we had received a call about a murder. Except when we played Tarzan, we never found it necessary to be characters. However, we always had names. In the detective game, we were usually Sam and Fred. We'd get a call telling us who was murdered, and then we'd go back to the bedroom and examine the corpse and question the suspects. I'd fire questions at an empty chair. Sometimes Edward would get tired of being my sidekick and he'd slip into the chair and be the quaking suspect. Other times, he would prowl around the room on his hands and knees with a magnifying glass while I stormed and shouted at the perpetually shifty suspect: "Where were you,

Mrs. Eggnogghead [giggles from Edward], at ten o'clock, when Mr. Eggnogghead [laughter, helpless with pleasure, from Edward] was slain with the cake knife?"

"Hey, Fred! *I found bloodstains.*" Edward's voice would quiver with a creditable imitation of the excitement of radio detectives.

"Bloodstains! Where, Sam? Where? This may be the clue that breaks the case."

Edward could sustain the *commedia dell' arte* for hours if I wanted him to. He was a precocious and delicate little boy, quivering with the malaise of being unloved. When we played, his child's heart would come into its own, and the troubled world where his vague hungers went unfed and mothers and fathers were dim and far away—too far away ever to reach in and touch the sore place and make it heal—would disappear, along with the world where I was not sufficiently muscled or sufficiently gallant to earn my own regard. (What ever had induced my mother to marry that silly man, who'd been unable to hang on to his money? I could remember when we'd had a larger house and I'd been happy; why had she let it get away?) It angered me that Edward's mother had so little love for him and so much for her daughter, and that Edward's father should not appreciate the boy's intelligence—he thought Edward was a queer duck, and effeminate. I could have taught Edward the manly postures. But his father didn't think highly of me: I was only a baby-sitter, and a queer duck too. Why, then, should Edward be more highly regarded by his father than I myself was? I wouldn't love him or explain to him.

That, of course, was my terrible dilemma. His apartment house, though larger than mine, was made of the same dark-red brick, and I wouldn't love him. It was shameful for a boy my age to love a child anyway. And who was Edward? He wasn't as smart as I'd been at his age, or as fierce. At his age, I'd already seen the evil in people's eyes, and I'd begun the construction of my defenses even then. But Edward's family was more prosperous, and the cold winds of insecurity *(Where will the money come from?)* hadn't shredded the dreamy chrysalis of his childhood. He was still immersed in the dim, wet wonder of the folded wings that might open if someone loved him; he still hoped, probably, in a butterfly's unthinking way, for spring and warmth. How the wings ache, folded so, waiting; that is, they ache until they atrophy.

So I was thirteen and Edward was seven and he wanted me to love him, but he was not old enough or strong enough to help me. He could not make his parents share their wealth and comfort with me, or force them to give me a place in their home. He was like most of the people I knew—eager and needful of my love; for I was quite remarkable and made incredible games, which were better than movies or than the heart could hope for. I was a dream come true. I was smart and virtuous (no one knew that I occasionally stole from the dime store) and fairly attractive, maybe even very attractive. I was often funny and always interesting. I had read everything and knew everything and got unbelievable grades. Of course I was someone whose love was desired. Mother, my teachers, my sister, girls at school, other boys—they all wanted me to love them.

But I wanted them to love me first.

None of them did. I was fierce and solitary and acrid, marching off the little mile from school, past the post office, all yellow brick and chrome, and my two locust trees (water, water everywhere and not a drop to drink), and there was no one who loved me first. I could see a hundred cravennesses in the people I knew, a thousand flaws, a million weaknesses. If I had to love first, I would love only perfection. Of course, I could help heal the people I knew if I loved them. No, I said to myself, why should I give them everything when they give me nothing?

How many hurts and shynesses and times of walking up the back stairs had made me that way? I don't know. All I know is that Edward needed my love and I wouldn't give it to him. I was only thirteen. There isn't much you can blame a boy

of thirteen for, but I'm not thinking of the blame;
I'm thinking of all the years that might have been
—if I'd only known then what I know now. The
waste, the God-awful waste.

Really, that's all there is to this story. The boy
I was, the child Edward was. That and the terrible
desire to suddenly turn and run shouting back
through the corridors of time, screaming at the
boy I was, searching him out, and pounding on
his chest: Love him, you damn fool, love him.

FIRST LOVE
AND OTHER
SORROWS

TOWARD the end of March, in St. Louis, slush fills the gutters, and dirty snow lies heaped alongside porch steps, and everything seems to be suffocating in the embrace of a season that lasts too long. Radiators hiss mournfully, no one manages to be patient, the wind draws tears from your eyes, the clouds are filled with sadness. Women with scarves around their heads and their feet encased in fur-lined boots pick their way carefully over patches of melting ice. It seems that winter will last forever, that this is the decision of nature and nothing can be done about it.

At the age when I was always being warned by my mother not to get overheated, spring began on that evening when I was first allowed to go outside after dinner and play kick-the-can. The ground would be moist, I'd manage to get muddy in spite of what seemed to me extreme precautions, my mother would call me home in the darkness, and when she saw me she would ask, "What *have* you done to yourself?" "Nothing," I'd say hopefully. But by the time I was sixteen, the moment when the year passed into spring, like so many other things, was less clear. In March and early April, track began, but indoors; mid-term exams came and went; the buds appeared on the maples, staining all their branches red; but it was still winter, and I found myself having feelings in class that were like long petitions for spring and all its works. And then one evening I was sitting at my desk doing my trigonometry and I heard my sister coming home from her office; I heard her high heels tapping on the sidewalk, and realized that, for the first time since fall, all the windows in the house were open. My sister was coming up the front walk. I looked down through a web of budding tree branches and called out to her that it was spring, by God. She shrugged—she was very handsome and she didn't approve of me—and then she started up the front steps and vanished under the roof of the porch.

I ran downstairs. "The bus was crowded tonight," my sister said, hanging up her coat. "I could hardly breathe. This is such a warm dress."

"You need a new spring dress," my mother said, her face lighting up. She was sitting in the living room with the evening paper on her lap.

She and my sister spread the newspaper on the dining-room table to look at the ads.

"We'll just have to settle for sandwiches tonight," my mother said to me. My father was dead, and my mother pretended that now all the cooking was done for my masculine benefit. "Look! That suit's awfully smart!" she cried, peering at the paper. "Montaldo's always has such nice suits." She sighed and went out to the kitchen, leaving the swinging door open so she could talk to my sister. "Ninety dollars isn't too much for a good suit, do you think?"

"No," my sister said. "I don't think it's too much. But I don't really want a suit this spring. I'd much rather have a sort of sky-blue dress—with a round neck that shows my shoulders a little bit. I don't look good in suits. I'm not old enough." She was twenty-two. "My face is too round," she added, in a low voice.

My mother said, "You're not too young for a suit." She also meant my sister was not too young to get married.

My sister looked at me and said, "Mother, do you think he shaves often enough? How often *do* you shave?"

"Every three days," I said, flushing up my neck and cheeks.

"Well, try it every other day."

"Yes, try to be neater," my mother said. "I'm sure girls don't like boys with fuzz on their chin."

"I think he's too proud of his beard to shave it," my sister said, and giggled.

"I feel sorry for the man who marries you," I

said. "Because everybody thinks you're sweet and you're not."

She smiled pityingly at me, and then she looked down over the newspaper again.

Until I was four, we lived in a large white frame house overlooking the Mississippi River, south of St. Louis. This house had, among other riches, a porte-cochere, an iron deer on the lawn, and a pond with goldfish swimming in it. Once, I asked my mother why we had left that earlier house, and she said, "We lost our money—that's why. Your father was a very trusting man," she said. "He was always getting swindled."

She was not a mercenary woman, nor was she mean about money—except in spells that didn't come often—but she believed that what we lost with the money was much of our dignity and much of our happiness. She did not want to see life in a grain of sand; she wanted to see it from the shores of the Riviera, wearing a white sharkskin dress.

I will never forget her astonishment when she took us—she was dressed in her best furs, as a gesture, I suppose—to see the house that was to be our home from then on and I told her I liked it. It had nine rooms, a stained-glass window in the hall, and neighbors all up and down the block. She detested that house.

As she grew older, she changed, she grew less imperious. She put her hair into a roll, wore dark-colored clothes, said often, "I'm not a young woman any more," and began to take pride in being practical. But she remained determined; she had seen a world we didn't remember too clearly, and she wanted us to make our way back to it. "I had it all," she said once to my sister. "I was good-looking. We were rich. You have no idea what it was like. If I had died when I was thirty, I would have died completely happy. . . ."

But being practical did not come easy to her. She was not practical in her bones, and every spring brings back the memory of my mother peering nearsightedly, with surprise, at the tulip shoots in her flower border. And it brings back her look of distraught efficiency during spring housecleaning. "You'd better clear your closet shelves tonight," she would warn me, "because tomorrow Tillie and I are going in there with a vacuum cleaner, and we'll throw out everything we find." Year after year, I would run upstairs to save my treasures— even when I was sixteen and on the verge of a great embarkation, the nature of which I could not even begin to guess. My treasures consisted of my postcard collection—twenty-five hundred cards in all, arranged alphabetically by states of the Union and countries of the world (the wonder was that *I* lived in St. Louis)—an old baseball glove, my leaf collection, two obscene comic books I had won in a poker game at a Boy Scout jamboree, my marble collection, and thirty-five pages of secret thoughts written out in longhand. All these had to be taken out to the garage and hidden among the tools until the frenzy of cleaning was over and I could smuggle them back upstairs.

After supper, as the season grew warmer, my mother and sister and I would sit on the screened porch in the rear of the house, marooned among the shadows and the new leaves and the odor of insect spray, the light from our lamps sticking to the trees like bits of yellow paper. Usually the radio was on, and my mother, a book on her lap, her face abstracted (she was usually bored; her life was moved mainly by the burning urge to rise once more along the thin edge of social distinction), would listen to the comedians and laugh. When the phone rang, she would get up and go into the house with long strides, and if the call was for my sister, my mother would call her to the phone in a voice mottled with triumph.

Sometimes in the evening my mother would wash my sister's hair. My sister would sit in front of the basin in Mother's bathroom, a towel around her shoulders, smiling. From my room across the hall I would hear my sister chattering about the men she knew—the ones she dated, the ones she wanted to date, the ones she wouldn't touch with a ten-foot pole. My mother would interrupt with accounts of her own cleverness, her sorties and successes when young, sometimes laughingly, but sometimes gloomily, because she regretted a lot of things. Then she and my sister would label my sister's suitors: one or two had family, one had money, one—a poor boy—had a brilliant future, and there were a few docile, sweet ones who were simply fillers, who represented the additional number of dates that raised my sister to the rank of a very popular girl.

In these conversations, my mother would often bring up matters of propriety. Late dates were improper, flirting with boys other than one's date, breaking dates. Then, too, she would try to instruct my sister in other matters, which had to do with keeping passion in its place and so preventing embarrassment for the boy and disaster for the girl. My sister would grow irritated. "I don't know why you talk like that—I behave very well," she would tell my mother. "Better than the other girls I know." Her irritation would please my mother, who would smile and say that only good-looking girls could afford to be good, and then they would both laugh.

I used to wonder why my mother didn't take my sister's success for granted. My sister was lovely, she had plenty of dates, the phone rang incessantly. Where was the danger? Why did she always lecture my sister?

Once, my mother said my sister ought not to dance with too many boys or she would frighten off the more serious ones. My sister was getting dressed for the spring dance at the country club. Arrogant and slender, she glistened like a water nymph, among her froth of bottles and jars and filmy clothes. She became furious; she screamed that she *liked* to dance. I closed the door to my room, but I could still hear the two of them. "Don't be so foolish," my mother kept saying, over and over again. "Please don't be foolish. . . ." Then my sister, on the verge of tears, said she just wanted to have a good time. My sister's date arrived, and I went downstairs to let him in, and by the time I came back upstairs, the two of them were laughing. My mother said she was just trying to be helpful; after all, my sister was impractical and her looks wouldn't last forever. My sister, as she opened the door of her room, said, under her breath, "They'll last a lot longer yet."

I'll never forget the wild rustling of her voluminous white skirt as she came down the hallway toward me. Her face was strangely still, as if seen by moonlight. Her hair was smooth and shining, her hands bent outward at the wrist, as if they were flowers. "How beautiful you look!" I cried. My sister smiled and then solemnly turned all the way around, and her huge skirt rose and fell like a splash of surf. She was so beautiful I could hardly bear it. I hugged her, and she laughed.

Later that night I asked my mother why she got so distraught. Wasn't my sister popular enough? My mother was sitting in the kitchen, in an old, faded yellow housecoat, drinking a glass of warm milk. "You don't know anything about it," she said, with such sadness that I rose from the table and fled to my room.

"I know what I'm saying!" my mother would cry when she argued with my sister. "You must listen to me. People talk. . . . You don't know who you'll meet on a date; it's good to accept even if you don't like the boy. . . . Girls have to be very careful. You're thoughtless. Don't you think in fifty years I've learned what makes the world go around? Now, listen to me. I know what I'm saying. . . ." But my sister's face was so radiant, her charm was so intense, she pushed her blond hair back from her face with a gesture so quick, so certain, so arrogant and filled with vanity, that no one, I thought, could doubt that whatever she did would be right.

I wanted to be arrogant, too. I didn't want to wear glasses and be one of the humorless, heavy-handed boys my sister despised. I was on her side as much as she'd let me be. She was the elder, and she often grew impatient with me. I didn't seem to understand all the things involved in being on her side.

Night after night I saw her come home from work tired—she had a secretarial job in a hospital and she hated it—and two hours later she would descend the stairs, to greet her date, her face alight with seriousness or with a large, bright smile, depending on her mood or on where her escort was taking her that evening. A concert or an art movie made her serious; one of the hotel supper clubs brought the smile to her face. She would trip down the stairs in her high heels, a light, flimsy coat thrown over one arm, one hand clutching a purse and gloves, her other hand on the banister. In the queer yellow light of the hall chandelier, her necklace or her earrings would shine dully, and sometimes, especially if she was all dressed up, in a black dress, say, with a low neck, because they were going out to a supper club, there would be an air, in spite of her gaiety, of the captive about her. It was part of her intense charm. In her voluminous white skirt, she went to the spring dance at the country club and brought back to my mother the news that she had captured the interest of Sonny Bruster, the oldest son of M. F. Bruster, a banker and a very rich man—more than interest, it turned out, because he started calling my sister up almost every day at work and taking her out almost every night. My mother was on the phone much of the afternoon explaining to her friends that my sister wasn't engaged. It was criminal the way some people gossiped, she said. My sister had only gone out with the boy ten or twelve times. They were just getting to know each other. Then my mother began to *receive* calls; someone had heard from a friend of Mrs. Bruster's that Mrs. Bruster had said her son was very serious about my sister, who was a very charming, very pretty girl, of good family. . . . My mother rubbed her hands with glee. She borrowed money from her brothers, and every week my sister had new clothes.

My sister would come home from work and run upstairs to change. Sonny would be due at seven, to take her out to dinner. My sister would kick her shoes off, struggle out of her dress, and dash around the upstairs in her slip.

"Mother, I can't find my earrings."

"Which earrings, dear?"

"The little pearls—the little tiny pearl ones that I got two Easters ago, to go with my black . . ."

My sister was delighted with herself. She loved being talked about, being envied.

"Mother, do you know what Ceil Johnson said to me today? She said that Beryl Feringhaus—you know, the real-estate people—was heartbroken because she thought Sonny Bruster was going to get engaged to her." My sister giggled. Her long hair was tangled, and my mother yanked a comb through it.

"Maybe you ought to cut your hair," my mother said, trying to hide her own excitement and to stay practical. During this period, my mother was living in the imminence of wealth. Whenever she stopped what she was doing and looked up, her face would be bright with visions.

That spring when I was sixteen, more than anything else in the world I wanted to be a success when I grew up. I did not know there was any other way of being lovable. My best friend was a boy named Preston, who already had a heavy beard. He was shy, and unfortunate in his dealings with other people, and he wanted to be a physicist. He had very little imagination, and he pitied anyone who did have it. "You and the word 'beautiful'!" he would say disdainfully, holding his nose and imitating my voice. "Tell me—what does 'beautiful' mean?"

"It's something you want," I would say.

"You're an aesthete," Preston would say. "I'm a scientist. That's the difference."

He and I used to call each other almost every night and have long, profound talks on the telephone.

On a date, Preston would sit beside his girl and stolidly eye her. Occasionally, toward the end of the evening, he would begin to breathe heavily, and he would make a few labored, daring jokes. He might catch the girl's hand and stare at her with inflamed and wistful eyes, or he might mutter incoher-

ent compliments. Girls liked him, and escaped easily
from his clumsy longing. They slipped their hands
from his grasp and asked him to call them up
again, but after a few dates with a girl Preston
would say disgustedly, "All she does is talk. She's
frigid or something. . . ." But the truth was, he
was afraid of hurting them, of doing something
wrong to them, and he never really courted them
at all.

At school, Preston and I had afternoon study
hall together. Study hall was in the library, which
was filled with the breathing of a hundred and
fifty students, and with the dim, half-fainting
breezes of high spring, and with books: it was the
crossroads of the world. Preston and I would sign
out separately, and meet in the lavatory. There we
would lean up against the stalls and talk. Preston
was full of thoughts; he was tormented by all his
ideas. "Do you know what relativity means?" he
would ask me. "Do you realize how it affects every
little detail of everyday life?" Or it might be Spi-
noza that moved him: "Eighteenth-century, but
by God *there* was a rational man." I would pace
up and down, half listening, half daydreaming,
wishing *my* name would appear on Preston's list
of people who had elements of greatness.

Or we talked about our problems. "I'm not
popular," I would say. "I'm too gloomy."

"Why is that, do you think?" Preston would ask.

"I don't know," I would say. "I'm a virgin. That has a lot to do with everything."

"Listen," Preston said one day, "you may not be popular but you're likable. Your trouble is you're a snob." He walked up and down the white-tiled floor, mimicking me. He slouched, and cast his eyes down, and jutted his chin out, and pulled a foolish, serious look over his face.

"Is that me?" I cried, heartbroken.

"Well, almost," Preston said.

Or, leaning on the window sill, sticking our heads out into the golden afternoon air and watching a girl's gym class doing archery under the trees, we talked about sex.

"It starts in the infant," Preston said. "And it lasts forever."

"Saints escape it," I said mournfully.

"The hell they do," Preston said. The girls beneath us on the hillside drew their bows. Their thin green gym suits fluttered against their bodies. "Aren't they nice?" Preston asked longingly. "Aren't they wonderful?"

After school, Preston and I went out for track. The outdoor track was a cinder oval surrounding the football field. A steep, grassy hill led up to the entrance of the school locker room. "Run up that hill every night, boys," the coach pleaded—Old

Mackyz, with his paunch and his iron-gray wavy hair—at the end of the practice period. "Run, boys, because when you're abso-lootly exhausted, that's when you got to give *more*. It's the *more*, boys, that makes champions." And then he'd stand there, humble, and touched by his own speech.

During our warmup sessions, we used to jog-trot the length of the field and back again, keeping our knees high. The grand inutility of this movement filled me with something like exaltation; and on every side of me, in irregular lines, my fellow-males jogged, keeping their knees high. What happiness!

"The turf's too springy," Preston would mumble. "Bad for the muscles." Preston was a miler. He was thickset and without natural grace; Mackyz said he had no talent, but he ran doggedly, and he became a good miler. I ran the 440. I was tall and thin, and even Mackyz said I ought to be good at it, but I wasn't. Mackyz said I didn't have the spirit. "All you smart boys are alike," he said. "You haven't got the *heart* for it. You always hold back. You're all a bunch of goldbricks." I tried to cure my maimed enthusiasm. As I ran, Mackyz would bawl desperately, "Hit the ground harder. Hit with your toes! Spring, boy! SPRING! Don't coddle yourself, for Christ's sake. . . ." After a race, I'd throw myself down on a knoll near the finish

line, under a sycamore tree, where the track manager dug a new hole every day for us to puke in.
Three or four others would join me, and we'd lie
there wearily, our chests burning, too weak to
move.

Among my other problems was that I was re-
duced nearly to a state of tears over my own looks
whenever I looked at a boy named Joel Bush. Joel
was so incredibly good-looking that none of the
boys could quite bear the fact of his existence; his
looks weren't particularly masculine or clean-cut,
and he wasn't a fine figure of a boy—he was merely
beautiful. He looked like a statue that had been
rubbed with honey and warm wax, to get a golden
tone, and he carried at all times, in the neatness
of his features and the secret proportions of his
face and body that made him so handsome in that
particular way, the threat of seduction. Displease
me, he seemed to say, and I'll get you. I'll make
you fall in love with me and I'll turn you into a
donkey. Everyone either avoided him or gave in to
him; teachers refused to catch him cheating, boys
never teased him, and no one ever told him off.
One day I saw him saying goodbye to a girl after
school, and as he left her to join me, walking
toward the locker room, he said to her, "Meet you
here at five-thirty." Track wasn't over until six, and
I could tell that he had no intention of meeting
her, and yet, when he asked me about some experi-

ments we had done in physics, instead of treating him like someone who had just behaved like a heel, I told him everything I knew.

He never joined us under the sycamore tree, and he ran effortlessly. He would pass the finish line, his chest heaving under his sweat-stained track shirt, and climb into the stands and sit in the sunlight. I was watching him, one afternoon, as he sat there wiping his face and turning his head from side to side. At one moment it was all silver except for the charred hollows of his eyes, and the next it was young and perfect, the head we all recognized as his.

Mackyz saw him and called out to him to put his sweatshirt on before he caught a cold. As he slipped the sweatshirt on, Joel shouted, "Aw, go fry your head!" Mackyz laughed good-naturedly.

Sprinkled here and there on the football field were boys lifting their arms high and then sweeping them down to touch their toes, or lying on their backs and bicycling their legs in the air. I got up and walked toward them, to do a little jog-trotting and high-knee prancing. I looked at Joel. "I'm cooling off," he said to me. I walked on, and just then a flock of crows wheeled up behind the oak tree on the hill and filled the sky with their vibrant motion. Everyone—even Preston—paused and looked up. The birds rose in a half circle and then glided, scythelike, with wings outspread, on a down current of air until they were only twenty feet or so above the ground; then they flapped their wings with a noise like sheets being shaken out, and soared aloft, dragging their shadows up the stepped concrete geometry of the stands, past Joel's handsome, rigid figure, off into the sky.

"Whaddya know about that?" Mackyz said. "Biggest flock of crows I ever saw."

"Why didn't you get your gun and shoot a couple?" Joel called out. Everyone turned. "Then you'd have some crow handy whenever you had to eat some," Joel said.

"Take a lap," Mackyz bawled, his leathery face turning red up to the roots of his iron-gray hair.

"He was only kidding," I said, appalled at Mackyz's hurt.

Mackyz looked at me and scowled, "You can take a lap too, and don't talk so much."

I took off my sweatshirt and dropped it on the grass and set off around the track. As soon as I started running, the world changed. The bodies sprawled out across the green of the football field were parts of a scene remembered, not one real at this moment. The whole secret of effort is to keep on, I told myself. Not for the world would I have stopped then, and yet nothing—not even if I had been turned handsome as a reward for finishing— could have made up for the curious pain of the effort.

About halfway around the track, Joel caught

up to me, and then he slowed down and ran along-side. "Mackyz isn't watching," he said. "Let's sneak up the hill." I looked and saw that Mackyz was lining up the team for high-jump practice. Joel sailed up over the crest of the hill, and I fol-lowed him.

"He's getting senile," Joel said, dropping to a sitting position, sighting over the crest of the hill at Mackyz, and then lying down. "Come on, jerk, lie down. You want Mackyz to see you?"

I was uneasy; this sort of fooling was all right for Joel, because he "made the effort," but if Mackyz caught me, he'd kick me off the team. I pointed this out to Joel.

"Aw, Mackyz takes everything too seriously. That's his problem," Joel said. "He's always up in the air about something. I don't see why he makes so much fuss. You ever notice how old men make a big fuss over everything?"

"Mackyz' not so old."

"All right, you ever notice how *middle-aged* men make a big fuss over everything?" A few seconds later, he said casually, his gaze resting on the underside of the leaves of the oak tree, "I got laid last night."

"No kidding?" I said.

He spread his fingers over his face, no doubt to see them turn orange in the sunlight, as children do. "Yeah," he said.

From the football field came the sounds of high-jump practice starting. Mackyz was shouting, "Now, start with your left foot—one, two, three— take off! TAKE OFF, GODDAMN IT! Spread your God- damned legs, spread 'em. You won't get ruptured. There's sand to catch you, for Christ's sake." The jumper's footsteps made a series of thuds, there was a pause, and then the sound of the landing in the sand. Lifting my head, I could see the line of boys waiting to jump, the lead boy breaking into a run, leaping from the ground, and spreading his arms in athletic entreaty.

"It was disappointing," Joel said.

"How?" I asked.

"It's nothing very special."

I was aroused by this exposé. "You mean the books—"

"It's not like that at all." He turned sullenly and scrabbled with his fingers in the dirt. "It's like masturbation, kind of with bells."

"Maybe the girl didn't know how to do it."

"She was a grown woman!"

"Yeah, but—"

"She was a fully grown woman! She knew what she was doing!"

"Oh," I said. Then, after a minute, "Look, would you mind telling me what you said to her? If I ever had a chance, I wouldn't know what to say. I . . ."

"I don't remember," Joel said. "We just looked

at each other, and then she got all tearful, and she told me to take my clothes off."

We lay there a moment, in the late afternoon sunshine, and then I said we'd better be getting back. We walked around behind the hill, and waited until Mackyz wasn't looking before we sprinted out onto the track.

The jumping went on for fifteen or twenty minutes more; then Mackyz raised his arms in a gesture of benediction. "All right, you squirts—all out on the track for a fast lap. And that includes you, goldbrick," he said to me, wagging his finger.

All the boys straightened up and started toward the track. The sun's light poured in long low rays over the roof of the school. Jostling and joking, we started to run. "Faster!" Mackyz yelled. "Faster! Whatsa matter—you all a bunch of girls! Faster! For Christ's sake, faster!"

Since Preston, in his dogged effort to become a good miler, ran three laps to everyone else's one, he was usually the last in the locker room. He would come in, worn out and breathing heavily; sometimes he even had to hold himself up with one hand on his locker while he undressed. Everyone else would long since have showered and would be almost ready to leave. They might make one or two remarks about Preston's running his legs down

to stumps or trying to kill himself for Mackyz'
sake. Preston would smile numbly while he tried
to get his breath back, and somehow, I was always
surprised by how little attention was paid to Preston, how cut off and how alone he was.

More often than not, Joel would be showing off
in the locker room—walking around on his hands,
singing dirty songs, or engaged in some argument
or other. Preston would go into the shower. I
would talk to Joel, dressing slowly, because I
usually waited for Preston. By the time I was all
dressed, the locker room would be empty and
Preston would still be towelling himself off. Then,
instead of hurrying to put his clothes on, he would
run his hand over his chest, to curl the few limp
hairs. "Oh come on!" I would say, disgustedly.

"Hold your horses," he would say, with his mad-
dening physicist's serenity. "Just you hold your
horses."

It took him half an hour to get dressed. He'd
stand in front of the mirror and flex his muscles
endlessly and admire the line his pectorals made
across his broad rib cage, and he always left his
shirt until last, even until after he had combed his
hair. I found his vanity confusing; he was far from
handsome, with his heavy mouth and bushy eyebrows and thick, sloping shoulders, but he loved
his reflection and he'd turn and gaze at himself in
the mirror from all sorts of angles while he but-

toned his shirt. He hated Joel. "There's a guy who'll never amount to much," Preston would say. "He's chicken. And he's not very smart. I don't see why you want him to like you—except that you're a sucker. You let your eyes run away with your judgment." I put up with all this because I wanted Preston to walk me part way home. It seemed shameful somehow to have to walk home alone.

Finally, he would finish, and we would emerge from the now deserted school into the dying afternoon. As we walked, Preston harangued me about my lack of standards and judgment. The hunger I had for holding school office and for being well thought of he dismissed as a streak of lousy bourgeois cowardice. I agreed with him (I didn't like myself anyway); but what was to be done about it? "We might run away," Preston said, squinting up at the sky. "Hitchhike. Work in factories. Go to a whorehouse. . . ." I leaned against a tree trunk, and Preston stood with one foot on the curb and one foot in the street, and we lobbed pebbles back and forth. "We're doomed," Preston said. "Doom" was one of his favorite words, along with "culture," "kinetic," and "the Absolute." "We come from a dying culture," he said.

"I suppose you're right," I said. "It certainly looks that way." But then I cheered up. "After all, it's not as if we were insane or anything."

"It wouldn't show yet," Preston said gloomily.

"It's still in the latent stage. It'll come out later. You'll see. After all, you're still living at home, and you've got your half-assed charm—"

I broke in; I'd never had a compliment from him before.

"I didn't say you were charming," he said. "I said you have a half-assed charm. You behave well in public. That's all I meant."

At the corner where we separated, Preston stood a moment or two. "It's hopeless," he said.

"God, do you really think so?" I asked.

"That's my honest opinion," he said.

He turned toward his house. I jogged a block or two, and then felt my stomach muscles. When I came to a maple with a low, straight branch, I ran and jumped up and swung from the branch, while a big green diesel bus rolled ponderously past, all its windows filled with tired faces that looked out at the street going by and at me hanging from the branch and smiling. I was doomed, but I was very likely charming.

I ran in the front door of my house and called out, "Mother! Mother!"

"What is it?" she answered. She was sitting on the screened porch, and I could see a little plume of cigarette smoke in the doorway. There was the faint mutter of a radio news program turned on low.

"Nothing," I said. "I'm home, that's all."

At the dinner table, I would try to disguise myself by slouching in my chair and thinking about my homework, but my mother and my sister always recognized me. "How was track today?" my sister would ask in a slightly amused way.

"Fine," I would say in a low voice.

My mother and my sister would exchange glances. I must have seemed comic to them, stilted, and slightly absurd, like all males.

Almost every evening, Sonny Bruster used to drive up to our house in his yellow convertible. The large car would glide to a stop at the curb, and Sonny would glance quickly at himself in the rear-view mirror, running his hand over his hair. Then he'd climb out and brush his pants off, too occupied with his own shyness to notice the children playing on the block. But they would stop what they were doing and watch him.

I would wait for him at the front door and let him in and lead him into the living room. I walked ahead of Sonny because I had noticed that he could not keep himself from looking up the stairs as we passed through the hallway, as if to conjure up my sister then and there with the intensity of his longing, and I hated to see him do this. I would sit in the high-backed yellow chair, and Sonny would settle himself on the couch and ask me about track, or if I'd picked a college yet. "You ought to think carefully about college," he would say. "I think

Princeton is more civilized than Yale." His gentle, well-bred voice was carefully inexpressive. In his manner there was a touch of stiffness to remind you, and himself, that he was rich and if some disrespect was intended for him he wouldn't necessarily put up with it. But I liked him. He treated me with great politeness, and I liked the idea of his being my brother-in-law, and I sometimes thought of the benefits that would fall to me if my sister married him.

Then my sister would appear at the head of the stairs, dressed to go out, and Sonny would leap to his feet. "Are you ready?" he'd cry, as if he had never dared hope she would be. My sister would hand him her coat, and with elaborate care he'd hold it for her. It would be perhaps eight o'clock or a little after. The street lamps would be on, but looking pallid because it wasn't quite dark. Usually, Sonny would open the car door for my sister, but sometimes, with a quick maneuver, she would forestall him; she would hurry the last few steps, open the door, and slip inside before he could lift his hand.

Sonny was not the first rich boy who had loved my sister; he was the fourth or fifth. And in the other cases there had been scenes between my mother and sister in which my mother extolled the boy's eligibility and my sister argued that she was too young to marry and didn't want to stop having a good time yet. Each time she had won, and each time the boy had been sent packing, while my mother looked heartbroken and said my sister was throwing her chances away.

With Sonny, the same thing seemed about to happen. My sister missed going out with a lot of boys instead of with just one. She complained once or twice that Sonny was jealous and spoiled. There were times when she seemed to like him very much, but there were other times when she would greet him blankly in the evening when she came downstairs, and he would be apologetic and fearful, and I could see that her disapproval was the thing he feared most in the world.

My mother didn't seem to notice, or if she did, she hid her feelings. Then one night I was sitting in my room doing my homework and I heard my mother and sister come upstairs. They went into my sister's room.

"I think Sonny's becoming very serious," my mother said.

"Sonny's so short," I heard my sister say. "He's not really interesting, either, Mother."

"He seems to be very fond of you," my mother said.

"He's no fun," my sister said. "Mother, be careful! You're brushing too hard! You're hurting me!"

I stopped trying to work, and listened.

"Sonny's a very intelligent boy," my mother said. "He comes from a good family."

"I don't care," my sister said. "I don't want to waste myself on him."

"Waste yourself?" My mother laughed derisively. I got up and went to the door of my sister's room. My sister was sitting at her dressing table, her hair shining like glass and her eyes closed. My mother was walking back and forth, gesturing with the hairbrush. "He's the one who's throwing himself away," she said. "Who do you think we are, anyway? We're nobodies."

"I'm pretty!" my sister objected angrily.

My mother shrugged. "The woods are full of pretty girls. What's more, they're full of pretty, rich girls. Now, Sonny's a very *nice* boy—"

"Leave me alone!" My sister pulled her hair up from her shoulders and held it in a soft mop on the top of her head. "Sonny's a jerk! A jerk!"

"He's nice-looking!" my mother cried.

"Oh, what do *you* know about it?" my sister cried. "You're old, for God's sake!"

The air vibrated. My sister rose and looked at my mother, horrified at what she had said. She took her hands from her hair, and it fell tumbling to her shoulders, dry and pale and soft. "I don't care," she said suddenly, and brushed past me, and fled into the bathroom and locked the door. There was no further sound from her. The only trace of her in the house at that moment was the faint odor in her room of the flowery perfume she used that spring.

"Oh, she's so foolish," my mother said, and I saw that she was crying. "She doesn't know what she's doing. . . . Why is she so foolish?" Then she put the hairbrush down and raised her hands to her cheeks and begin to pinch them.

I went back to my room and closed the door.

When I came out again, an hour later, my mother was in bed reading a magazine; she looked as if she had been wounded in a dozen places. My sister sat in her room, in front of the mirror. Her hair streamed down the back of her neck and lay in touching, defenseless little curls on the towel she had over her shoulders. She was studying her reflection thoughtfully. (Are flowers vain? Are trees? Are they consumed with vanity during those days when they are in bloom?) She raised her finger and pressed it against her lower lip to see, I think, if she would be prettier if her lip, instead of being so smooth, had a slight break in the center as some girls' did.

Shortly after this, my mother, who was neither stupid nor cruel, suggested that my sister stop seeing Sonny for a while. "Until you make up your mind," she said. "Otherwise you might break his heart, you know. Tell him you need some time to think. He'll understand. He'll think you're grown-up and responsible."

Sonny vanished from our house. In the evenings now, after dinner, the three of us would sit on the screened porch. My sister would look up eagerly when the phone rang, but the calls were never for her. None of her old boy friends knew she had stopped dating Sonny, and after a while, when the phone rang, she would compose her face and pretend she wasn't interested, or she would say irritably, "Who can that be?" She began to answer the phone herself (she never had before, because it wasn't good for a girl to seem too eager) and she would look sadly at herself in the hall mirror while she said, "Yes, Preston, he's here." She tried to read. She'd skim a few pages and then put the book down and gaze out through the screens at the night and the patches of light on the trees. She would listen with my mother to the comedians on the radio and laugh vaguely when my mother laughed. She picked on me. "Your posture's no good," she'd say. Or "Where do you learn your manners? Mother, he behaves like a zoot-suiter or something." Another time, she said, "If I don't make a good marriage, you'll be in trouble. You're too lazy to do anything on your own." She grew more and more restless. Toying with her necklace, she broke the string, and the beads rolled all over the floor, and there was something frantic in the way she went about retrieving the small rolling bits of glitter. It occurred to me that she didn't know what she was doing; she was not really as sure of everything as she seemed. It was a painfully difficult thought to arrive at, and it clung to me. Why hadn't I realized it before? Also, she sort of hated me, it seemed to me. I had never noticed that before, either. How could I have been so wrong, I wondered. Knowing how wrong I had been about this, I felt that no idea I had ever held was safe. For instance, we were not necessarily a happy family, with the most wonderful destinies waiting for my sister and me. We might make mistakes and choose wrong. Unhappiness was real. It was even likely. . . . How tired I became of studying my sister's face. I got so I would do anything to keep from joining the two women on the porch.

After three weeks of this, Sonny returned. I was never told whether he came of his own accord or whether he was summoned; but one night the yellow convertible drove up in front of our house and he was back. Now when my mother would watch my sister and Sonny getting into Sonny's car in the evenings, she would turn away from the window smiling. "I think your sister has found a boy she can respect," she would say, or "They'll be very happy together," or some such hopeful observation, which I could see no basis for, but which my mother believed with all the years and memories at her disposal, with all the weight of her past and her love for my sister. And I would go and call Preston.

I used to lie under the dining-room table, sheltered and private like that, looking up at the way the pieces of mahogany were joined together, while we talked. I would cup the telephone to my ear with my shoulder and hold my textbook up in the air, over my head, as we went over physics, which was a hard subject for me. "Preston," I asked one night, "what in God's name makes a siphon work?" They did work—everyone knew that—and I groaned as I asked it. Preston explained the theory to me, and I frowned, breathed heavily through my nose, squinted at the incomprehensible diagrams in the book, and thought of sex, of the dignity of man, of the wonders of the mind, as he talked. Every few minutes, he asked "Do you see" and I would sigh. It was spring, and there was meaning all around me, if only I were free— free of school, free of my mother, free of duties and inhibitions—if only I were mounted on a horse. . . . Where was the world? Not here, not near me, not under the dining-room table. . . . "Not quite," I'd say, untruthfully, afraid that I might discourage him. "But I almost get it. Just tell me once more." And on and on he went, while I frowned, breathed hard, and squinted. And then it happened! "I see!" I cried. "I see! I see!" It was air pressure! How in the world had I failed to visualize air pressure? I could see it now. I would never again not see it; it was there in my mind, solid and indestructible, a whitish column sitting on the water. "God damn but science is wonderful!" I said, and heaved my physics book into the living room. "Really wonderful!"

"It's natural law," Preston said reprovingly. "Don't get emotion mixed up with it."

One evening when my sister and Sonny didn't have a date to go out, my mother tapped lightly on my foot, which protruded from under the dining-room table. "I have a feeling Sonny may call," she whispered. I told Preston I had to hang up, and crawled out from beneath the table. "I have a feeling that they're getting to the point," my mother said. "Your sister's nervous."

I put the phone back on the telephone table. "But, Mother—" I said, and the phone rang.

"Sh-h-h," she said.

The phone rang three times. My sister, on the extension upstairs, said, "Hello. . . . Oh, Sonny. . . ."

My mother looked at me and smiled. Then she pulled at my sleeve until I bent my head down, and she whispered in my ear, "They'll be so happy. . . ." She went into the hall, to the foot of the stairs. "Tell him he can come over," she whispered passionately.

"Sure," my sister was saying on the phone. "I'd like that. . . . If you want. . . . Sure. . . ."

My mother went on listening, her head tilted to one side, the light falling on her aging face, and then she began to pantomime the answers my sister ought to be making—sweet yesses, dignified noes, and little bursts of alluring laughter.

I plunged down the hall and out the screen door. The street lamps were on, and there was a moon. I could hear the children: "I see Digger. One-two-three, you're caught, Digger. . . ." Two blocks away, the clock on the Presbyterian church was striking the hour. Just then a little girl left her hiding place in our hedge and ran shrieking for the tree trunk that was home-free base: "I'm home safe! I'm home safe! Everybody free!" All the prisoners, who had been sitting disconsolately on the bumpers of Mr. Karmgut's Oldsmobile, jumped up with joyful cries and scattered abruptly in the darkness.

I lifted my face—that exasperating factor, my face—and stared entranced at the night, at the waving tops of the trees, and the branches blowing back and forth, and the round moon embedded in the night sky, turning the nearby streamers of cloud into mother-of-pearl. It was all very rare and eternal-seeming. What a dreadful unhappiness I felt.

I walked along the curb, balancing with my arms

outspread. Leaves hung over the sidewalk. The air was filled with their rustling, and they caught the light of the street lamps. I looked into the lighted houses. There was Mrs. Kearns, tucked girlishly into a corner of the living-room couch, reading a book. Next door, through the leaves of a tall plant, I saw the Lewises all standing in the middle of the floor. When I reached the corner, I put one arm around the post that held the street sign, and leaned there, above the sewer grating, where my friends and I had lost perhaps a hundred tennis balls, over the years. In numberless dusks, we had abandoned our games of catch and handball and gathered around the grating and stared into it at our ball, floating down in the darkness.

The Cullens' porch light was on, in the next block, and I saw Mr. and Mrs. Cullen getting into their car. Eleanor Cullen was in my class at school, and she had been dating Joel. Her parents were going out, and that meant she'd be home alone —if she was home. She might have gone to the library, I thought as the car started up; or to a sorority meeting. While I stood there looking at the Cullens' house, the porch light went off. A minute later, out of breath from running, I stood on the dark porch and rang the doorbell. There was no light on in the front hall, but the front door was open, and I could hear someone coming. It was Eleanor. "Who is it?" she asked.

"Me," I said. "Are you busy? Would you like to come out for a little while and talk?"

She drifted closer to the screen door and pressed her nose against it. She looked pale without make-up.

"Sure," she said. "I'll have to go put my shoes on. I'm not in a good mood or anything."

"That's all right," I said. "Neither am I. I just want to talk to somebody."

While I waited for Eleanor to come out, Mattie Seaton appeared, striding along the sidewalk. He was on the track team. "Hey, Mattie," I called out to him.

"Hi," he said.

"What's new?"

"Nothing much," he said. "You got your trig done?"

"No, not yet."

"You going with *her*?" he asked, pointing to the house.

"Naw," I said.

"Well, I got to get my homework done," he said.

"See you later," I called after him. I knew where he was going: Nancy Ellis's house, two blocks down.

"Who was that?" Eleanor asked. She stepped out on the porch. She had combed her hair and put on lipstick.

"Mattie Seaton," I said.

"He's pinned to Nancy," Eleanor said. "He likes her a lot. . . ." She sat down in a white metal chair. I sat on the porch railing, facing her. She fumbled in her pocket and pulled out a pack of cigarettes. "You want a cigarette?" she asked.

"No. I'm in training."

We looked at each other, and then she looked away, and I looked down at my shoes. I sat there liking her more and more.

"How come you're in a bad mood?" I asked her.

"Me? Oh, I don't know. How did you know I was in a bad mood?"

"You told me." I could barely make out her face and the dull color of her hands in the darkness.

"You know, I think I'm not basically a happy person," Eleanor said suddenly. "I always thought I was. . . . People expect you to be, especially if you're a girl."

"It doesn't surprise *me*," I said.

A breeze set all the leaves in motion again. "It's going to rain," I said.

Eleanor stood up, smoothing her yellow skirt, and threw her cigarette off the porch; the glowing tip landed on the grass. She realized I was staring at her. She lifted her hand and pressed it against her hair. "You may have noticed I look unusually plain tonight," she said. She leaned over the porch railing beside me, supporting herself on her hands.

"I was trying to do my geometry," she said in a low voice. "I couldn't do it. I felt stupid," she said. "So I cried. That's why I look so awful."

"I think you look all right," I said. "I think you look fine." I leaned forward and laid my cheek on her shoulder. Then I sat up quickly, flushing. "I don't like to hear you being so dissatisfied with yourself," I mumbled. "You could undermine your self-confidence that way."

Eleanor straightened and faced me, in the moonlight. "You're beautiful," I burst out longingly. "I never noticed before. But you are."

"Wait," Eleanor said. Tears gathered in her eyes. "Don't like me yet. I have to tell you something first. It's about Joel."

"You don't have to tell me," I said. "I know you're going with him. I understand."

"Listen to me!" she said impatiently, stamping her foot. "I'm *not* going with him. He—" She suddenly pressed her hands against her eyes. "Oh, it's awful!" she cried.

A little shudder of interest passed through me. "O.K.," I said. "But I don't care if you don't tell me."

"I want to!" she cried. "I'm just a little embarrassed. I'll be all right in a minute—

"We went out Sunday night . . ." she began after a few seconds. They had gone to Medart's, in Clayton, for a hamburger. Joel had talked her into drinking a bottle of beer, and it had made her so drowsy that she had put her head on the back of the seat and closed her eyes. "What kind of car does Joel have?" I asked.

"A Buick," Eleanor said, surprised at my question.

"I see," I said. I pictured the dashboard of a Buick, and Joel's handsome face, and then, daringly, I added Eleanor's hand, with its bitten fingernails, holding Joel's hand. I was only half listening, because I felt the preliminary stirrings of an envy so deep it would make me miserable for weeks. I looked up at the sky over my shoulder; clouds had blotted out the moon, and everything had got darker. From the next block, in the sudden stillness, I heard the children shouting, uttering their Babylonian cries as they played kick-the-can. Their voices were growing tired and fretful.

"And then I felt his hand on my—" Eleanor, half-drowned in shadow was showing me, on her breast, where Joel had touched her.

"Is that all?" I said, suddenly smiling. Now I would not have to die of envy. "That's nothing!"

"I—I slapped his face!" She exclaimed. Her lip trembled. "Oh, I didn't mean—I sort of wanted —Oh, it's all so terrible!" she burst out. She ran down the front steps and onto the lawn, and leaned against the trunk of an oak tree. I followed her. The pre-storm stillness filled the sky, the air be-

tween the trees, the dark spaces among the shrub-
bery. "Oh, God!" Eleanor cried. "How I hate
everything!"

My heart was pounding, and I didn't know why.
I hadn't known I could feel like this—that I could
pause on the edge of such feeling, which lay
stretched like an enormous meadow all in shadow
inside me. It seemed to me a miracle that human
beings could be so elaborate. "Listen, Eleanor," I
said, "you're all right! I've *always* liked you." I
swallowed and moved closer to her; there were two
moist streaks running down her face. I raised my
arm and, with the sleeve of my shirt, I wiped away
her tears. "I think you're wonderful! I think you're
really something!"

"You look down on me," she said. "I know you
do. I can tell."

"How can I, Eleanor. How *can* I?" I cried. "I'm
nobody. I've been damaged by my heredity."

"You, too!" she exclaimed happily. "Oh, that's
what's wrong with me!"

A sudden hiss swept through the air and then
the first raindrops struck the street. "Quick!"
Eleanor cried, and we ran up on her porch. Two
bursts of lightning lit up the dark sky, and the
rain streamed down. I held Eleanor's hand, and
we stood watching the rain. "It's a real thunder-
shower," she said.

"Do you feel bad because we only started being

friends tonight? I mean, do you feel you're on the rebound and settling on the second-best?" I asked. There was a long silence and all around it was the sound of the rain.

"I don't think so," Eleanor said at last. "How about you?"

I raised my eyebrows and said, "Oh, no, it doesn't bother me at all."

"That's good," she said.

We were standing very close to one another. We talked industriously. "I don't like geometry," Eleanor said. "I don't see what use it is. It's supposed to train your mind, but I don't believe it. . . ."

I took my glasses off. "Eleanor—" I said. I kissed her, passionately, and then I turned away, pounding my fists on top of each other. "Excuse me," I whispered hoarsely. That kiss had lasted a long time, and I thought I would die.

Eleanor was watching the long, slanting lines of rain falling just outside the porch, gray in the darkness; she was breathing very rapidly. "You know what?" she said. "I could make you scrambled eggs. I'm a good cook." I leaned my head against the brick wall of the house and said I'd like some.

In the kitchen, she put on an apron and bustled about, rattling pans and silverware, and talking in spurts. "I think a girl should know how to cook,

don't you?" She let me break the eggs into a bowl
—three eggs, which I cracked with a flourish. "Oh,
you're good at it," she said, and began to beat
them with a fork while I sat on the kitchen table
and watched her. "Did you know most eggs *aren't*
baby chickens?" she asked me. She passed so close
to me on her way to the stove that, because her
cheeks were flushed and her eyes bright, I couldn't
help leaning forward and kissing her. She turned
pink and hurried to the stove. I sat on the kitchen
table, swinging my legs and smiling to myself. Suddenly we heard a noise just outside the back door.
I leaped off the table and took up a polite position
by the sink. Eleanor froze. But no one opened the
door; no one appeared.

"Maybe it was a branch falling," I said.

Eleanor nodded. Then she made a face and
looked down at her hands. "I don't know why we
got so nervous. We aren't doing anything wrong."

"It's the way they look at you," I said.

"Yes, that's it," she said. "You know, I think
my parents are ashamed of me. But someday I'll
show them. I'll do something wonderful, and
they'll be amazed." She went back to the stove.

"When are your parents coming home?" I asked.

"They went to a double feature. They can't possibly be out before eleven."

"They might walk out on it," I said.

"Oh no!" Eleanor said. "Not if they pay for
it . . ."

We ate our scrambled eggs and washed the dishes, and watched the rain from the dining-room windows without turning the light on. We kissed for a while, and then we both grew restless and uncomfortable. Her lips were swollen, and she went into the kitchen, and I heard her running the water; when she returned, her hair was combed and she had put on fresh lipstick. "I don't like being in the house," she said, and led me out on the porch. We stood with our arms around each other. The rain was slackening. "Goodbye, rain," Eleanor said sadly. It was as if we were watching a curtain slowly being lifted from around the house. The trees gleamed wetly near the street lamps.

When I started home, the rain had stopped. Water dripped on the leaves of the trees. Little plumes of mist hung over the wet macadam of the street. I walked very gently in order not to disturb anything.

I didn't want to run into anybody, and so I went home the back way, through the alley. At the entrance to the alley there was a tall cast-iron pseudo-Victorian lamppost, with an urn-shaped head and panes of frosted glass; the milky light it shed trickled part way down the alley, illuminating a few curiously still garage fronts and, here and there, the wet leaves of the buses and vines that

bordered the back yards and spilled in such profusion over the fences, hiding the ashpits and
making the alley so pretty a place in spring. When
I was younger, I had climbed on those ashpits,
those brick squares nearly smothered under the
intricacies of growing things, and I had searched
in the debris for old, broken mirrors, discarded
scarves with fringes, bits of torn decorated wrap-
ping paper, and such treasures. But now I drifted
down the alley, walking absently on the wet as-
phalt. I was having a sort of daydream where I
was lying with my head on Eleanor's shoulder—
which was bare—and I could hear the slow, even
sound of her breathing as I began to fall asleep.
I was now in the darkest part of the alley, the very
center where no light reached, and in my daydream I turned over and kissed Eleanor's hands,
her throat—and then I broke into a sprint down
the alley, slipping and sliding on the puddles and
wet places. I came out the other end of the alley
and stood underneath the lamppost. I was breathing with difficulty.

Across the street from me, two women stood,
one on the sidewalk, the other on the front steps of
a house, hugging her arms. "It's not a bad pain,"
the woman on the sidewalk said, "but it persists."

"My dear, my dear," said the other. "Don't take
any chances—not at our age . . ."

And a couple, a boy and a girl, were walking

up the street, coming home from the Tivoli Theatre. The girl was slouching in order not to seem taller than the boy, who was very short and who sprang up and down on the balls of his feet as he walked.

I picked a spray of lilac and smelled it, but then I didn't know what to do with it—I didn't want to throw it away—and finally I put it in my pants pocket.

I vaulted our back fence and landed in our back yard, frightening a cat, who leaped out of the hedge and ran in zigzags across the dark lawn. It startled me so much I felt weak. I tucked my shirt in carefully and smoothed my hair. Suddenly, I looked down at my fingertips; they were blurred in the darkness and moist from the lilac, and I swept them to my mouth and kissed them.

The kitchen was dark. There was no sound in the house, no sound at all, and a tremor passed through me. I turned the kitchen light on and hurriedly examined myself for marks of what had happened to me. I peered at my shirt, my pants. I rubbed my face with both hands. Then I turned the light off and slipped into the dining room, which was dark, too, and so was the hallway. The porch light was on. I ran up the front stairs and stopped short at the top; there was a light on in my mother's room. She was sitting up in bed, with pillows at her back, a magazine across her lap, and a pad of paper on the magazine.

"Hello," I said.

I expected her to bawl me out for being late, but she just looked at me solemnly for a moment, and then she said, "Sonny proposed to your sister."

Because I hadn't had a chance to wash my face, I raised one hand and held it over my cheek and chin, to hide whatever traces of lipstick there might be.

She said, "They're going to be married in June. They went over to the Brusters' to get the ring. He proposed practically the first thing when he came. They were both so—they were *both* so *happy!*" she said. "They make such a lovely couple. . . . Oh, if you could have seen them."

She was in a very emotional state.

I started to back out the door.

"Where are you going?" my mother asked.

"To bed," I said, surprised. "I'm in training—"

"Oh, you ought to wait up for your sister."

"I'll leave her a note," I said.

I went to my room and took the white lilac out of my pocket and put it on my desk. I wrote, "I heard the news and think it's swell. Congratulations. Wake me up when you come in." I stuck the note in the mirror of her dressing table. Then I went back to my room and got undressed. Usually

I slept raw, but I decided I'd better wear pajamas if my sister was going to come in and wake me up. I don't know how much later it was that I heard a noise and sat bolt upright in bed. I had been asleep. My sister was standing in the door of my room. She was wearing a blue dress that had little white buttons all the way down the front and she had white gloves on. "Are you awake?" she whispered.

"Yes," I said. "Where's Mother?"

"Downstairs," my sister said, coming into the room. "Sending telegrams. Do you want to see my ring?" She took her gloves off.

I turned the bedside-table lamp on, and she held her hand out. The ring was gold, and there was an emerald and four diamonds around it.

"It was his grandmother's," my sister said. I nodded. "It's not what I—" she said, and sat down on the edge of the bed, and forgot to finish her sentence. "Tell me," she said, "do you think he's really rich?" Then she turned a sad gaze on me, through her lashes. "Do you want to know something awful? I don't like my ring. . . ."

"Are you unhappy?" I asked.

"No, just upset. It's scary getting married. You have no idea. I kept getting chills all evening. I may get pneumonia. Do you have a cigarette?"

I said I'd get her one downstairs.

"No, there's some in my room," she said. "I'll

get them. You know, Sonny and I talked about you. We're going to send you to college and everything. We planned it all out tonight." She played with her gloves for a while, and then she said, looking at the toes of her shoes, "I'm scared. What if Sonny's not good at business?" She turned to me. "You know what I mean? He's so young. . . ."

"You don't have to marry him," I said. "After all, you're—"

"You don't understand," my sister said hurriedly, warding off advice she didn't want. "You're too young yet." She laughed. "You know what he said to me?"

Just then, my mother called out from the bottom of the stairs, "Listen, how does this sound to you? 'Dear Greta—' It's a night letter, and we get a lot of words, and I thought Greta would like it better if I started that way. Greta's so touchy, you know. Can you hear me?"

"I have to go," my sister whispered. She looked at me, and then suddenly she leaned over and kissed me on the forehead. "Go to sleep," she said. "Have nice dreams." She got up and went out into the hall.

" '—Dodie got engaged tonight,' " my mother read. "Is 'got engaged' the right way to say it?"

"Became engaged," my sister said, in a distant voice.

I put on my bathrobe and slippers and went out into the hall. My sister was leaning over the banister, talking to my mother at the bottom of the stairs about the night letter. I slipped past her and down the back stairs and into the kitchen. I found a cold chicken in the icebox, put the platter on the kitchen table, and tore off a leg and began to eat.

The door to the back stairs swung open, and my sister appeared. "I'm hungry, too," she said. "I don't know why." She drifted over to the table, and bent over the chicken. "I guess emotion makes people hungry."

My mother pushed open the swinging door, from the dining-room side. "There you are," she said. She looked flustered. "I'll have to think some more, and then I'll write the whole thing over," she said to my sister. To me she said, "Are you *eating* at this time of night?"

My sister said that she was hungry, too.

"There's some soup," my mother said. "Why don't I heat it up." And suddenly her eyes filled with tears, and all at once we fell to kissing one another—to embracing and smiling and making cheerful predictions about one another—there in the white, brightly lighted kitchen. We had known each other for so long, and there were so many things that we all three remembered. . . . Our smiles, our approving glances, wandered from face to face. There was a feeling of politeness in the air. We were behaving the way we would in railway stations, at my sister's wedding, at the birth of her first child, at my graduation from college. This was the first of our reunions.

THE QUARREL

I CAME to Harvard from St. Louis in the fall of 1948. I had a scholarship and a widowed mother and a reputation for being a good, hard-working boy. What my scholarship didn't cover, I earned working Wednesday nights and Saturdays, and I strenuously avoided using any of my mother's small but adequate income. During the summer between my freshman and sophomore years, my grandmother died and willed me five thousand dollars. I quit my part-time job and bought a gray flannel suit and a pair of white buck shoes, and I got on the editorial board of the college literary magazine. I met Duncan Leggert at the first editorial meeting I attended. He had been an editor for a full year, and this particular night he was infuriated by a story, which everyone wanted to print, about an unhappy, sensitive child. "Why shouldn't that child be unhappy?" Duncan shouted. "He's a bore." The story was accepted, and Duncan stalked out of the meeting.

Two nights later, as I was walking along Massachusetts Avenue in the early dusk, I saw Duncan peering into the window of a record store at a display of opera albums. He was whistling "Piangi, piangi," from "La Traviata," and he looked, as usual, wan, handsome, and unapproachable. I stood beside him until he looked up, and then I told him I thought he'd been right about the story.

"Of course I was right," he said, looking down at me from his patient, expectant eyes. "Those people confuse being sordid with being talented."

We went to a tavern and sat in a booth that was illuminated by one of those glowing juke-box things in which you deposit a nickel and push a button, and the Wurlitzer, a mile away, plays the tune. At first, I was nearly asphyxiated with shyness, but I asked Duncan what he was planning to be when he graduated (substituting "graduated" for "grown up" at the last minute), and he said "Nothing." I looked blank, and he took his cigarette and stared at the glowing coal for a moment and then said quietly, with a good deal of sadness in his voice, "I'm rich." Then he raised his head, looked me in the eye—he was half smiling—and added, "Filthy rich." I was utterly charmed. I asked him how rich. He said, airily, "Oh, a couple million if the market holds." The idea of talking to someone that rich pleased me so much I burst into idiotic laughter. He asked me why I was laughing, but I didn't tell him.

We talked warily at first, as men—or, rather, as boys imitating men—will; but then, impelled by the momentum of some deep and inexplicable sympathy, we went on talking until one o'clock. Duncan said the college literary magazine was a mere journal of self-pity, and those parts of it that weren't amateurish were grubby. He firmly believed, he said, that most unhappiness was a pose. "It's a way of getting out of being interesting."

Even at his most arrogant, Duncan always had a note of despair in his voice. "People get what they deserve," he said. "Why should I believe in tragedy? I've never seen any. Stories ought to have happy endings; people ought to be more interesting; everyone ought to have better taste.

"The important thing," he said as he slouched in his corner of the booth and sketched faces in the sugar he had poured on the table, "is to have quality. No one cares if your mother loved you or not if you're dull. And most people are dull," he added sadly.

"This is a democracy," he said later. "I'm supposed to consider everyone my equal. Well, I don't. Dull people give me a pain. I think Whitman is a lousy poet and Willa Cather is feeble-minded, and old Huckleberry Twain gives me the creeps. What's more, if there's anything I can't stand, it's a lot of pointless good nature." I quenched my smile.

It seemed to me he was saying everything I had always thought and never expressed.

From that first night, we were friends. I suppose any friendship must have a core of mutual need. I was tired of what I had been. I was full of Midwestern optimism about my ability to change. From that very first night, I fully intended to live my life in line with the doctrine Duncan was expounding. But it wasn't his ideas that I admired and wanted. What I wanted was his Eastern Shore of Maryland manner, and his honesty, and his faith that what he thought was important. And I wanted to look like him. He was very tall. He had a wan, smooth face, elongated and arrogant. He walked with a slouch and often sat for hours among people without saying a word, sometimes without an expression crossing his handsome countenance. But then he might suddenly begin to talk, especially if there was a discussion going on, and he would talk overexcitedly, gesticulate, occasionally not even making sense, and then later he would be inconsolable because he thought he had made a fool of himself. I thought he was charming at those moments. What did dismay me was the way he had of being rendered speechless by a color, or a pretty woman's gesture of welcome, or an automobile, or the way a girl's hair blew. He would stand, quite tense and excited, held by a kind of surprised rapture. When he had these quiet transports, I was embarrassed—for myself, because I was unable to share a friend's emotion. But as I knew Duncan longer, the beauty that seemed to electrify him touched me, too. Duncan was always showing me shapes in the clouds.

Everything he said explained me to myself or else put a weapon in my hand, and his bitterness struck me like a surge of sunlight, bringing crispness and definition, drenched as I was in the foggy optimism of my home. I was discarding my traditions as fast as I could, but it was difficult work; I had first to locate the roots and then to get them up. And Duncan's disillusion—any disillusion, in fact—was infinitely helpful. I did my best to speak as Duncan did, with frequent, entrancing pauses, and with small curlicues of contempt.

Yet if Duncan felt it was a moment for kindness, his entire soul and bank account, his car, his wardrobe, his time were yours. I used to worry about people taking advantage of him; but although he had a terrible memory for telephone numbers and people's names, he never forgot how much he spent, where, and with whom.

Girls fell in love with him often. They seemed to find his mixture of melancholy and arrogance irresistible. At first, Duncan would be overwhelmingly chivalrous to them, light their cigarettes, take them out when they asked him. But sooner or later he would begin to feel cornered; he'd cease lighting cigarettes; he'd stop answering the telephone.

The number of people we saw that year steadily dwindled as we decided they were doomed to be ordinary or as they disagreed with us; and they were struck from our list of acquaintances. He and I both believed that if we were careful and did the right thing, we could escape turning out as our elders had. "They give you advice," Duncan pointed out, "and never stop to think of what you think of what they turned out to be." We thought if you travelled far enough and long enough, you would come to a place where everyone liked the things you liked and talked the way you talked, where everyone knew your value without your having to get undignified and nervous in proving it. In this place that we were looking for, you would never have to boast or to make conversation out of pity for an ugly girl or to feel sorry for your parents. One January night when Duncan and I were walking along the Charles—it was cold and foggy—we swore never to hide the truth from each other, always to admit our faults, to admire each other's virtues, to become men of stature, true stature, and to go to Europe together that summer for a year, leaving college, no matter what our parents said or did about it. We would take bicycles and be frugal and healthy, and we would deepen our culture and our refinement.

My mother objected violently when I told her I was going to Europe with Duncan. She said I

was wasting my inheritance and going to the bad
out of sheer obstinacy, and that it was all Duncan's
bad example. Duncan said that, of course, she was
right. I got drunk and told Duncan that my mother
could go to hell, and he watched me, as I recall,
with eyes glassy with admiration. How could my
mother compete with Duncan? All I wanted, that
year, was to be like him.

We sailed from Halifax in June, on the Aqui-
tania, for Southampton. Almost as soon as the
green hills around Halifax receded and the ship
was in open water, Duncan said to me, "I think
you ought to write your mother a good letter. You
were quite unpleasant to her over the phone.
That's one of your faults," he added, and he
grimaced to show that he didn't like to talk this
way but that he had to, in accordance with our
vow. "You have so little tact. On the other hand,
you're much more dynamic than I am. I wish I
were more like you."

"But you're not," I said, candid at any cost.
"You mustn't worry about it," I went on quickly,
"because I like you very much the way you are
now . . ."

We were free from college and observation; we
were molding each other, protecting each other
from being ordinary. Duncan put his hand on my

shoulder briefly and smiled, and then we paced each other around the deck of the ship to get our exercise in before dinner. The statured figure had to be physically attractive, too.

We stayed in England just long enough to see the Tower of London, the National Gallery, and Scott's, and to decide the food was inedible, and then we took the channel steamer from Newhaven. Standing at the rail, we saw the shores of France rise from the waves, green and promising.

When we landed in Dieppe, my delight—let me say that my delight rose like a flock of startled birds. Everything I saw or heard—the whole pastel city, the buildings as serene and placid as the green water of the harbor—touched off another flutter of the white wings. At one wharf, a group of fishing boats huddled in a confusion of masts, the hulls green and black and purple, arched like slices of melon. Along the waterfront was a row of buildings, with here and there a gap and a pile of rubble or a portion of a wall. But these were the colors of the buildings: pale green and mauve, light yellow like wispy sunlight, faded pink, gentle bluish gray. And then, perched on a hillside, the immemorial hulk of a castle.

Duncan's gaze moved lovingly around the scene. "Every town should have a castle," he said.

Our hotel room was old, with a sloping floor and a single, huge brass bed. There were no rugs on the wooden floor and no curtains on the high

French windows, which wouldn't quite close, because of their crooked frames. Outside our window,
three streets converged and formed a triangular
island, planted with plane trees and patterned
beds of yellow flowers. Workmen in gray clothes
and thick boots were sitting on stone benches and
drinking wine. The fronts of the houses along the
street were decorated with heavy lintels and occasionally with stringy caryatids, at once frivolous
and orderly. In the distance an elegant spire rose,
and the sound of bells floated down to us. We
washed our faces and brushed our teeth and
changed our clothes, singing the entire time—and
then, since we were in France, we set out to find
some women.

First, we walked along the beach and saw the
collection of Grand and Univers and Windsor
hotels; they were shattered, and workmen scurried
in and out of their rubbled interiors carrying
bricks. Other workmen were fitting dumpy concrete columns into the balustrade that ran along
the street, separating it from the rocky beach; as
the workmen finished one section, another crew
of workmen, with large pneumatic machines, came
along and drilled holes in the columns, chipped
the edges, and scarred the fluting. Duncan and I
stared, fascinated, and then realized that they were
making the balustrade look old. Within a few
years, people would forget that the balustrade had
been repaired after the war; they would see it

ancient-looking and indestructible and a tie to an earlier time.

Duncan and I picked our way over the upper beach, which was mostly rock, and down to the narrow ridge of sand that bordered the ocean. The beach was almost empty, but a few groups of people sat or lay on blankets. The people seemed strangely solid and fleshy. The only sound was that of the pneumatic machines busily restoring time.

The channel was gray and empty of ships; it was rather like a border of sky in a faded tapestry. Duncan said that as soon as we shipped our trunk to Paris we ought to set out on our bicycles to see Mont-Saint-Michel. "It's quite a small island," he said. "They've been working on it for a long time. It must be quite perfect by now."

On our way back to the hotel, we passed many women. Only one girl was pretty, and she was running, with her thin print dress whipping around her muscular figure and her arms pumping, and nothing short of a pistol shot would have stopped her.

In a moment of self-assertion, I said I had no particular interest in Mont-Saint-Michel and it was out of the way, to boot; I didn't want Duncan to know I was his follower. To my surprise, he gave in, and the next morning, on our bicycles, we set off for Paris. We each had two knapsacks and a sleeping bag. We rode through Arques-la-Bataille and Neufchatel, through Forges-les-Eaux and Gournay-en-Bray. The countryside was green, and we passed the dried-lavender granite spires of old, weather-beaten churches. Duncan told hideously funny, embarrassing stories about himself as a child. One he told me as we swam in a small pond near the road. I laughed so loud a farmer with a seamed face and huge dusty hands came to see who we were.

At Pontoise, we sat on a terrace above the Oise and watched the rockets of Bastille Day in the night sky over Paris. The day we entered Paris, we spent hours bicycling through endless suburbs, and then at noon, at last, we burst into the Place de la Concorde, with the fountains playing and the gardens of the Tuileries in bloom. And one morning we wakened in a wheat field, surrounded by pale stalks of spiked wheat, and saw on the horizon, shadowy and dim, the spires of Chartres. And at Beaugency we spent a whole day idling on a sandbar in the Loire with a family of seven girls, all of them blond, all of them charming, all of them in love with Duncan. ("You will write to us, yes?")

I don't know exactly when we each decided that the other wasn't worthy of this paradise. What I do remember is that it became increasingly difficult to decide which hotel we would stay at, which restaurant we would eat in, which road we would take.

The moments multiplied when one of us would draw his breath and turn away, confront the scenery and remark, "Well, whatever you want . . ." Against the sound of strained politeness in the background, I remember the sunset at Blois flooding crimson through the sky, and the long allées at Chambord; in such a manner I remember two swallows skimming low over the Loire, chirruping and beating their bent pointed wings. I remember Duncan's voice at Chenonceaux—the sky was filled with domed white clouds—saying "I don't care really. . . . I suppose we ought . . ." and his voice quivered with resentment.

We had decided to see the west of France— mostly it was my idea—because there would be fewer Americans there. But actually I had another reason. So far as I knew, it was barren of difficult places like Chartres. At Chartres, I'd had all the wrong reactions. Who would have known that the thing to do with the cathedral was to go into a pâtisserie and buy a bag full of chocolate éclairs and cherry tarts and then sit down on the grass plot in front of the entrance and stare at the towers while eating oneself into a chocolate coma? Duncan didn't like it when I said the cathedral was beautiful; you were supposed to feel these things so deeply you couldn't express yourself, and wouldn't even *want* to express yourself.

Duncan enjoyed Pernod. It made me sick. Duncan hated talking to people. I talked to everyone. My French vocabulary was better than Duncan's. His pronunciation was better than mine. I became terribly adept at not irritating Duncan before breakfast. I couldn't see that he appreciated any of this, or that he responded with any similar awareness. For the fiftieth time, I thought him unfair. The moment came when I could no longer stand the sound of his voice, or his ideas. After travelling with him day and night, without a break, for fifty-three days, I felt my senses suffocating in an awareness of Duncan.

We rode through the flat Vendéen landscape, with its bright-yellow marsh grasses and wheat and green meadows, its white farmhouses, and its tiny drawbridges over canals and streams—two college boys, sun-tanned and healthy, in T-shirts and shorts, so angry with each other that we rode our bicycles ten or fifteen feet apart. When an infrequent car passed us, I would wonder if Duncan would see it in time, but he always did.

There was a moist, sticky quality in the air. The villages were far apart, and when we came to one, the houses were shuttered and unfriendly. The French were barricaded in their cool, high-ceilinged rooms, cutting into ripe pears with tiny pearl-handled knives, while we bicycled the hot and dusty streets, only to emerge, on the other side of the gray church and white stucco café, back in the flat open country.

The heat was unbearable. At Luçon, we turned off the main road and headed toward the sea again, to a village on the map called La Tranche, which turned out to be three or four buildings along the highway. Just beyond La Tranche, our road climbed to the top of a ridge, and we saw that the flat, grassy countryside humped into the ridge we were on and then flowed into the Bay of Biscay, with no beach, or wall of rocks. The grass of the meadows, green and glowing, waved in the salt sea breezes and melted into the water. One could see the grass continuing underwater out of sight, probably to the rim of the low tide. Cows squooshed through their pasture; around their hoofs bubbles clung like necklaces. French boys and girls, their bicycles lying in the grass, swam over the submerged meadow. A few yards offshore, fishing boats with blue and yellow painted hulls swung to and fro at their moorings.

I stopped and called to Duncan, who continued a few yards and then stopped. I walked toward him, wheeling my bicycle. "It's really lovely, isn't it—" I began.

Duncan turned to me, and in a voice shaking with fury he said, "Do you always have to say something? Do you feel it's like dropping a coin in the box at church?"

We rode the rest of the day in silence. At sunset, we stopped in La Rochelle, where the old Huguenot fortifications still surround the tiny harbor, and we found a room in a strange old hotel near the railroad station. Our bedroom had two huge brass beds with swollen mattresses, which rustled whenever we moved. The back of the building contained a stable. The smell of horses permeated our room, and there was a vast rose trellis outside our window. The roses were blooming. All night long, we drifted on the ebb and flow of the oddly complementary odors; and every hour or so we could hear a train arriving or departing.

The next day, we bicycled on to Bordeaux. By midafternoon, we were racing, with neither slowing down or asking to rest. We reached Bordeaux at seven in the evening, and we went at once to a café and ordered a bottle of wine and began to quarrel. Several times, the waiter, a fat, black-browed Basque, came running on his toes, one pink round finger to his lips, and we nodded and said, "*Pardon, pardon*," and lowered our voices.

It seemed that Duncan could not stand the way I whistled when I shaved, the way I talked to waiters, the fact that even when I felt bad I smiled. "Is it something the corn belt does to the disposition?" he asked.

I told Duncan, at the top of my lungs, that he was childish, an arty son of a bitch, and a snob.

"You're ill-bred," he said. "You're yelling in a café."

He said that he'd always thought of me as an intelligent vulgarian but he'd had no idea how really ill-bred I was.

"All right," I said, rising to my feet. "That's it! That's *it*! Let's fight."

Solemnly we walked out of the café. The waiter ran after us and waved his bill in our faces. We had to figure out the bill and pay it; as usual, we were overcharged. I hadn't realized until that minute how dear Duncan was to me or how much he'd taught me. It also occurred to me that Duncan outweighed me by fifteen pounds.

We walked along, wheeling our bicycles. "All my friends have turned out to be no good," Duncan said bitterly, at one point. And then later he said, under his breath, "Once, I wanted to be like you—" I thought he was lying just to make me feel worse.

We came to a deserted street lined with warehouses. Duncan leaned his bicycle against a wall. I threw mine to the pavement. We faced each other and advanced. "I'm so angry that I'm going to try to hit your face," Duncan said.

We traded five or six blows, and then our eyes met. Shamefacedly, we backed away, and our hands dropped. Duncan sat down on the curb and pulled out his cigarettes and offered me one.

"You hurt my feelings," I said.

"I meant to."

"You meant what you said?"

"Of course," he said. "Didn't you?"

"Of course."

We agreed that we would have to separate.

"Where will I meet you in Biarritz?" Duncan asked; we had shipped our clothes there, in a trunk.

"At the railroad station," I said.

"When?"

I got out my map and tried to figure how long it would take us. "The hell with it," I said, finally. "It's too hard to figure out. We'll bicycle there together."

"Oh!" Duncan was disappointed. "Well, whatever you say. . . ."

We rose from the curb and got our bicycles.

"Your knapsack is loose," Duncan said politely.

"Thank you," I said.

We were much too depressed to find our way by our Michelins, and Bourdeaux, like Paris, is afflicted with endless suburbs. At one o'clock in the morning, we were still hopelessly lost, and we were worn out with the strain of our emotional predicament. Finally, after giving up hope that we might find an open field to sleep in, we settled in the graveyard of a church, next to a flowering hedge and beneath a small apple tree. We spread our sleeping bags and lay down. In a few moments, we began to itch. I suppose we were lying on an anthill. At any rate, in no time at all our sleeping bags were swarming with insect life. We talked about getting up and moving on, but the thought of bicycling was too much for us both. We lay inert, now and then scratching ourselves, immersed in the odor of the flowers, the silence of the grave-yard, the buzz of insects. Above us loomed the church. Out on the street, an occasional truck would lumber by, but they were diesel mostly, and diesels rumble with a pleasant noise.

Finally, Duncan began to talk. He said that now, since we were going to part, he could tell me that he hadn't meant anything at the meeting of the literary magazine. He had been ashamed of never saying anything at the meetings; he'd thought up a line of argument and his little witticism, and he'd planned to use it no matter what might be under discussion. He'd been very pleased when I agreed with him, but he had found it a little stifling trying to live up to my admiration. "I find it difficult to think," he told me. Anyway, he'd always thought his snobbery was something psychological, which he would have cured in time, and it upset him to have me always taking it so seriously and turning it into a doctrine. Much of what he said, he told me, he said just to be saying something. "You can't be silent all the time." It bothered him, he said, that I hadn't seen through him. It convinced

him that I was a fool. He felt both guilty and superior. He was sorry if he'd misled me, but actually he
had wanted to come to Europe mostly to get away
from schoolwork, which bored him. He was sorry
that we had come to hate each other so much, but
he guessed it was inevitable, because he was so
worthless a person.

A truck rumbled by on the cobble-stones, back-
firing strenuously. Through the filigree of tree
branches above me I could see the stars.

I told him I forgave him. He said he was grateful, and he added that he was sorry if he'd hurt
my feelings. He was sure my habit of talking in
front of a piece of scenery or a national monument
would undoubtedly please most of the people I'd
have to deal with in my life.

I called him a bastard, under my breath.

We wound up confessing that we were both
irretrievably dishonest, incapable of a true relationship, faulty as people. Finally, after a long
silence, I spoke up and said we ought to try to
get along, but I couldn't persuade him. Alter-
nately he would berate himself and insult me. It
was amazing, though, how much affection was in
the air, how sad we both felt, how hopeless it all
seemed.

The next morning, we found our way out of the
city by daylight, both of us depressed and silent. I
discovered that there is a kind of embarrassment
that has no boundary. Every hour revealed new

and hitherto unexplored regions. At lunch, in a small café set beneath trees at a crossroads, we drank two bottles of wine, and our constraint broke enough for us to talk—but with difficulty and a great many migrant smiles, and without ever really looking each other in the face.

We clambered onto our bicycles and began to ride, weaving back and forth in our drunkenness. The road was crowded with trucks carrying young Bordelais to the seashore for the weekend. Their faces were fresh and unsuspecting, sharp-nosed, bright-eyed. They leaned from the back of their trucks and clutched at our shirts, so that their trucks would pull us up hills, and they roared with excited laughter when they discovered I was ticklish. When Duncan sang all of "Le Poisson dans l'Eau," which he'd learned from an old Trenet record, the French youths, crammed in their open trucks under the hot August southern sky, applauded, yelling, *"C'est joli, ça!"*

On one long hill, my shirt tore. We had fallen behind, from truck to truck; this was the last truck in the procession. My shirt was almost ripped off my back, the truck grunted up the long hill and disappeared over the crest, and Duncan and I were alone in the middle of a birchwood. I looked at Duncan and was disappointed that I was there with him. The birchwood was lovely. Through the pale and fragile leaves, beams of sunlight fell in all directions. As I wobbled from one side of the road to the other, it seemed the trees leaned toward me, brushed my face with the tips of their branches, and then swung away; or, going downhill, I thought the trees leaned backward like a child's drawing of speed. Around a curve the trees seemed to take off, soar upward at the sky. Suddenly we were in the midst of a horde of yellow butterflies; they filled the air; their wings beat and trembled; they were everywhere. They beat on our foreheads and on our eyelids, tangled in our clothes, died on the wheels of our bicycles. With horror, Duncan stopped his bicycle and then slowly began to thread his way through the yellow cloud. "Try not to touch them," he said. "Their wings won't work if you touch them; they die." I was too drunk even to be able to slow my bicycle. I rode blindly through the butterflies, blinking my eyes, cursing when one lit on the wheel and was crushed. At the very last, a butterfly blundered against my eye, and my eye remained open with abrupt pity; between it and the sky was a yellow film laced with airy veins; the film beat, came apart. I closed my eyes and rode blindly into a tree.

Duncan helped me up, silently. We rode side by side, still drunk, but not as drunk as we had been. Occasionally, our bicycles lurched into each other. Duncan's hand was cut where it had scraped against my handle bars on one of the lurches. My torn shirt flapped in the wind.

At four, we reached Arcachon. It was a small

resort with several public beaches and miles of
tiny villas. We could smell the sea, the stiff, salty
odors from the bay, the wisteria, the pinewoods
on the surrounding hills. We rode through the
village and came to a large red brick villa, square
and Victorian, with a large glass conservatory facing southward, by the sea. Its garden was filled
with gardenia bushes and small lemon trees. We
lifted our bicycles over a low wall, made our way
through some trees, and climbed over another wall
to the white beach.

I sank on the sand, and Duncan, beside me,
muttered, "A resort is a resort is a resort." The
beach curved outward from us to a sandspit, where
there was a picnic party, and southward out of our
vision. Up the beach from us, a few people were
sprawled beneath a pink-and-yellow umbrella. I
said, "Do you want to swim out to the spit and see
if we can join the party?" Duncan looked at me,
frightened. He began to tremble. I turned away.

The waves of the bay were sparkling and blue.
Small sailboats with tinted sails swooped about
in the wide waters. The tide was out, and stranded
on the sand lay, seemingly, hundreds of small craft,
some with masts, some without, some the size of
dinghies, some good-sized, with the rounded,
almost voluptuously shaped hull of shallow-water
craft.

Duncan was so embarrassed that he began to
build a sand castle. I reached into the pouch on

the back of my bicycle and took out a pad of paper and began a letter to my mother.

DEAR MOTHER,

We have just come to Arcachon, a small French town which is a resort and very interesting. Duncan and I are having a wonderful time and learning a good deal which is what I told you would happen and why I wanted to come to Europe. You see, I was right about the trip and—

I threw the pad down and crawled over to Duncan and started to help him build his castle. He still wouldn't look me in the eye. I got on my bicycle and rode into the village and brought back ham sandwiches, two bottles of Evian water, and two bottles of *vin ordinaire*. We had to get through the evening somehow.

The party on the spit packed up their hampers and disappeared. The pink-and-yellow umbrella was folded up and whisked away. We were alone on the beach. Duncan scooped out a place for his shoulders and piled the sand in a mound behind his head, so that he could watch the boats on the water. We drank steadily, pausing only now and then to run into the water and swim a few strokes, through the seaweed that was close to the surface at low tide. We decided that that—the low tide—was the reason the beach was so empty.

"Oh God!" Duncan said suddenly. "This is sheer hell!" In desperation, we began to work on the sand castle. The towers multiplied, the moats and bridges; spires arose, Babylonian ziggurats, Egyptian pyramids, Mayan pyramids, Christian steeples, and Moslem minarets. Our castle became a city. The city began to spread over the beach, foot by foot, more and more grandiose, more and more wistful.

In the cool of the evening, a small blond boy came out of the red brick villa and began to play by himself in the garden. He was wearing a blue sailor blouse and short pants and a tiny pair of sandals.

Duncan was admiring the castle. We were quite drunk again. "It's really a nice castle," he said sadly. "If I had a camera, I'd take a picture. It's worth saving, don't you think?"

I felt that it was a wonderful castle, but I was damned if I knew what to do with it. "We could throw rocks at it," I suggested.

The little boy wandered down the wall and peered at us through the gate; one arm encircled one of the iron bars and the other arm lay over the top. He hung there, occasionally drawing lines with the tip of his sandal in the sand that had blown into the garden. He saw the castle; his eyes grew round. He and Duncan stared at each other. Then the little boy turned away and sat down behind the wall. We could see only a portion of his leg.

"He's bored," Duncan said desperately. "He's unhappy. I can't stand it."

I remember we tiptoed—we must have confused the little boy with the butterflies—to the wall and stuck our heads over it.

"Hi," Duncan said.

"*Bonjour*," the child said.

"I can't remember any French," Duncan said to me. He leaned over the wall anxiously. "*Voulez-vous*—What's the word for play?" he cried, turning to me. I didn't know. I was leaning on the wall for support.

The little boy looked at us; he was polite, unfrightened, and mystified. Finally, Duncan reached down and lifted the child over the wall. The little boy's face went pale. "*Les brigands?*" he asked, in a tiny voice. Duncan didn't hear; he carried the little boy over to the castle-city and placed him in front of it. "Yours," he said grandly. "All yours." The little boy looked at Duncan and then gave him a wan smile. "Go ahead," Duncan said patiently. "Play with the castle. Wreck it if you want. I don't care."

The child's head, cocked to one side, stayed motionless. The small hands grasped each other. Duncan fell to his knees and, with a face suffused with emotion, said, "I don't frighten you, do I? I'm a coward. I can't frighten you. Can I?"

"Comment, Monsieur?" the little boy said. He was quite close to tears.

Duncan gently took the child's hand and patted one of the ziggurats. A few grains of sand crumbled off. Duncan pointed to the little boy, then to the castle. Then, still holding the little boy's hand, he walked him all around the castle. The little boy began to smile. He looked up at Duncan.

"Oui," Duncan said excitedly. "For you. *Votre,"* he shouted in triumph. *"Pour vous, s'il vous plaît,* or whatever."

"Pour moi, Monsieur?"

"Oui," Duncan said. *"Oui."*

"Tout château? Vraiment?" The child clapped his hands.

A little later, just as we were finishing a new super three-way tunnel, just as Duncan was asking me, "He's happy now, isn't he? I haven't hurt his feelings, have I?" we heard a woman's voice. The little boy cried out in reply, and a woman came running—a tall, fair woman, with large, intent, genteel blue eyes. She swept down on the little boy and scooped him up, and when he was safe in her arms, she turned and glared suspiciously at us. We were drunk and unshaven, with bloodshot eyes and dirty clothes. Duncan made a bow of sorts, and explained that we were Americans. The woman exclaimed, and then a smile came over her face. She stepped forward and shook Duncan's hand. *"Enchanté, Monsieur,"* she said brusquely, and then, *"Enchanté,"* as she shook my hand, too. She stood a moment, holding her child, talking to us slowly and kindly, in careful French. She asked us where in America we came from, and nodded at our replies. She asked us if we planned to be in France long, and when we said a year, she nodded her head again and said we were *très sage.* Her voice was both grave and soft, and at first Duncan and I stared at her; Duncan caught himself up, and sent me a dirty glance, and then we both, shyly, stared at the ground. If we needed water, she said, we could come to the back door and get it. She had to cook dinner for the boy's grandparents. Her husband was working late in Bordeaux. She shook hands with us again, and then, still carrying the child, she went back into the garden. She was wearing a light-blue skirt that blew back and forth against the iron bars of the gate as she closed it.

Our wine was gone. The sunset was beginning, its pink splendor reflected in Duncan's bony kneecaps. He sat back on the sand, talking, piling the sand over his legs. "You know what makes their figures so beautiful? Work. They don't use these lousy labor-saving devices. They bend, they walk, they ride bicycles. Did you see how small her waist was? There's no use pretending that American women are as charming."

"That's not true," I said. "France is fine, but—"
All around me the air was perfumed, and the sunset was unraveling its tinted streamers across the sky. "You know. We're seeing it for the first time. I'm sure America—"

Duncan grew quite fierce. He told me I was being stubborn, defensive. Just because I didn't fit. After all, I hadn't even said a word to the woman.

"That's true," I admitted lazily. "But that's because I was so impressed I couldn't speak." I propped myself on my elbow and looked at him. I was smiling—a little uncertainly, it's true, as one does at an elder brother, or at someone inexpressibly dear, whose approval one longs for. Duncan gave me a sidelong glance. Then, several seconds after I'd spoken, we both laughed, as if I'd been quite witty.

The shadows, blue, liquid, were gathering across the beach. There we were, the two of us, with all of our fears and flaws, and our hopes that we didn't really believe in, and our failures; there we were, nineteen and twenty. From one of the houses along the beach came the strains of a phonograph playing "La Vie en Rose." Duncan began to hum the song. The kindness of France spread around us like the incoming night. I listened to Duncan and the distant phonograph and the dreamlike rush of the waves, and I knew I would survive my youth and be forgiven.

SENTIMENTAL
EDUCATION

IT was eight o'clock on a warm September evening, and all the bells of Harvard were striking the hour. Elgin Smith, tired of studying, was standing on the steps of Widener Library—those wide, Roman, inconvenient steps—blinking his eyes and staring into the distance, because that was supposed to refresh the corneas and the retina. He was thinking, but not of his schoolwork. He was thinking of what it would be like to fall in love, to worship a girl and to put his life at her feet. He despised himself, because he feared he was incapable of passion and he believed that only passionate people were worth while and that all other kinds were shallow. He was taking courses in English Literature, in German Literature, in Italian Literature, in History, ancient and medieval, and every one of them was full of incidents that he thought mocked him, since they seemed to say that the meaning of life, the peak of existence, the core of events was one certain emotion, to which he was a stranger, and for which he was very likely too rational. Therefore, he stood on the steps of Widener, so cracked by longing that it seemed only gravity held him together.

He was very tall, six feet three, and gangling. He had a small head, curiously shaped (his roommate, Dimitri, sometimes accused him of looking like a wedge of cheese), and a hooked nose. He wanted to be a professor in the field of comparative philology, and he believed in Beauty. He studied all the time, and there were moments when he was appalled by how hard he worked. He was known for his crying in movies. He was not unathletic.

Somehow, he had become convinced that he was odd and that only odd girls liked him, pitiable girls who couldn't do any better, and this singed his pride.

It was his fate that this particular night he should see a girl walking up the steps of Widener Library. She was of medium height and had black hair cut short; she was wearing a light-colored coat that floated behind her because she was walking so fast, nearly running, but not quite; and the curve of her forehead and the way her eyes were set took Elgin's breath away. She was so pretty and carried herself so well and had a look of such healthy and arrogant self-satisfaction that Elgin sighed and thought here was the sort of not odd girl who could bestow indescribable benefits on any young man she liked—and on his confidence. She was that very kind of girl, that far from unhappy, that world-contented kind, he believed would never fall for him.

She carried her books next to her bosom. Elgin's

eyes followed her up the steps; and then his head turned, his nostrils distended with emotion; and she was gone, vanished into Widener.

"Surely this year," he thought, looking up at the sky. "Now that I'm almost nineteen." He stretched out his arms, and the leaves on the trees, already growing dry at the approach of autumn, rustled in the breezes.

He thought about that girl once or twice in the days that followed, but the longing for her didn't really take root until he saw her again, two weeks later, at a Radcliffe Jolly-Up in Cabot Hall. It was in one of the dimly lit common rooms, where couples were indefatigably dancing in almost total darkness. Elgin was swaying in place (he was not a good dancer) with a girl who helped him on his German when he caught sight of his Widener Library vision. When the next dance began, he wound through the couples looking for her, to cut in on her, but when he drew near her, he turned and walked over to the wall, where he caught his breath and realized he was frightened.

This was the stroke that fatally wounded him. Knowing he was frightened of that girl, he longed for her, the way men who think they are cowards long for war so they can prove they're not. Or perhaps it was some other reason. The girl had a striking appearance; there was her youth and her proud, clean look to recommend her.

But whatever the reason, he did begin to think

about her in earnest. She rose up in clouds of brilliant light in his head whenever he came across certain words in his reading. ("Mistress" was one, "beautiful" another; you can guess the rest.) He did a paper on "The Unpossessable Loved One in Troubadour Poetry." When he walked through the Yard on his way to classes, his eyes revolved nervously and never rested, searching all the faces on all the walks in the hope of seeing her. In fact, on his walks to classes he looked so disordered that a number of his friends asked him if he was feeling ill, and it pleased Elgin, after the first two times this happened, to reply that he was. He was ill with longing.

At night, before going to the dining hall for supper, he would put on his bathrobe and slip down to the pool in the basement of Adams House. There, under the wooden beams, he would swim angrily from one end of the pool to the other, faster and faster, until his arms ached. Then he would take a cold shower.

When he slept, he dreamed of carnage, horses, and speeding automobiles. He went to French movies and ground his knees against the seat in front of him. He laughed at himself, and decided to break this absurd habit he had got into of thinking all the time about this girl he had never met, but he didn't quite succeed. At last, he admitted to himself that he was in love with her;

and one night, sleeping in his lower bunk while
Dimitri breathed heavily over his head, he had
tears in his eyes because he was so foolish and did
desire that girl whom he had seen the two times
mentioned and only twice more besides.

Having resigned himself—in imitation of Dante
—to a state of perpetual longing, he felt calmer
and looked at the world with sad, scholarly eyes.
But his equilibrium was delicate, and in December
Dimitri began having an affair with a Radcliffe
girl named Felicia. Upperclassmen could have
girls in their room in the afternoon if they signed
them in with the campus policeman who sat in a
little room near the main entrance of their house,
and signed them out when they left. There was
always the chance the policeman would come to
the room and check up, but even so on gray December afternoons Dimitri, all bundled up, would
come searching through Widener for Elgin and
ask him not to come home until after six o'clock
because Dimitri was taking Felicia to the room.
Then Elgin would sit in front of his books,
numbed, unable to read, with fine beads of sweat
standing out on his upper lip and forehead.
Once he came back to the room and found
Dimitri lying in front of a fire in the fireplace;
the fire was being fed by Dimitri's lecture notes.

"Oh God, it's you. How I hate your ugly face!"
Dimitri said, but Elgin knew what he meant; at
that moment, being Elgin and not Felicia was a
blasphemy. He tiptoed through the room to hang
up his coat and tiptoed out again.

In January, immediately after exams, Elgin
came down with flu. He was exhausted. When he
was well again, it seemed to him that he had been
washed clean and purified. He hardly thought
about that girl at all.

But one sunny, cold morning in February Elgin
saw her standing in front of Sever Hall. She was
wearing long blue woolen socks, and she was talking
to a pock-marked boy in a raccoon overcoat. Elgin
suddenly turned and went into Sever and waited in
in the hall until the bell rang. The girl came in,
and Elgin followed her upstairs and into a class-
room; he sat three rows in back of her. It was a
course given by Professor Bush on Metaphysical
Poets of the Seventeenth Century. And that afternoon Elgin went and got permission to transfer
from The Victorian Novel to that class.

The girl's name was Caroline Hedges and she
came from Baltimore. She was a horsewoman of
considerable ability. She spent a good deal of her
time on clothes, not ever being quite sure where
true elegance lay. She was inclined to buy pale

colors, blouses one size too large for her, and tweeds. She was easily embarrassed. She read a good deal, her favorite books being "The Charterhouse of Parma," "Anna Karenina," and "Madame Bovary."

She was very proud and easily moved by appeals to her courage. She considered she'd had a happy childhood, and she liked her family (although she could not help looking down on them a little because their name was not famous in the history of America). When she was ten, she had briefly loved a cousin of hers, who was twelve, and who had taken her to the National Museum of Art in Washington and told her the names of the great painters.

At Radcliffe, her freshman year, she discovered that she had been sheltered, compared to most of the other girls, and she felt young and slightly ashamed of herself. This gave her a look of great purity, and she was something of a belle. But late in the spring of her freshman year she stayed up all one night, obsessed and genuinely moved by the fact that she was intelligent and hadn't really known it before. She had just found it out by noticing that section men and assistant professors and sometimes full professors liked to hear her talk in class. From that night on, she limited her dating and threw herself into studying.

"It is poetry that I love," she wrote in her diary.

"It is hard for me to explain why. Once when I was staying with Aunt Kitty in New York I went for a walk in Central Park when it was snowing. In the zoo I saw the Bactrian camel standing in the middle of its pen. It was holding its head straight up in the air with its mouth open and its tongue out and the snowflakes were falling on it. Perhaps he never saw snow before. I'm not exactly sure where Bactria is or what its climate is like— perhaps it was remembering snow. That is how I feel about poetry."

Another entry read, "My mother writes and asks me if I still see Louis Du Pont whom she thought such a charming boy. How can Mother think any-one so plump is charming?"

Early in April of her junior year, she wrote, "Today in Metaphysical Poetry, we discussed the tradition of Platonic Love in Jacobean England. A boy named Elgin Smith spoke brilliantly, I thought. He described the winters the young peo-ple spent in those vast country houses, twenty or so young people visiting in one house, with two or three chaperons, and snow everywhere. They sang and gave masques and such things. Because young people are so hot-blooded, it was necessary to devise a code of courtship to restrain them, for marriages of alliance had to be made later. Need-less to say, it didn't work, Platonic Love, I mean, and it was much more often written about than observed. I do so admire brilliance and wish that I had some. This young man had the oddest voice. It is positively nasal and twangs and twangs. I wanted to put my hand over his mouth and tell him 'Sh-h-h.' He is terribly intense and nervous. He has borrowed a pencil from me several times, and he asked me to have coffee with him once. I said I couldn't, but next time he asks, I will accept. I long for some really intelligent friends."

When you consider the combustibility of the emotions of these two young people, it is hardly surprising that within two weeks of their first long conversation together they were trembling when they talked, and found themselves oppressed whenever silences fell. The impulse to discuss this state of affairs with each other kept recurring, but they fought it, until one afternoon when they were sitting in the Cambridge Common and having a cigarette together before separating for dinner.

All through the Common, young mothers were sitting, bored, by baby carriages, and beneath the trees, newly come to leaf, children were climbing on the old cannon. Abraham Lincoln was brooding under his canopy, and trolleys clanged on Massachusetts Avenue.

"Elgin," Caroline said, "we've talked about a hundred things, a thousand things, I bet."

"Yes."

"But we've never talked about what we think of each other."

"No," he said, twisting his fingers together. "I guess we never have."

"I—I don't approve of it, actually," Caroline said. "Analyzing things and all. Some things are better left unsaid."

"I agree," Elgin said. The words seemed to explode on his lips, leaving a faintly surprised look on his face.

"Do you?" Caroline said. For her part, she was having difficulty hanging on to her poise.

"There isn't much people can say that hasn't been said before," Elgin said with finality. Then he added, "It's my reading. I've read so much I guess I'm a little jaded."

"I see," said Caroline. "Well, it's a fascinating subject."

"Yes," said Elgin, "it is."

They sat in silence for several seconds, both of them on the verge of speaking, but Elgin was frightened and Caroline was disconcerted, as if her ideas of what could happen had been trampled on and left for dead.

"Let's get started back," Elgin said. Caroline rose and the two of them walked on toward Radcliffe, past the Hotel Continental. At the corner, Caroline said, "You coming by this evening?"

Elgin nodded.

Caroline reached out and shook Elgin's hand, which was a strange thing for her to do.

"Caroline!" Elgin said sharply.

"Yes."

"Let's go have dinner together."

"Where? I thought you were broke."

"The Chinese restaurant."

"All right, if I have enough money." She opened her purse and looked; she and Elgin went Dutch most places. "I've got two dollars and some change." They linked arms and walked back to the Common.

"I think Vaughan is a little bit of a bore," Caroline said. "Really, the language has deteriorated so much since Donne."

They sat down on the same bench where they had sat before.

Elgin said, "I assume since our conversation fifteen minutes ago it would be terrible if I talked about the way I feel about you."

"Oh, no," said Caroline. "Go right ahead."

"Well, they're very strong."

"I'd more or less guessed that," Caroline said, unable to make her voice sound normal.

"But I never mentioned it before," Elgin said, "because I didn't want anything to come up that might make you want to stop seeing me."

"I understand," Caroline said. "That was very subtle of you."

"Please shut up," Elgin said. "I'm trying to get

something out and it's very hard. I want you to
know I'm not just chasing you or anything like
that."

"Oh?"

"I saw you last fall. You were going into Widener. It was—you know—at first sight."

"Elgin!"

"It was. I only took Metaphysical Poetry because
you were taking it. Caroline, I have deep feelings
about you."

Caroline felt an intense sense of relief. "Well,
I always thought so," she said. "But I wasn't sure."
Then she realized Elgin was trembling. "Elgin,
what's wrong?"

A child ran by with a red disintegrator pistol.
"You're not angry?" Elgin asked.

"Of course not!" she said ringingly.

"You're not going to tell me that the most I can
expect is your friendship? And if I expect more
we oughtn't to see each other any more?"

There was silence. "I hadn't thought this far,"
Caroline said. She thought it was much more
decent if she didn't have to mention her feelings;
she felt trapped. "Well, Elgin, I'll tell you, I certainly don't want to stop seeing you." She moved
her legs until they were spread ungracefully. "But,
really, I think . . . we ought to be careful and not
get, oh, I don't know, sloppy, if you know what I
mean."

"I don't mind that," Elgin said. He swallowed.

"But is it all right—Is it all right, Caroline, if I show how I feel a little more?" His voice rose and quivered with longing.

"I don't know what you mean."

"You do."

"Honestly, Elgin, I—"

"You do!"

"I suppose so. . . . Yes. Do show it. Let's be honest. For God's sake, who can it hurt? Yes, let's not be priggish."

To her astonishment and delight, Elgin caught her hand and pressed it to his lips.

They hadn't kissed then, nor did they kiss each other for several days afterward. It was a tacit confession that they suspected the presence of passion, and in such cases, if one is at all practical, one stands back, one dawdles, one doesn't rush in to confront the beast in its lair. Or to put it another way, one doesn't go tampering with the floodgates. What they did, after this conversation, was suddenly to become lighthearted. They made jokes; Caroline stole Elgin's notebook from his hands and made him chase her; they discussed Metaphysical Poetry. And when this lightness and gaiety had eased their suspicion and their fright was in abeyance, Caroline decided she wanted Elgin to kiss her.

She was walking up Garden Street in late after-

noon, and the sunlight was clear and golden. There
was a light wind that ruffled her hair, and she was
striding along, passing any number of couples,
Harvard boys and Radcliffe girls, some with their
arms around each other's waist, some holding
hands, some just walking side by side. Caroline
decided then, in a single flash; and the next minute
her cheeks began to glow and she pushed happily
at her hair, which kept blowing across her eyes.

At seven o'clock that evening, Elgin arrived at
Cabot Hall to pick her up. He was wearing his
shabby tweed jacket and khaki pants and a striped
tie. Caroline came downstairs wearing her prettiest
sweater, a pink cashmere. Her hair was carefully
brushed and she wore lipstick, so Elgin knew
something was up.

"I'd sort of like to go to a movie tonight," she
said. "I've got enough money for both of us if
you're flat."

Elgin told her he had a little cash. They settled
on the U.T.—the University Theatre in Harvard
Square.

"I'm in the mood for gangsters," Caroline said as
they emerged from Cabot into the spring evening.

The sky between the trees was purple, a deep,
stirring plum color. Caroline put her arms through
Elgin's, and they strode briskly through the Quad
toward Garden Street, and then through the Common—one of a number of couples, in a long, irreg-

ular procession stretching from the Radcliffe dormitories to Harvard Square.

"I finished my paper on Donne," Elgin said.

Caroline laughed inconsequently, and Elgin laughed, too, for no good reason.

They passed through the middle of the Common, by Lincoln's statue, where a lamp cast a ghostly white glare on leaves and benches and the surface of the walk. Caroline's charming face swam into the light, shadows fell across it, and Elgin closed his eyes.

Caroline pressed his hand. They hurried.

All during the movie, they sat holding both of each other's hands, and their shoulders touching. Entwined and tangled like that, they giggled together whenever the movie became particularly violent. They couldn't stop giggling after a while, as the death toll in the movie mounted. When the movie ended, they left and Elgin bought Caroline a chocolate ice-cream cone at St. Clair's and they walked down to the Charles River.

The Charles looked placid, and glimmered as it quietly flowed under its bridges; the lights of Eliot House were reflected in its surface. Caroline put her head on Elgin's shoulder. They breathed in unison, the two of them, standing on the bank of the river, and then Elgin said, "It's clumsy to ask, but Caroline, do you really . . . or . . . would I . . ." He missed her lips, kissing her cheek instead, and he was holding her so tightly that she couldn't move and correct his mistake. But a minute later he corrected his error himself. They both had difficulty breathing. "I love, I love you, I love you," he whispered.

It sounded beautiful in the moonlight, the river ran quietly beneath the bridge, and Caroline was glad she had let him kiss her.

After that they took to kissing each other a good deal. They met every afternoon at Widener. When one of them broke off work, the other would break off, too, and they would both go downstairs. Along either side of the steps rose large stone arms, which looked as if they should be surmounted by statues, but they were bare, and in spring, in the afternoons, on both of them there would usually be people sitting, sometimes alone, sometimes in pairs. Here Elgin and Caroline would sit and look out over the Yard toward the Chapel.

At four-thirty, they would go to Massachusetts Avenue and have a cup of coffee in one of the luncheonettes. Usually they separated then, Caroline to go to Cabot Hall, Elgin to Adams House, for supper, but some evenings, when they had the money, they had dinner together at a Chinese restaurant near the Square, where the food was very cheap. (Elgin didn't like taking her to Adams

House on the nights when girls were allowed in the dining hall, because it reminded him that he was young and ineffectual and under the control of an institution.) In the evenings, they studied, either in the library or in one of the common rooms at Cabot, and at nine o'clock when the library closed, they would walk down to the riverbank. Elgin had an old raincoat that he wore, and they used that to spread on the grass, to sit on. They sat side by side and shared long, rather tender kisses. At first on these expeditions they talked about poetry, but after a while conversation began to seem disagreeable, and they sat in silence.

Then they began to leave off studying at Widener earlier in the afternoon, at three-thirty, or even three. Caroline liked going with Elgin to the Boston Museum of Fine Arts, and they would look at the pictures and, when their feet were tired, go and sit in the Fens, the park just behind the Museum, which has a rose garden at one end of it. Caroline wanted Elgin to lose his Middle Western pronunciation, and the excuse they used for these jaunts was that this was time spent in teaching Elgin how to speak. He would bring a book, Bacon's "Essays," or Montaigne's, or Jeremy Taylor's "Sermons," or Johnson's "Rasselas"—good, sturdy books, with sentences so rich that sometimes Elgin's voice grew fuzzy with the pleasure he felt reading them.

"Always, all-ways, not oll-wez," Caroline would say.

"Wait, Caroline, just wait a bit, listen to this," and he would read another rolling, rhetorical period. "Isn't that gorgeous?"

"Not gorgeous," Caroline would say. "That's not the right word somehow."

"Oh, it is in this case," Elgin would say. "It's absolutely exact."

And Caroline, struggling not to be moved, would say, "I suppose. I suppose, just barely."

Then Elgin started reading Colette and Boccaccio. Now, when silence fell, something seemed to be lying beside them on the grass, breathing softly. Glances, trees, the movements of people in the park suddenly split off from the commonsensical, taken-for-granted world and became strange. Caroline frowned more and more often, turned into something very like a nag. She made Elgin buy new ties and have his shoes reheeled. Often, in the afternoons, she would take him to St. Clair's and make him drink freshly squeezed orange juice. When it was raining, she still insisted they go for walks because it was good for Elgin. She took to proof-reading all his papers and typing them over for him because he was a poor and careless typist. One day, Elgin read to her the story in Boccaccio of the young girl who used to tell her mother that she wanted to sleep in the garden in order to hear the nightingale sing, but the girl met her lover in the garden—*he* was the nightingale. Elgin read this story to Caroline in an intense and quavering voice. For a week afterward, Caroline walked back and forth to classes hearing in her head the phrase "listening to the nightingale." Finally, the phrase came to stand for so much, it aroused such deep tumult in her and made her feel so lonely and deprived, that one night Elgin came back to his room, woke Dimitri from a sound sleep, and asked him to stay away from the room the next afternoon.

It turned out that Elgin and Caroline were both virgins.

Their first dip in sensual waters left them nonplussed. They didn't know what to make of it. They tried to persuade themselves that something had really happened, but the minute it was over, they couldn't believe they had ever done such a thing. They rushed into further experiences; they broke off in the middle of embraces and looked at each other, stunned and delighted. "Is this really happening?" they both asked at different times, and each time the other said, "No," and they would laugh. They knew that nothing they did was real, was actual. They had received a blow on the head and were prey to erotic imaginings, that was all. But at the same time they half realized it was true,

they *were* doing these things, and then the fact
that they, Caroline and Elgin, shared such intimacy dazed and fascinated them; and when they
were together, they tried to conceal it, but this
indescribable attraction they felt for each other
kept making itself known and draining all the
strength from their bodies. They tried to make
jokes about themselves and this odd little passion
they felt. "We're unskilled labor," Elgin said. "You
know, I'm just giving in because you're irresistible," Caroline said. She always pretended that she
was completely dispassionate about sex. It just
happened that she was susceptible to Elgin's en-
treaties. But he was too shy to entreat unless she
encouraged him, and Caroline often felt like the
worst kind of hypocrite. The truth of the matter
is, they were caught up in a fever of their senses.

Caroline would have her lunch in Cabot Hall,
locked in an impenetrable haze of daydreaming,
not even hearing the girls chattering around her.
She would walk to Widener, and if boys she knew
stopped her to talk, she would stare at them stonily,
afraid the boy might guess her feelings for Elgin
and think they applied to him. She would run up
the stairs of Widener, past the Sargent murals,
petrified that Elgin might not be waiting for her.
Every day this fear grew worse; but every day he
was there, sitting at one of the long wooden tables
in the reading room, beneath the great coffered
ceiling, and the look on his face when he caught

sight of her would make Caroline smile giddily, because she had never known before what a miraculous power she had over men.

They managed a wry stiffness when they were in public. They spoke to each other in tones of the crudest good-fellowship. Elgin called her "Girl." "Girl, you finished with that book?" Caroline called Elgin "Cheese." "No, Cheese. Don't rush me." They didn't hold hands or touch. They thought they fooled everyone, but everyone who knew them guessed, and they both told their roommates. In fact, they wanted to talk about what was happening to them to everyone; this news was always on the tip of their tongues; and so they got into the habit of suddenly breaking off conversations with their friends when the impulse to confess grew too strong to be contained a moment longer, and all their friends thought they were becoming very queer and difficult indeed.

Each afternoon that they met in Widener started on this high level of confusion and rapidly ran downhill. The minute hand of the clock over the door of the reading room jerked every sixty seconds, marking off a whole minute in one movement, and at two-thirty they were no longer capable of speech. Elgin would be pale or flushed. He would draw breath irregularly through a mouth he couldn't quite close, or through distended nostrils, and this phenomenon would fascinate Caroline, except that she couldn't look at him for too long without feeling the most awful pain in her head. Finally, Elgin would gasp, "Well?"

"I'm finished," Caroline would say in the weakest voice imaginable.

They would walk in silence to Adams House, and Elgin would sign Caroline in at the policeman's room. In silence they would mount the stairs, and Elgin would unlock the door of his room, and then they would fall into each other's arms, sometimes giggling with relief, sometimes sombre, sometimes almost crying with the joy of this privacy and this embrace.

Then, later, both of them dressed and their faces scrubbed, Caroline, like an addict, would descend on Elgin's bureau and haul out his torn and buttonless shirts. She didn't know how to sew, but she thought she did, and she sat on Elgin's couch, smiling to herself, softly humming, and sewed buttons on wrong. Elgin tried to study, but his moods whirled and spun him around so that one minute he'd be reading quietly and the next minute he'd be striding up and down the room on the worn carpet, wringing his hands or else waving them aloft and denouncing the College and the American Educational System, full of rage, but not knowing with what or why, and forced to let it out any way he could, while Caroline, faintly bored, ignored him mostly and sewed.

Every once in a while, Caroline would cry. Then

she would be unable to dress properly, and she'd drag around the room with her hair badly combed, her shoes off, looking slatternly, and say, "I don't know what's wrong with me. Actually, nothing's wrong with me." But every few minutes tears would course down her cheeks. Nor did she know why she cried; she was as innocent of understanding herself as she was of understanding Elgin.

Sometimes they quarrelled. Once, it was because Caroline wouldn't use Elgin's towel.

"If you loved me, you'd use it."

"I'd adore to use *your* towel," Caroline said, "but *this* towel is dirty."

Elgin thought her preposterous; she called Elgin a boor and slammed out of the room. She reached the bottom of the stairs and started back up and heard Elgin coming down. Neither of them said a word; they didn't apologize or mention this episode again. They went for a walk along the riverbank and talked about Metaphysical Poetry.

On Saturdays, Elgin took Caroline to the Harvard courts to play tennis. Caroline had fine ankles and legs, and while they walked to the courts, Elgin kept stealing glances at them, which made Caroline nervous. She was a good tennis player, as good as Elgin, but he could throw her off her game by charging the net and yelling at her, "I've got you now!" This would rattle her so she'd completely miss the ball, and then she would laugh with exasperation.

When he served, he made a point of calling the score in a loud, cheerful, teasing voice: "Thirty-love!" He'd say the "love" in such a way that Caroline would blush, and then she would try to drive the ball directly at him, and most of the time it went out of bounds.

One afternoon, they were in each other's arms in Elgin's room. Elgin was whispering, "I love you, Caroline. I love you so much," and someone knocked on the door. The sound seemed to blind Elgin, who squeezed his eyes closed, as tightly as he could. The knock was repeated second time, and a third, echoing in the small room. Then the footsteps retreated.

Elgin got up and fetched cigarettes and towels for them both. They leaned back on the couch, at opposite ends, wrapped in towels, and smoked. They didn't mention the fact that they were afraid it had been the campus policeman and they would be expelled. They discussed whether or not they were depraved.

"We are," Caroline said. "Otherwise, we wouldn't be so ashamed."

We don't have to be ashamed," Elgin said. "We only pretend we are anyway, to be polite."

"You're a rebel," Caroline said gloomily. "You can say that. But I'm a conformist. I'm basically a nice girl. I *am* ashamed."

The pressure of details, the maze of buttons,

hooks, and zippers that they had to make their way through to that condition which pleased them best, kept forcing them to be self-conscious. They couldn't believe that what they were doing was real, and yet it was real, as they well knew the minute they separated, when the memory of their last encounter would descend on both of them, occupying their minds, and unfitting them for any occupation except dreaming of the next encounter. At night, lying in his bunk, Elgin would try to sleep, but he'd think of Caroline, and slowly, like a leaf curling in a salt solution, he would twist under his covers until his knees were even with his chest, and this was a tortured, involuntary movement of longing he could no more control than he could control his thoughts. He would try to do his reading for his courses: "In the early years of this century, I moved to London, feeling that Ireland and my love for Ireland were too distracting for my poetry." And then right on the printed page would appear "CAROLINE," in capital letters, and Elgin would rub his face foolishly with both hands, twisting his mouth and his cheeks and his nose.

He didn't believe that Caroline loved him as much as he loved her, or at least that she desired him as much as he did her, and this made him sullen. He picked on her. He told her she wasn't as smart as she thought she was; people treated her as if she were intelligent only because she was pretty. He would accuse her of pettiness, and she would agree with him, confess that she had an awful character, and while he was consoling her, their embraces would begin.

Elgin would be hurt whenever Caroline was the first to point out that it was time to go and have dinner. Caroline would eye the clock, but Elgin would pretend he was so entranced with Caroline he didn't know what time it was. The minutes would tick by, and Caroline would grow gayer and gayer, trying to ignore the time, while Elgin, beetling, thin, and sardonic, refused to say the words that would release her.

Elgin became frightened. He was so frightened he couldn't eat. He was afraid of losing Caroline, of failing his courses because he couldn't study unless she was sitting beside him where he could reach out and touch her every few minutes. The thought of what it would be like if any of the quarrels they had should turn serious worried him until he was sick. Finally, looking gray and haggard, he suggested to her one afternoon that the two of them should run off and get married.

"Elgin, don't. Don't let's talk about that. You know we can't."

Elgin shrugged and looked disheartened. "I don't like self-pity," he said. "But I admit I have some. Oh, yes. I pity myself a lot, Imagine, here I am, in love with a common, ordinary, conventional girl like you."

Caroline supported her head with her hands. "Oh, Elgin," she said, "you're being cruel. You know we're awfully young. And just because we got carried away—there's no need, really, to . . . It's our animal appetites mostly, you know. . . ."

Elgin wanted to say something bitter but her last remark stopped him. "*Your* animal appetites, too?"

"Yes."

He was so happy he forgot his feelings had been hurt.

Sometimes, she and Elgin went out with Felicia and Dimitri. Caroline could not now bear girls she thought were virgins; they made her uneasy, and she would not go on a double date with Dimitri and Felicia until Elgin swore they were lovers, too. Elgin spent more than one afternoon telling her that almost all the girls at Radcliffe and all other colleges had slept with somebody. "The percentage is very high," he said.

They went boating twice at Marblehead. Dimitri had a car, which Elgin borrowed—an old, weak-lunged Ford—and they would wheeze up to Marblehead and rent a dinghy and be blown around the bay, with the sunlight bright on Caroline's hair and the salt air making them hungry and the wind whipping up small whitecaps to make the day exciting.

Caroline wrote in her diary, "His back is so beautiful. It has such a lovely shape. It's so defenseless. I like to put my ear against his back and listen to his heart—I think it's his heart I hear. It's funny he is not more handsome in his clothes, but that only makes him seem more beautiful to me, I think. I feel I would like to give birth to him. Sometimes, I want to crawl into his pocket and be carried like a pencil. I never let him see how strongly I feel. I am a dreadful person, dreadful. . . ."

Elgin wrote her a letter.

"Dear Caroline, Isn't it funny to have me writing a letter to you when I see you every day? But just imagine how it would seem later if we looked back and saw that we had never written each other how we felt.

"You, Caroline Hedges, are the greatest love of my life, just as you are the first.

"I don't suppose, you being a girl, that you know what it's like to love a girl like you, but if you knew how dependent men are on women, you might understand. Not that men can't survive alone, but they don't seem to really amount to anything until they have a woman they love.

"Reading over what I have just writen, I see that everything I've said applies only to the selfish side of love. I guess that's a dead giveaway about me. But as for you, kid, just knowing you is rather awe-inspiring."

Sometimes, there would be birds singing in the

ivy outside the window of Elgin's room. Sometimes, Elgin would sing to Caroline; he had a sweet, insecurely pitched voice, and his singing would give them both pleasure. Sometimes, seeing Elgin walk across the room unclothed would make all the breath leave Caroline's body, and she would not even be conscious of her gasp or that he heard her. One afternoon, Elgin went into the bathroom to get Caroline a glass of water. She was lying in the lower bunk, lapped in shadows, and she saw him come back into the room and she said weakly, "I love you, Elgin." It was the first time she had said it, that proud, stubborn girl. Elgin heard her; he stopped in his tracks and he put his head back. "God," he said. "This is the happiest moment I ever had."

Now there was no bar to their intimacy, and they talked. Elgin was relentless about asking questions: "What do you think about money? What is your father like? Are you fond of him?"

At first, Caroline was cautious. "Well, I think there's a minimum amount of money people should have. . . . My father is sort of nice. He's shallow, I guess. He doesn't seem to have very strong emotions. He works for an insurance company. I used to like him a lot; I still do. . . . I think I feel sorry for him."

"What do you mean by that?" Elgin asked. He handed her a cigarette and lit it for her. "Tell me everything about yourself. Be honest. I've never known anyone as well as I know you."

Caroline cupped her hands over her mouth. "I think he loves me, and now I love you, and I think that's sad. That he's older . . . Should we be talking like this, Elgin?"

"Why not? Who else can we talk to?"

Then it all began to come out, her feelings toward her father, toward her mother, toward money. Caroline wanted a nice house and a large family; she looked down a little on people who weren't well off. When she felt exhausted from telling Elgin these things, she asked him questions.

"My mother's very possessive," he said. "If we got married, I think we'd have in-law problems. I want to be a famous scholar. I don't disapprove of campus politics. I know I should, but I don't. Isn't that shameful?"

"This isn't dignified, talking like this," Caroline said. "I don't want to do it any more."

She was frightened. Having admitted she loved Elgin, she felt naked, and these conversations only made her feel worse. She kept hoping she and Elgin would reach some stability together, but it never came. She still was frightened when she ran up the stairs of Widener that he wouldn't be waiting for her. She wondered why she couldn't get used to this situation, why the pleasures she was drawn into didn't lose their elements of pain—indeed, why the elements of pain grew steadily worse, until she dreaded seeing Elgin and had to force herself to get out of bed in the morning and go through her day. She couldn't help thinking that what she was with comparative strangers was much pleasanter than what she was with Elgin. With him she was capricious, untruthful, often sharp-tongued, giddy with emotions that came and went, and while one emotion might be ennobling, having six or seven in the space of an hour was undignified and not decent at all. She had always believed that a woman ought to walk very straight, write a firm hand, keep house and entertain well—in short, be like those friends of her mother's whom she most admired. The fact that she was young didn't seem any excuse at all for her not being like those women, and now she said to herself, "I'm wild. That's all there is to that."

She decided she was inordinately sexual. Elgin caught her in Widener reading a book describing the great courtesans of the nineteenth century, La Belle Otero and Lola Montez. She believed that Elgin would inevitably forsake her because she had lost all her dignity and mystery, and she boasted to him that he would never forget her, even if he married some pasty-faced virgin. Elgin couldn't calm her; in fact, he was more than half persuaded that she *was* unusually passionate when she said she was, and he became uneasy with her. Caroline

began to wear a little too much lipstick and to walk
not in her habitual erect fashion but slouching and
swaying her hips. She drank and smoked more, and
when she got high, she would look at Elgin through
lowered eyelids and kiss him in a knowing—a
childishly knowing—way. And all of this humbled
Elgin, who felt Caroline was a great enigma and
that she was drawing away from him. One night,
they were sitting on the riverbank and Caroline
put her hands on Elgin's head and drew him to
her, and Elgin pulled away desperately. "I don't
want you to kiss me like that!"

"What's wrong?" Caroline asked haughtily. "Am
I too much woman for you?"

Elgin's eyes grew moist. "I don't know what you
do to me," he said miserably. "I'm ready to cry. I
didn't think we were having *that* kind of an affair."

In the darkness, he saw Caroline's eyelids descend. Then a shudder passed over her face. He
decided to stake everything rather than have Caroline frighten him into helplessness.

He grabbed her arm. "Listen, you've got to get
hold of yourself. You're acting like an ass."

Caroline was motionless.

"You're ruining everything," Elgin said.

"You have too many illusions about me," Caroline said coldly. She pulled away from his grasp and
lay down on his old, battered raincoat and put her
hands under her head. "There are a lot of things
you don't know about me. I didn't want to tell you

I loved you because I wanted to hold you. There, what do you think of that?"

Elgin hit himself on the chest. "You think that's bad? Well, I always intended to seduce you, right from the beginning. God!" He lay down, too, on the damp grass, two feet away from her, and he put his hands under his head.

Lying like that, they quarreled in this peculiar way, libeling themselves, lowering the object of love in the other's eyes.

"I think it's loathsome that we sleep together," Caroline said. "I feel like a you-know-what."

"I hate seeing you every day," Elgin said. "Not because of you but because I'm always afraid you'll see through me. Also, I miss having free time to study—that's how cold-blooded I am."

There was a full moon that night, and its light was no chillier than what these two young people said about themselves. But after a while Elgin rolled over and took Caroline in his arms. "Please don't hate me."

"I don't hate you. I love you."

"I love you, too. God, it's hell!"

They decided to be more sensible. The next day they didn't meet in Widener. Elgin stayed in his room, and at three o'clock the phone rang.

"It's me—Caroline."

"Oh God, you called. I was praying you would. Where are you?"

"In the drugstore on the corner." There was

silence. "Elgin," she said at last, "did you have any orange juice today?"

He ran, down the stairs, along the sidewalk, to the drugstore, to have his orange juice.

One day, Elgin told Caroline he was going to stay home and play poker with some of the boys in his entry. Caroline said that was a good idea. She had to write her mother; for some reason, her letters home had got her mother all upset, and she wanted to take some time and calm the old biddy down. "Poor thing," said Caroline. "She's had such an empty life, and I'm so important to her." Then she smiled a thin, nervous smile. "Of course, when I think how stupid she is, I wonder what I'll find to say to her."

Elgin played poker. He lost four dollars and sixty cents. At eleven-thirty, he excused himself from the game and went out on the street. He walked hurriedly, jogging part of the distance, until he stood on the sidewalk across from Cabot Hall, looking up at the light in Caroline's room. Finally, a shadow passed over the window, and Elgin felt what he could only describe as anguish.

He looked in the gutter until he found a pebble, and then he hurled it at Caroline's window. It struck. The shadow appeared again, standing quite still. At that moment, a policeman rounded the corner. Elgin thrust his hands in his pockets and walked up the street. The policeman stopped him.

"Hey, buddy, did you just throw something at that building?"

"No, Officer." Elgin was sweating and looked so pitiable the officer said, "I guess it was a trick of the light."

When Caroline asked him if he had come by Cabot the night before, he denied it.

The next day, he and Caroline went up to his room. As Elgin closed the door, Caroline threw herself onto the couch. She looked pale and unhappy, and she was making a face, preparing herself for what was coming. But Elgin walked over and stood next to the couch and said, "Caroline, we've got to be chaste. God!" he cried. "It's not easy to say this, and if your feelings get hurt, I don't know what I'll do!"

"They're not hurt."

"I want you to be happy," he said, looking down at her. "I think we ought to get married."

"We're under age, Elgin—you know that. Our parents won't let us."

"We'll tell them you're pregnant. We'll do something."

Caroline jumped up. "But I don't want to marry you! You won't make me happy. I'm scared of you. You don't have any respect for me. I don't know how to be a good wife."

"Listen, Caroline, we haven't done the right thing. You want to have children?"

A pink, piteous flush covered Caroline's face. "Oh," she said.

"We ought to get married," he said doggedly. "It won't be easy, but otherwise we'll never be happy. You see, what we didn't figure out is the teleology of the thing. We don't have a goal. We have to have a goal, do you see?"

"Elgin, we can't be foolish. If we really love each other, we have to be very practical or else we'll just cause each other very needless pain."

They looked at each other, pure at last, haloed by an urge to sacrifice.

"I may not be right for you," Caroline whispered. "We'll wait. We'll wait until fall. We'll have the summer to think things over."

Elgin frowned, not liking to have his sacrifice ignored. "I'm willing to marry you," he said.

"No, it's not right," said Caroline. "We're too young. We couldn't have children now. We're too ignorant. We'd be terrible parents." How it pained her to say this!

"If you feel that way," Elgin said, "I think we ought to plan to break up. Nothing sudden," he added, to ease the sudden twinge that was twisting his stomach. "When school's over."

Caroline hesitated, but it seemed to her dream-like and wonderful to be free of this febrile emotion. And atonement would be so wonderful. . . . At the same time, she was hurt. "All right," she said with dignity. "If you want."

Elgin turned away from her. "Caroline, tell me one thing," he said with his back to her. "Emotionally, would you like to marry me?"

"Yes."

"God!" he said. "You're so practical!"

"I'm not!" she cried. "I can't help it." She wrung her hands. "If you tried to carry me off, I wouldn't resist," she said. "But if you ask me, I think—I think—"

He didn't have to marry her; he wouldn't have to worry about supporting her; he hadn't lost his career. Elgin felt irrepressible relief welling up in him. "God, how we love each other."

Caroline laughed. "It's true." She laughed a little more. "It's so true!" She threw her arms around his neck and kissed him.

Of course, they didn't stick to Elgin's plan of breaking up when school ended. They decided they would take a vacation from each other, and meet in the fall, when college began again, as friends. This agreement seemed to remove a great weight from them. They had only two weeks of the reading period and three weeks of exams left to be together, but they resumed some of their old habits—the walks between classes, for instance, and the trips to the Boston Museum of Fine Arts—and they even took to reading stories aloud again, preferring Chekhov and Colette. The sweetness and the sadness of their predicament were what they loved, and they threw themselves into the role of well-disciplined lovers with all their energy. Hardly a day passed without their thinking of some new gesture toward each other. Elgin gave flowers to Caroline; she bought him cuff links and books of poetry. Elgin left off suspecting that he was being made a fool of, and was actually gentlemanly, opening doors for Caroline and lighting her cigarettes. Caroline was ladylike and concealed her moods. They engaged in roughhouse; Elgin pulled her hair and she pummelled him when they sat on the riverbank. They were chaste. They referred sometimes to the times when they had listened to the nightingale, and while the chastity didn't come easily to them, the act of sacrifice did. Elgin put on weight, and his face regained its color. "My goodness," Caroline said. "I think knowing me has improved your looks." It seemed they had found the secret of being happy together, in the imminence of separation, and while they didn't understand the paradox, they knew it was true.

But as their five last weeks passed, they discovered why it was true. All the pain of the relationship was now bound up with the parting and not with the things they did to each other. "It's dreadful," Caroline said. "I have feelings. They're like heavy mice that come out of holes and sit in my stomach and weigh me down."

They had been so proud of themselves, so free and relaxed and peaceful together, and now, when they saw what this parting was going to be like, all their vivacity and happiness flagged, they lost interest in talking to each other, and all they wanted was to get it over with.

On the last day of exams, they went up to Elgin's room at six o'clock. Elgin had bought a bottle of champagne and rented two glasses. Caroline was all dressed up because she was going to catch a train for Baltimore at nine o'clock. She had on a small hat, which she kept eying in the mirror. Poor Elgin was nervous about opening the champagne. "It's imported," he said. "I don't want to sound tight, but if half of it explodes or comes out in foam, I won't be happy." Caroline laughed, but when the cork popped, she turned very serious. She was afraid of what Elgin would toast; she was afraid it would ruin her self-possession.

Elgin slowly poured the champagne into the two glasses. Then the two young people, alone in the room, picked up their glasses and held them together. "To our reunion in the fall," Elgin said. "God knows what it will be like." They drank.

Caroline put her glass down. "Let's play a record and dance," she said. Elgin put on a Cole Porter L.P., and he and Caroline circled around the room, dodging the furniture, pausing to take occasional sips of their champagne. At six-thirty, they went downstairs and ate in the dining hall.

By seven-fifteen, they were back upstairs in

Elgin's room, sitting on the bunk, kissing each other with a dry, intense helplessness. At quarter of eight, Caroline said she had to go. Elgin pulled away from her; she had taken off her hat, and her dress, made of some pretty gray-blue material, was hopelessly rumpled. With his hands, he set her just so on the bunk. Then he took out his pocket comb and combed her hair. "There," he said.

"Do I look prettier now?" Caroline asked.

"Yes," Elgin said.

They walked downstairs and out the door of Adams House. When they reached the sidewalk, Caroline said, "I don't want you to come with me. I want to go back to the dorm alone. All right?"

Elgin nodded.

"I'll write you from Europe," Caroline said. "Goodbye," she said and walked away, up the sidewalk; she tried to walk crisply but her feet dragged because she felt tired. Slowly, the hoped-for sense of relief was coming; she was free of Elgin, she had herself back, but not all of herself. Elgin still held some of her, and she would never get it back except when he was beside her.

Elgin sat on the steps in front of Adams House and buried his face in his hands. "God!" he said to himself. "I love her." And he wondered what would become of them now.

LAURIE DRESSING

LAURIE leaned toward the mirror on her dressing table and carefully drew the outline of her lips on her mouth. Her tiny pearl-handled brush moved without wavering. She studied the outline for a moment and then decided it was too passionate. Laurie was nineteen, a junior at Wellesley. She was wearing a virulent-purple bathrobe her favorite cousin, a would-be actor named Vergil, had given her when she was sixteen. It was, as Laurie said, a woman of the world's bathrobe, even though by now it was a little faded and stained. In the cleft of the bathrobe was the lacy top of a black slip. Laurie's brush hovered over the points of her lips. Innocence, she thought —a sort of ripe innocence, for a Chestnut Hill White. But, how the hell do you design ripe innocence? Laurie's more familiar mouths wouldn't do at all—the one she called "sullen juvenilia," for instance, or "it's springtime and time to laugh." Henry White was taking her home to meet his mother, and even though Laurie had no intention of becoming engaged, still Henry was rich enough that she might change her mind. It would make her mother very happy. Her mother would say gravely, "Laurie, I hope you'll be very happy." But if she became engaged to Martin, whose father was not rich, her mother would cry softly and say, "Laurie, how could you?" It wasn't that her mother was a conscious snob; as far as Laurie knew, her mother wasn't conscious of anything much. It was just a matter of playing by pitch; some things sounded right to Mama, and some things didn't. Laurie had a tendency toward the somethings that didn't and so she was forced to think of herself as a rather racy young girl.

She raised her upper lip and painted a faint lurking smile at the corners. There, she thought, I'm good-natured. With her eyebrow pencil she drew a line on the rim of her eyelids, to darken her eyelashes. Her blondish hair was cut short and fluffy around her head. She pushed at her hair and moved it around. The face in the mirror smiled at her wanly. Laurie's nose was large, her lips full, her eyes kind and shining. When she looked in the mirror, she invariably dilated her eyes and pulled in her lips, and so she thought she had a blank, polite face. But she was wrong. She had an asymmetrical face, a strangely dignified, knowing girl's face, bright with a peculiar dazzle, perhaps of health, perhaps of carelessness.

The trouble was, she thought, that if you married someone poor, it was obviously lechery. But if you married someone rich, everyone congratulated you as if you had performed some act of unusually intricate virtue. Even liberals. Laurie rose from the mirror, and the minute she did so, her face flowed back to its normal expression, brighter and more wary. Of course, if you were enclosed in the sort of physical envelope she was, people thought of you as lecherous anyway, no matter what you did, Laurie thought hopefully. Men fell in love with you, older men, younger men, little boys.

She took off her bathrobe and backed up to the mirror on her closet door. Her back was straight, her rear ample (too ample; with sudden savagery, she swatted it), her legs acceptable. She slid into a daydream where she was a musical-comedy star who made lots of money and didn't have to marry. Laurie gave an exploratory bump and grind, and then burst out laughing at herself. It had been such a very dignified bump and grind. With one hand on her stomach and the other gyrating in space, she closed her eyes and tried to do better.

Her roommate, Carey, came in. "Laurie, what the hell you doing?"

"Shaking my tail. It's good for the waistline. You ought to try it. You're a little thick in the middle."

Carey was a tall, flat-chested, athletic girl with protruding teeth, who loved horses. She frowned. "You're not very witty," she said. "You're not even funny."

Laurie opened her closet door and looked at her dresses. Carey opened a drawer, made a few angry noises, and then left the room. Laurie relaxed. She began to lift dresses out of the closet and hold them in front of her. Then, suddenly, she felt like crying. After all, tonight might be the night when she became engaged, when she pledged her honor to marry a man, and in her family the women stayed married. She would be obliged to spend an entire lifetime with this one man. . . . She quickly grabbed another dress and held it up. It was brown silk, with tiny black figures on it, and it had sleeves that went only to the middle of her forearm. It was her sophisticated dress (Laurie, defenseless and alone, puckered her lower lip and pressed the dress against her body); her mind swam with memories. In that dress she had sipped her first Martini. . . . At the Plaza, too. It was with Roy Delbert and his father and his father's third wife. The men had leaned across the table and lit her cigarettes, and Mrs. Delbert had persistently, *gallantly,* asked her questions about her college courses. But nothing could have turned Laurie back into a mere college girl that day, nothing could touch her. She remembered clearly only the beating of her heart . . . and slipping her shoes off under the table, her new high heels, green I. Millers with pointed, uncomfortable toes. Roy's face was a blur. Though he'd been the one who cried . . . Laurie flung her dress on her bed and fell down beside it. How could he expect her to promise to marry him? She had been seventeen at the time. He had called her a cruel bitch. Laurie ran her hands wonderingly over her face. Was she a bitch? Was she coarse and cruel? It was terribly important to know. But Laurie's mind refused to enter into a discussion. She felt sick and unhappy, but her mind did nothing. She would be late; she would make Henry White wait and wait and wait. She lit a cigarette.

The first time she'd ever been called a bitch was at practically her very first dance. It was her first *big* dance. In Philadelphia. She'd gone down from New York on the train to her cousin Phyllis's. Phyllis had an expensive formal of white tulle; it was someone's coming-out party. Laurie had a rather bargain-type dress, calico and proper, from Best's. What her mother called reasonable and what Laurie called cheap. Fourteen ninety-five and with plenty of material at the seams. She'd been pudgy then, but her skin had the healthy glaze that comes from sunshine and ten hours of sleep a night. She had always hoped she would be attractive, and it was very likely she would find out that night. Phyllis had been hateful from the moment they started dressing for the party. She said Laurie's humming got on her nerves. She said Laurie hogged the mirror. And when the boys had arrived and Phyllis and Laurie were about to start downstairs, Laurie took one last hopeful look at herself in the mirror and then she threw her head back and laughed with delight. Phyllis grabbed her by the arm and yanked her toward the head of the stairs. Phyllis was seventeen then, two years older than Laurie, and thin; she looked well in suits. "You fat little bitch!" she muttered as they went down.

Laurie sat up. She had been pretty bad at that party. She'd tucked her bodice a little lower than it had been at Best's. And the boys. Laurie, on her bed, in her college room, shivered with delight. She's been stared at and pleaded with and cut in on and kissed. . . . "Oh, goodness me!" Laurie said aloud. "I certainly liked that," she whispered to herself. "And the flowers. So many boys sent me flowers that weekend, and I promised to write them all, and I never wrote a single one."

The buzzer sounded in the hall: three long and a short. Laurie went to the doorway of her room, frowned, and then slowly, graciously, sauntered down the hall to the telephone. It was Henry. Laurie told him she wasn't nearly dressed. Maybe he'd better go have coffee and come back in twenty minutes.

"But Mother's waiting for us!" Henry said.

Laurie stared coldly into the telephone. "This speaks ill for the future," she said; she felt herself becoming more and more of a great lady. She said soothingly, "Now, Henry . . . Well, if you must know, the showers were crowded."

She wandered back to her room, her eyes blank. Martin, who was tall and serious and in the third year of law school, would never have put up with that. He would have slammed the phone in her ear. Laurie had never known anyone who studied with the ferocity Martin did. He could even cross his legs ferociously when he was reading. Martin counted so much on the future that when Laurie was with him, she could feel it, those hours of getting ahead, those days, and years, glittering like gold.

"What kind of boy is he?" her mother had asked. Sweetly. "Is he of good family?" That meant that Martin had little value. He was no catch, no treasure. And truthfully, Laurie had to admit, his manners were poor; he was sulky at the drop of a hat; he was easily hurt. He could be very, very foolish. And what was worse, any girl could get him: she had only to be nice, to be a little tender, and a little curious about the law.

Laurie surrendered. She decided to wear her pale-blue dress for Henry; it was innocent, to go with her lips. She took the dress out of her closet and began to slip it over her head. The strange thing was how few men had cut in on her at the law-school dance. Perhaps Martin had been fierce-looking and scared the other men off. Or perhaps, with Martin, she hadn't been so eager to attract all the men; maybe it was something you turned off and on, being a bitch. . . .

Laurie threw her head back, her blue dress still unfastened. What in hell were you supposed to do with your looks? Collect just one man, very rich, with a number of houses, and have everyone look up to you? Be a good girl, date nice boys, not say mean things to the Careys and Phyllises, not make the Roy Delberts cry?

She zipped up her dress savagely. No: she'd rather be mean and bad and have a foul character. She'd sleep with Martin. Her mother could go to hell.

She savagely unzipped her dress and pulled it over her head. She threw it on the floor, where it would irritate Carey, who didn't have a date. She reached into the closet and pulled out her new black dress. Her mother had said she was too young for black. Laurie laughed, showing her teeth. She wasn't going to wear a girdle, either. Her behind was going to shake its heart out. The dress fit very well. Laurie sighed and patted her hair, pushing one strand over her forehead. Then with a Kleenex she wiped the curve off the corner of her lips. Sullen juvenilia, that was her. Bad world. Bad Laurie.

LAURA

LAURA was bending over, trying without much hope to touch her toes, when the baby began to cry again. Laura's eyes, always warm and luminous, turned warmer and more luminous; at that moment, with her back bent, arms hanging straight down, and her head cocked to one side, she slid back into her childhood and its pleasantly queer perspectives. Somehow, her mother had always managed to be irritated when Laura assumed such postures (of course, her mother had been practically the only person who was impervious to her beauty); Laura could almost feel the vaguely desperate maternal hands pulling at the back of her dress. "Stand up, Laura. Stand up this instant. You're making a spectacle of yourself." But that was precisely what Laura had wanted to do; she would look at all the faces turned toward her, and she would *know* that she, Laura, was bending over imitating a monkey. She could almost feel her tail. "It's me, Mother!" she'd say, delighted and surprised, and afterward her mother could go on scolding her for hours without ever penetrating the wonderful foliage of reveries and thoughts that had sprung up from her successful maneuver.

The baby's voice in a series of faint cries announced that hunger, like the tide, was coming in.

"If that damn child doesn't shut up, I'll strangle it!" Laura said. Hardly a second passed before she jerked upright in a spasm of guilt. Oh, you are a terrible person, she thought, and fled to the mirror, but no, her face was the same—kind, gentle, and infinitely calm. Laura leaned forward and touched the spot on the mirror behind which her lovely lips so provokingly lurked untouchable. Soon the cries would be demanding, but now they were gentle—little invitations to her mother to fondle her, to wade in the baby's need. Laura, refusing to give up the mirror, sighed because she would never know the pleasure that others had touching her lips. The trouble with beauty was that one could never enjoy it all by oneself in private, and one couldn't go on forever imitating a monkey in public, and so what was one to do?

"Be an actress," Laura crooned, standing beside her daughter's crib. "Be an actress, wee thing, and be lovely on the stage, where it earns you money," she sang, in soft lullaby tones. The baby bent its tiny six-week-old body in an arch, and the eyes flashed open for an instant, but the figure at the edge of the crib wasn't bending down. "Poor poverty-stricken child!" Laura said. The baby began to bawl. Her pink hands grew purplish and knotted with tension; her wrinkled eyelids pressed into her cheek; her almost nonexistent nose distended in hungry rage.

"Grow up tough," Laura whispered. "Grow up tough and mean. Learn to get your own way. Cry harder. Make me pick you up." She bent over the crib, staring at her tiny daughter, hardly breathing, waiting for the coercive power of the other's life to force her to touch her, to calm her. But the baby was simply crying in some lonely universe where tire irons float in space. Poor Laura watched, being a Theban—no, Spartan—woman staring at her offspring exposed on a deserted hill while the moon watched and said nothing.

Laura was waiting for a sign from God or one of the gods (any omen would do) or a flash of inspiration—something mystical, like Saint Theresa—that would tell her what to do. The baby's very destiny was at stake. Surely a child of hers would have a destiny—a bird that came and watched over it, a guardian fairy with no other duties, who lurked in the shadows until midnight and then carried the child to Oberon's palace, where the walls were woven of vines and inlaid with grapes and ripe fruit. . . . No, Laura thought, her large, square hands joined in the peasant's gesture of hopelessness, she didn't want a guardian spirit; she wanted to devote her entire existence to the child.

The baby cried on, still in its lonely void just

before Genesis, before the earth is formed, where nothing has been named yet, and there is only the mother's face and the mother's breast, like the sun and the moon. But the crying was softer now, temporarily eased by the orbital warmth of another presence, and Laura looked down, aware that she was afraid. Her hands moved upward and pressed against her eyes, but the fear oozed through, in brighter and brighter streams. Laura impulsively reached for the baby. But I musn't pick it up when I'm disturbed, she thought. I'll frighten it. Her hands lay twitching near the crying baby's head. Just holding it will comfort me. *Why can't I think?*

Tears streamed down Laura's face. She withdrew her hands from the baby's crib and pressed them one into the other, for warmth. She knew she was overtired. Every three hours, all through the day and night, Laura nursed the baby. In bright light, her face was gray with fatigue, and sometimes parts of her body would begin to twitch, as her hands were doing now; sometimes it was her leg, and sometimes her shoulder, and she couldn't control them.

"But I wanted to be a mother!" Laura cried. "At least, I think I did." She let herself sink wearily to the floor until her face peered at the baby's through the bars of the crib. "Baby, don't cry. Mother's here. And you just ate. I can't feed you again. I haven't enough milk yet, anyway. Look, baby,

Mummy's making faces at you." The baby cooed faintly between sobs. "Please tell me you're crying just for exercise. Please? Tell me I haven't ruined you."

There were bottles for supplementary feeding in the icebox downstairs. You take the bottle and loosen the cap so the bottle won't explode, and put it in a pan of water and heat it. Then you test it on your wrist. . . . No, Laura thought grimly, I won't. The baby and I'll work it out together. A voice in the back of her mind said, "You're being romantic, Laura. You're being silly. Your baby's crying, and you think silly thoughts about motherhood and how you're going to be a natural mother." The voice was her husband's.

"That's not true," Laura said desperately. "I don't think anything. I don't know how to think. That's my whole problem."

Once, her husband had told her (they'd been lying side by side in bed, looking out their window at a particularly large and beautiful moon), "Darling, you're so absurdly romantic. No one else says 'I belong to you' and means it, the way you do. Do you know what I think?"

"What?" Laura had said, with an expression of hurt but secretly feeling pleasure at being the subject of the discussion.

"When you were little, you never developed defenses, the way normal people do. You were too spoiled. You never had to save yourself. You could always run to someone and smile at them, and they'd love you—as I do."

"That's not so," Laura said. But she remembered how her father's face had softened when she clambered on his knee and raised her pudgy hands for him to kiss. ("Mummy says I'm a bad girl." "Maybe you are," her father had said, but he had laughed.)

"I was a very lonely child," Laura said to her husband, lying there in the bright moonlight. *How pure it is,* she thought; *if only I could wear it.*

"Laura," her husband cried, "you only say that because you read it somewhere!" Tears gathered in her eyes, in the moonlight—because he was right, and it was depressing.

Since her husband hated her to cry, she stuffed her hand into her mouth so he couldn't hear her. And then, because she feared that he might not understand that she didn't blame him for anything, she bit her ring finger—pressed her teeth as hard as she could until the skin broke and the blood welled out warm and soothing. Laura lay for a moment savoring the pleasure of sacrifice, and then she turned and held out her hand to her husband. "See how much I love you."

"Laura!" he cried in exasperation, but the exasperation disappeared in laughter, and he rolled over so she could put her arms around him—she was almost as big as he was—and stroke him as one strokes a dog, until he stopped worrying and lay warm and placid on her shoulder. "I deserve you because I put up with you," he murmured.

But he *is* right, Laura thought now. I have a bad character; I have flaws. The baby was entranced with her faces. It reached out its tiny hand and gripped her nose. The fingernails were sharp and scratched at the tender membrane in her nostrils. Laura smiled and made noises at the baby. Surreptitiously, with one hand, she tested her breast, but there wasn't enough milk.

"Please don't cry any more," Laura said. "The milk is almost here. Just a few more minutes."

She stood up and lifted the baby and held it on her shoulder and began to walk around the room with it, singing nonsense songs. Outside, the sky was turning purple and the locust trees down the block were swaying delicately. Soon her husband would come home and tell her what to do, persuade her to use the bottled supplement. Laura was perspiring gently. But the baby was already ruined, of course; she didn't love it. It was too much trouble. She didn't love anything. The baby was riding on her shoulder, a strange little lump that made noises. Laura began to stride around the room, and the song she was singing suddenly marched into a menacing minor key:

"Lumpen, lumpen, little lumpen
On my shoulder you are bumpen . . ."

The telephone rang. The baby gave a startled little leap. In sudden distaste, Laura half slung, half dropped the baby in its crib and ran to the telephone; she was going to talk to the outside world. How wonderful telephones were! She flew down the steps. Behind her, the baby began to make small noises. "She's just exercising," Laura said aloud, to the hall mirror. She picked up the telephone. "Oh, it's you, Mother." Cars moved up and down the street, the shadows were sliding eastward, and out of the dining-room window the sun lay in the west, ripe and glowing. "No, I'm not tired, Mother. I don't want you to come over and help. . . . Mother, please. . . . Yes, that's the baby crying. . . . Mother, I don't want that awful nurse back. . . . I don't care if my waist hasn't gone back to normal. I mean I *do* care, but not now. . . . Mother, I have to go. . . ."

The baby was bawling again, and her mother was in the middle of an expostuation, but nothing mattered, thank God, because her breasts were full. Dreamily, not thinking, or even knowing what she was doing, she slipped the receiver on its hook. It was important to tiptoe, to move very quietly, in order not to spill the happiness. You have to be happy when you feed your baby; otherwise, the milk is poisoned or something.

The crying had such a needy sound, but how could it be desperate or frightened when she had her milk full in her breasts? Laura's hands unfolded into the crib, like flowers opening, and nestled the baby. Laura's sloppy dress slithered on her shoulders as she wiggled, and finally it fell free. One was supposed to wash the nipple with boiled water and antiseptic cotton, but "After all," Laura whispered, "Mother's germs are nice germs." The tiny head cradled itself in her hand; the tiny mouth clutched the nipple. Laura giggled amiably, aimlessly, and settled herself in the rocker she'd bought in a junk shop for two dollars, over her husband's objections. The chair began to move gently. The baby sucked. Laura smiled down at her nether heart and said, "You'll give me back to me, won't you? When you don't need me." And then she laughed, because her daughter looked so fierce clutching at the nipple and eating.

TRIO FOR THREE GENTLE VOICES

FAITH skittered out of the narrow hall-way into the living room, her red telephone hanging around her neck, a toothbrush clutched in one hand. She swaggered to the desk, her telephone bumping against her chest. "Don't go in the desk drawers," Laura called warningly from the back room where she was folding diapers. "And don't you dare touch the ink." Faith opened the desk drawer and took out the ink bottle, which she placed in the crook of her arm. She closed the desk drawer, her tongue creeping out between her lips in concentration. She considered the drawer for a moment; then she pulled it out about an inch. That pleased her and she tottered into the kitchen. "What are you doing, Faith?" Laura called.

Faith, fifteen months old, didn't talk yet; or rather, she didn't say anything except words like hot dog, bye-bye, Mommee and Daddee. Now she pulled open the cabinets under the sink and took out a large aluminum pan, into which she dropped the bottle of ink. She took a paper napkin out and put it on the top of her head. It blew off. She put it on again. It blew off. Her lip quivered contemptuously and she wedged it under the ink bottle in the aluminum pan. Her mother's purse was lying on the kitchen table, its strap hanging over the edge. Faith walked over on tiptoe, gripped the edge of the table and peeked; she saw that the purse was still on the other end of the strap. She yanked the strap and the purse tumbled to the floor. Faith bent and fumbled in the purse until she found her mother's wallet. "Munn," she whispered, "munn-munn."

"Faith, come see what Mother's doing," Laura called from the back room. "Come help Mummy fold diapers." Faith tucked a dollar bill into the top of her overalls and put a ten in the aluminum pan, which she picked up, grunting slightly. She had two ones and a five clutched in her hand. Fully loaded, she staggered down the hallway toward her mother, "Momm-ee, Momm-ee, I come."

Laura looked at her daughter and sighed. As far as she was concerned her daughter was a nearly flawless thing; Laura would look at her and think to herself, Isn't she rare? And she would shiver with a kind of delight. She could see her daughter at twenty, tall, slender, with curly hair and brilliant eyes—brave, honorable, dashing, appealing, intelligent. . . . The great problem with such a child was to keep the fine mechanism from being damaged; not that Faith couldn't take care of herself under most circumstances. "She copes," Laura was fond of saying, "she copes all the time." But Laura didn't want her child subjected to the more frequent childhood horrors—the maid that beat her, the cruel playmate. Laura investigated and watched Faith's playmates; the mean ones Faith was allowed to see only once or twice a month; the nice ones, the kind and jolly ones, Faith played with almost every day.

However, maids and baby sitters were a different problem. Martin, Laura's husband, insisted often on short notice that Laura get a baby sitter; and Laura would be desperate, her news-gathering and -reporting system being useless without a good deal of time. "Do you know a goodhearted, playful sort of sitter?" she'd ask her friends one by one. "The kind that doesn't curdle a child? A responsible one?" Sometimes they did; sometimes they laughed at her. Whenever a new sitter came Laura had her come either a day before to play with Faith or else early on the same day. If the sitter was difficult Laura, in tears, would refuse to go out and nothing Martin could do would move her. However, on this particular day Martin was going to a cocktail party at his biggest client's new apartment. Martin was a lawyer and he had laid down the law. Laura's usual baby sitter, Mad Margaret, a somewhat re-tarded but very gentle woman who lived in the neighborhood, was busy; and all of Laura's emer-gency girls were unavailable. Laura was going to try a girl named Cora, whom she had never met but who had been recommended by Mary Ellen Cabany, her dearest friend, from Wellesley.

Cora arrived at ten minutes after three. She was a tall, handsome colored woman, with fine eyes and a firm mouth. Cora got paid by the hour and she didn't mind being trained at all. She straightened her back, pushed her full breasts toward the door, and she looked down across this passionate topography at the earnest and ladylike Laura.

"Oh, come in, come in. You must be Cora."

"You hit it, ma'am," Cora said. "Right on your very first try."

"Well, I'm very glad to see you. My name is Laura Andrews and this is my daughter, whose name is Faith. Won't you say 'Hi' to the nice lady, dear?" Laura desperately wanted Faith to do something charming, to win over the solemn and warlike colored woman, who stood impassive and slightly mocking by the door. Faith, rosy and cheerful, refused to say anything, but her face, distended with good feeling and smiles, was fixed on Cora like an obedient searchlight.

Cora sauntered into the living room, smoothing her cherry red skirt over the tumult of her hips. "Hi, Little Mouthful," Cora said, "how ya doing?"

Faith, flushed with coquetry, hurled herself to the floor and squirmed under the couch. She stuck her head out and looked up seriously at Cora; Cora refused to look down.

Laura, distraught by Cora's coldness, said: "Cora, would you like a cup of tea? Or coffee?"

"Coffee, ma'am," Cora said casually, "good and black." From her purple bodice Cora fetched a package of cork-tipped Tareytons. She reached into the pocket of her skirt and pulled out a wooden match, which she lit with her thumbnail. She blew a prodigious cloud of smoke.

"O do [hot dog]," said Faith. "O do, o do."

"You like that, do you, Little Mouthful?" Cora blew a smoke ring.

Faith watched for a minute and then turned to her mother. "Mommee—ooop." That meant pick me up.

Laura swooped down, relieved to be able to hold her daughter, and hauled her out from underneath the couch. Faith looked at the last smoke ring and let out a squeal of uncontrollable pleasure.

"Has a good time, don't she?" Cora said.

Faith, still smiling in her mother's arms, leaned over and swatted Cora on the side of her head.

Cora remained impassive.

"You mustn't do that," Laura said desperately to her daughter. She felt perspiration bead her upper lip. Faith held out her hand for her mother to slap.

"Don't hit her," Cora said suddenly. "Let me hold her. Y'all treat your baby rough?"

Laura closed her eyes and held out her child. It was Martin's fault: where there was no trust, no love existed, and she had to love this sitter before five o'clock.

Cora ruffled Faith's curls. "Y'all kinda pretty," she said dispassionately. She threw Faith into the air; Faith giggled. Cora looked at the baby, squinting slightly. Then she threw her again; Faith laughed. Cora put her cigarette in the corner of her mouth and threw Faith again. "O do!" Faith said breathlessly. Cora sighed and lay down on the floor, placing Faith on the firm knoll of her stomach. Cora began to bump up and down on the floor. Laura looked at Cora in her red skirt and purple blouse on the yellow rug. That rug's a mistake in the city, Laura thought. She poured the coffee.

Faith gripped Cora's purple blouse; she rolled and tumbled on Cora's grinding stomach. Her laughter broke off into nearly soundless gasps. Cora sat up. Faith's arms encircled Cora's neck and hugged it. "You sure a damn nice Little Mouthful," Cora said.

Cora and Laura sat down with their cups of coffee. Laura asked, "How many sugars?" "Four or five," Cora said. "I don't pay no mind to getting fat the way some women do." Laura asked Cora to tell her a little about herself. Cora said she was from Baltimore, her husband was no good and she had left him. "Your husband any good, ma'am?"

"Oh, yes," Laura said, conscious of Faith being in the room. "Very good," she added piously. Faith was down on her stomach hiding spoons under the rug. "Is he good-looking?" Cora asked. "I can't abide men who aren't good-looking." "He has a very Italian quality in dim light," Laura said absently. "Faith, not with Mamma's sterling. You can play with the plate, not the sterling." Laura reached on the coffee table for a cigarette and placed it unlit in her mouth. Once, in college, she had learned to strike wooden matches with her thumbnail, and now she looked Cora in the eye and asked for a match. Cora handed her one impassively. Laura, anxious to love, to be loved, to show her friendliness, hoped her thumbnail wouldn't break. The match lit on her first try and Laura held it to her cigarette. But Cora didn't smile. Laura wondered if Cora disliked her. She wondered how she would ever get such a fierce woman to like her.

Faith lifted the rug and swept out the five spoons she had hidden. She sat up, her back straight, her small neck holding the rosy weight of her head; her mouth was open, the upper lip curling like a bud. She could get two spoons in each hand and a fifth in her mouth. She stood up and walked away. Then guilt seized her. "No, no, no," she muttered and dropped the spoons. She toppled to the floor and lay on her back; idly she kicked her heels.

"Otsee wahwah," she said. "Otsee poosfah." She sat up and put two spoons down the front of her overalls. She took two more spoons in her left hand and the last one in her right hand. She rolled over until she was on all fours; it was the only way she could rise. Then she stood up. She glided toward the kitchen, leaning slightly to one side, perhaps because the spoons inside her overalls tickled. Then she stumbled and looked down and saw that a spoon had fallen down her pants leg. "Oh," she breathed, "oh." She bent, straight from the rump, and tried to push the spoon back up her pants leg. "Mamma," she said angrily. The spoon slipped down again. "Mamma." Faith lifted her head and gazed at the ceiling, then swooped and shoved at the spoon again; she was chortling as she fell forward; her head bumped on the floor and Faith collapsed. "Mamma!" Faith cried, "Maa-maa!" Laura came running and started to pick her up. "Aagh," said Faith and took a swipe at her mother's nose. "Oh, you want me to take out the spoon," Laura said and removed it. Faith burst into screams of rage. Laura looked blank.

"She wants you to shove it up her pants leg," Cora said calmly. "Don't you, Little Mouthful?"

At quarter of four Cora began to dress Faith in her snowsuit. Laura thought it was time for her to take her shower and begin to get ready. She was planning to wear the black dress that made her look indecent and with that dress she felt she had to be perfectly groomed. Cora sat Faith on the bureau and began to work the baby's legs into the snowsuit pants. Faith laughed and swung her legs around. "Put your legs in before I pound you," Cora snarled. Faith stunned, looked up and then slipped her legs into the snowsuit. Cora looked grim.

"O do?" Faith tried, experimentally.

"Hot dog yourself," Cora said, forcing Faith's strangely limp arms into the sleeves of the jacket.

Faith laughed happily. "O do," she caroled. "O do do," she went on. Then she played dead. She rolled backward with her mouth open and her entire body limp.

"Where's your ear," said Cora. "I'm roaring hungry." Faith sat up and tugged at her ear and looked at Cora. Cora said, "I'm gonna chew the damn thing off," and with a deft motion slipped Faith's cap on and fastened the strap.

Faith, encased in her snowsuit, waddled toward the front door. Laura stuck her head out of the bathroom and said to Cora: "Don't worry about whether she's warm enough. She's very warm in that suit. It's made of the same cloth Admiral Byrd wore when he flew over the South Pole."

Cora nodded sagely and followed Faith out the

front door. A minute later the doorbell rang. Laura slipped to the peephole and looked out and saw Cora. "What's the matter?" Laura asked.

"She's walking funny," Cora said.

"She always walks funny," Laura said. "She's built like me."

"Open the door," Cora said wearily. "I got to give your child a medical examination."

Laura swung the door open. Faith waddled into the house. With every third step she listed noticeably to port.

"Well, that's new," Laura said.

"It hasn't got much chance of getting popular," Cora snapped.

Faith seemed undisturbed. She waddled on into the living room, lurching regularly but seemingly paying no attention to it. She circled the coffee table once.

"Maybe her shoes are too tight," Laura said thoughtfully.

"Well, go and look at them," Cora said.

Laura knelt by her child. "You sound just like my husband," she muttered under her breath. "Everybody's smarter than I am."

Faith leaned forward, holding out her arms toward her mother; then she gave a cry of pain and clutched her side. "Mamma!" she said rebukingly.

"Don't panic," Cora cried and came running.

Laura said, half-laughing with relief that Cora cared: "Oh, Cora, I don't know what I'd do without you."

"I'm here, I'm here," Cora said, squatting down beside mother and daughter. Laura poked at her daughter for a moment and then unzipped her jacket. She reached a maternal hand down the front of Faith's overalls and pulled out a spoon that had stuck in the diaper.

It was time for Laura to leave. She leaned out the window and called Cora. At the sound of her mothers voice Faith came running up the sidewalk. She was pulling a small yellow Holgate toy that had three pegs sitting in three holes in it; one peg was yellow, one blue, one red. Faith yelled, "Toot-toot-toot—" The toy hit a crack in th the sidewalk and the pegs spilled out. "Oh," said Faith, stopping. "O dee, o dee [oh dear]." She bent and carefully replaced the pegs one by one. As she lifted the red one, she murmured—affectionately— "Dadd-ee, Dadd-ee." She pounded the peg on the sidewalk for a moment. Then she worked it into its hole.

"Are you going now?" Cora asked Laura.

"Yes, bring her in and I'll kiss her goodbye."

"You'll do nothing of the sort. Get the Little mouthful all upset . . . no, indeed. You just sneak out when she's not looking. That's what you do. I'll call you at your party when she goes to sleep."

Laura protested.

"Don't try to think, you'll just get yourself all upset," Cora said, "and you'll give the Little Mouthful distresses."

Faith ran down the street, her feet flying in odd rhythms, her arms outspread, her toy slamming along behind her. "Toot," came from the distance, "Toot-toot, toot-toot."

PIPING DOWN
THE VALLEYS WILD

ALL she said was that the little delft bowl she had bought for an ashtray was a bargain, and Martin started to get angry. He had just come home from work, having walked the half mile from the railway station, and he looked warm and uncomfortable. "A bargain!" he said loudly. "How can an ashtray be a bargain? We don't need any more ashtrays. Saving money is a bargain. But another ashtray!"

Laura knit her brows and stiffened her chin—but what came out was a half-smothered laugh. "Oh, Martin, don't say anything more about that ashtray. You'll only make a dreadful gulf between us," she said, feeling terribly witty. "A dreadful gulf," she repeated, smiling.

Without another word, Martin started up the stairs to the second floor of their apartment, a garden duplex in Pelham. He took off his coat as he went, and Laura saw that his shirt was damp in places. But it was only May, and Martin claimed it wasn't proper to wear a summer suit until June. Laura called after him, "You haven't time for a shower. Stu's coming in fifteen minutes."

Martin groaned, and continued up the stairs. A few seconds later, Laura heard a drawer being dragged open, then banged shut.

She bit her lip. She was a tall, blond girl of twenty-seven, with a handsome, rosy face, so healthy and high-colored that people—strangers on the street, salesgirls, teachers—tended to smile at her with pleasure. Long ago she had decided that she was somehow unthinkingly comic; all her talk was brightened by this feeling. "I don't think you're made of money!" she shouted up the stairs, grinning. She heard another drawer being jerked open. "Oh dear," she murmured. She headed for the stairs, paused, turned, and hurried to the kitchen and stuck her head out the back window. "Faith!" she called to her three-year-old daughter, who was sitting, playing intently, in her sandbox. "Faith, don't you dare leave that sandbox!" Then she ran back to the stairs, and halfway to the top she slowed to a walk. Martin, in the bedroom and shirtless, was pawing through a drawer. "I just straightened that drawer," she said querulously— actually it had been two weeks before. "Please don't mess it up." His mouth set, Martin continued to rummage. "I can't help it if your suit's too hot," Laura said. "Someday you'll be glad we have a delft ashtray."

Martin looked at her, still angry.

"You oughtn't to get mad at me so often," Laura said, and her eyes filled with tears.

"Are you really crying?" he asked suspiciously.

"Oh!" Laura said. "Oh! You're impossible!" She flung herself on the bed.

Martin drifted nearer to her. "Laura?" he asked delicately. Laura sniffled. "Laura, we have to save our money if you want another child next spring."

"The money came out of my food budget."

"But you could have put that money in a savings account. Even if it's the food budget, it's still money."

"It only cost two dollars," Laura said, sitting up. "Two measly, dirty dollars. And it's real delft. You know what? You're only mad at me because you got hot on the train. Well, I'll tell you something," she said, beginning to smile in spite of herself. "You're not slaving your life away for me; I'm slaving my life away for you." She thought that outrageously funny; she roared with laughter.

Martin stared down at her. "Yeah?" he said. "Women outlive men." He stalked into the bathroom and turned on both taps in the basin.

Laura rose and trailed after him and leaned against the doorjamb. "We could practice suttee," she said, "if you wanted." Then she added slyly, "Your life isn't so hard. I see you're putting on weight."

"God *damn* it!" Martin howled, bent over the washbasin. "Do you have to insult me?" But his back quivered. Laura saw he was on the verge of laughing.

Faith, at the foot of the stairs, called up, "Mommy, why do I have to stay in my sandbox?"

Laura thought for a moment, and said, "I'm coming," and started down the hallway. Martin flicked his washcloth at her. Laura let out a squeal and ran down the stairs, her husband pursuing her as far as the landing. There he halted, leaned over the banister, and squeezed the last drops in the washcloth over her head.

"Not in front of the child!" Laura said.

"I'm infantile," Martin said, looking at her in a funny way, confused and tender. "I'm too young to have a wife," and he turned back up the stairs.

Laura had scooped up her daughter and started toward the kitchen. A horn honked—a little, wizened, foreign horn. "Stu's here," she called up to her husband, and hurried into the kitchen to take care of the dinner.

Martin rushed into the bedroom and resumed his search in the bureau for a comfortable shirt. "Ah!" he said, and hauled out of the bottom drawer an old red-and-white faded cotton shirt with slightly ravelled sleeves. He had bought it his second year in college, the year he and Stu became roommates. Stu had been tall, gangling, irretrievably gloomy then, whereas Martin had been cheerful, athletic, and, though he didn't suspect it, almost deliriously happy. Martin played baseball for the college and basketball for the fraternity; he drank a little too much, because everyone did; every fall, he fell in love—in a way—and if that romance didn't last through until summer, he fell in love again in the spring. Stu had looked up to him. Stu had daydreams in which he saved Martin from drowning. And he had other daydreams in which Martin drowned and he sent a telegram to Martin's parents. Now Martin stood in front of the mirror, in a faded sport shirt that was a little tight under the arms.

The self he saw was six feet tall, with broad shoulders and a squarish, amiable face, and twenty-eight years old.

He broke away from the mirror still buttoning his shirt. He had two buttons to go as he burst out of the house onto the front stoop. Stu had turned around in the traffic circle at the end of the dead-end street, and was trying to maneuver into a tiny parking place between two cars—this even though there were empty places all along the curb big enough to hold trucks.

Through the opening in the roof of the little foreign car Stu's hand appeared, making a circle with thumb and forefinger, and there sounded a challenging whistle. Martin watched Stu whip his car backward, forward, throw the wheel back and forth, and make it on the third try. "No over-size American tub could do that," Stu called out as he closed the panel in the roof.

Martin finished buttoning his shirt and stood with his hands in his pockets, smiling vaguely toward the street, remembering college, hardly conscious that he was doing so.

Two little boys about seven years old wandered up to the car and began to talk to Stu. Stu, trying to ignore them as he climbed out of the car, managed to wedge himself between the steering wheel and the seat. He turned pink. One of the little boys said, "But why do you drive such a little car, Mister?" Martin turned and went into the house; he didn't want Stu to know he had seen the episode.

A minute later, Stu appeared at the front door, his face still pink with irritation. "Scrofulous bastards," he muttered, and with Wagnerian rage stamped up the stairs to the bathroom.

Martin ambled out to the kitchen. Laura had set out two cans of beer on the top of the ice box. "Don't we have any whiskey we can offer our guests?" he asked plaintively.

"We're saving money."

Faith sat in a chair at the table, eating spaghetti and cucumbers, her favorite meal. "Tony threw sand in my eyes," she told her father.

"Again!" Martin exclaimed. He looked so large and concerned, so vague and helpless before the mystery of rearing a daughter, that Laura suddenly arched her back and felt quite passionate. Martin leaned over and kissed her.

"You might try *kissing* me sometime," Laura said, enraged. "Peck, peck, peck, nothing but pecks. It's a wonder I stay faithful."

"You damn well better not talk like that!" Martin cried, his face turning dark.

Laura huddled against his chest. "You're jealous," she said. Placatingly, she added, "I'm glad you're jealous." Martin's heart slowed its beating; Laura could hear it through the faded old sport shirt.

"I'm not jealous," he said. "Is that lamb chops I smell? How wonderful."

"They're cheap," Laura told him. "They're probably stringy."

Martin picked up the cans of beer and put them on a tray with two glasses and an opener; he walked into the living room carrying the tray, chanting "Poverty, poverty, poverty."

Stu was halfway down the stairs. He was carrying his jacket and he had begun to loosen his tie. He looked bitterly at Martin. "If you tease me about my car, I'll kill you."

"My God!" Martin exclaimed. "Everyone's so fierce. What for? What does it get you?"

"I don't know," Stu said. "It's ego, I guess." He sounded slightly ashamed of himself. He dropped his coat and tie on a chair and then looked questioningly at Martin. He was asking if Laura would mind the coat on the chair. Martin shrugged. Stu shrugged, too, and the two of them sat down. Stu selected a small modern chair with wooden arms. He groaned. "This is the world's most uncomfortable chair, right here, under me, at this very minute."

"It was cheap," Martin informed him. "How's the job going?"

"I went through hell today," Stu said. "My boss's secretary is a bloodsucker. She hates me."

"I know, I know," Martin said, feeling almost paternal. "Secretaries are sheer hell. My boss's girl does a lot of work with the eyes, you know. And she has this fake accent, as if she just escaped from the daisy chain."

"What daisy chain?" Stu asked.

"The one at Vassar, I think," Martin said. "Hey, Laura!" he called out. "Where do they have the daisy chain?"

"The daisy chain?" said a voice filled with incredulity. "Oh, the daisy chain. I think it's Bryn Mawr."

Stu lowered his voice. "My secretary's not a bad girl. She's young," he said deprecatingly. "She's nice."

"Pretty?" Martin asked, unconsciously lowering his voice, too.

"So-so," Stu said. "She's built, though. She's really built."

Laura appeared in the doorway. "I can't hear what you're saying. Please talk a little louder."

Stu blushed and mumbled something about the hydrogen bomb.

"Yeah," Martin said. "That was some blast. Did you see the photographs in the papers?" Laura disappeared into the kitchen.

"Sure," Stu said. "The big boom-boom."

Martin was slouching so much he was practically recumbent. He supported his glass of beer on his belt. "I guess we're as good as done for," he said gloomily. "All those crazy slobs in the Pentagon."

"I know, I know," Stu said. "But our National Honor is at stake. We'll all be half rotten with radiation in a few months. Children with two heads—"

"Hey!" Laura called out. "Either you two talk louder or I'll come in there and let the lamb chops burn."

"Talk louder, Daddy," Faith echoed.

"Let's change the subject," Martin whispered.

Stu nodded. "Sure."

"Tell me," Martin said, "why don't you sell that car if it makes you so mad?"

"I can't sell it," Stu said. "It was too big a bargain."

There was a sudden, nearly insane peal of laughter from the kitchen. Martin started to laugh, too.

"What is it?" Stu asked, baffled.

"Never mind," Martin said. "If we explained it, you wouldn't think it was funny."

"You know who I saw in Best's the other day?" Laura asked from the kitchen. "Mary Lou Glover. From Smith. You remember Mary Lou, don't you?"

"You know what I wonder?" Stu said. "I wonder where all the shlunks come from. You at least have a family to come home to. I'll tell you what," he said, suddenly brightening. "Let's go talk to your daughter. . . ."

Faith was polishing off a bowl of pudding. She looked up somberly at Stu. "Hello, Stu," she said.

"Uncle Stu," her mother corrected her.

Stu cupped one hand to his mouth and the other to his ear.

"*Brrring*," he said. "*Brrring*. Your telephone is ringing."

"Mommy, Uncle Stu is calling me on the telephone," Faith said ecstatically.

"Hello," Stu said. "Are you there?"

"Hello," said Faith, with rapture. "I'm here."

They were sitting around the dining-room table. It was eight o'clock, and Faith was getting sleepy. Two lighted candles stood on the table, and their flames swayed in the current of air that came through the open windows. The candlelight made Faith and Laura look exactly alike.

"Gee, that was a good dinner," Stu said. "I can't tell you how I enjoy being here. All week I've been nervous."

"The chops were a little tough," Laura remarked, "but they had a nice taste, I thought." She clapped her hand to her mouth. "I'm not supposed to say that, am I?"

"Sure you are," Stu said hurriedly. He thought she really was embarrassed, and his face was concerned. "You're an awfully good cook."

Laura smiled. She sighed. "Faith," she said to her daughter, "you have bags under your eyes. I think we should start getting ready for bed."

Faith pouted. "I don't want to." She was glassy-eyed with the long-drawn-out pleasures of the evening. She leaned forward and put her arms around her mother's neck. "I don't want to, Mommy."

"It's bedtime," Laura said.

"It's all right," Martin said. "Let her stay up another minute or two. I couldn't bear it if she started to cry just now."

There was a sudden silence all around them. The candles flickered. Stu sighed.

"The fireflies will be out soon," Laura said. "It always seems like summer to me then."

"You put them in a jar," Stu murmured. "Faith will chase them and catch them."

"What in a jar?" Faith asked. One small hand rubbed at her eye.

"I used to collect beetles," Martin said. "I wonder if the rosebush we put in is going to bloom."

Faith yawned. The moment seemed to spread out around the four people and pause and hold them all.

"I have to put her in bed. She'll be overtired in another minute." Laura straightened up in her chair, placed her hands on the table edge, and blinked her eyes. "I have to let the maternal force build up," she said. "All right, Pumpkin. Bedtime. Allez-oop." And she stood up, lifting her daughter at the same time in her arms. Faith attempted to cry out, but she was too sleepy and made a tiny drawling sound instead. Her head spilled forward on her mother's shoulder. Laura carried her upstairs.

The two men looked at each other, almost shyly. "You know," Martin said, "I have some Scotch. I've been saving it."

He went out to the kitchen and returned with two glasses, a bowl of ice cubes, and the Scotch. He and Stu moved to the couch and made themselves drinks. After a time, Laura tiptoed down the stairs. She cleared the table without looking at the men, and carried the dishes out and piled them in the sink, not bothering to turn on the kitchen light. She stood by the back window and looked out into the dark back yard. She could almost see the fireflies glowing among the leafy branches. Faith would chase them and cry, "Look, Mommy! Look!" Stu's voice droned on. In a little while, he would get up and go, because he had to drive back to the city. Laura decided she would kiss Stu goodbye. She was filled with emotion; the emotion had haunted her all day. She peered into the darkness to distract herself. And then she would turn to Martin and say—But as she stood there, she realized there wasn't anything she wanted to say. She just wanted this day to go on forever and ever, unending, with all its joys intact, and no one changing, nothing new happening, just these same things occurring over and over. Because how did you know happiness would come back? Or if it came back, that it would be as good as this? Laura sighed and wiped her eyes surreptitiously. The trouble with being happy was that it made you frightened.

THE DARK
WOMAN OF
THE SONNETS

LAURA ANDREWS was one of those tall, big-bodied young women who look so serene. Because of the way her eyes were set, deep, beneath sensible eyebrows, and because of the calm light in them, it was difficult to think of her as moody or frightened or as anything, as a matter of fact, except warm and wise. She also had a certain comic flair, which made people laugh at her even when she was upset, and when they laughed, she became frantic because she believed no one would ever understand her; and her eyes would narrow, and she would quite determinedly set out to prove just how upset she was. Not on purpose, of course, but driven, you might say, by the thought that no one was taking her suffering seriously.

It was six-thirty on a hot August day that had not gone well for Laura. She was pottering around the kitchen, glancing occasionally out the back window to keep an eye on her four-year-old daughter, Faith, who was playing in the sandbox. The third time Laura looked out the window, it seemed to her there were insects in the air everywhere, and, clutching a bottle of insect repellent, she ran out and encased Faith in a thick oily film.

"Mommy, I don't like this stuff," Faith cried.

"It's good for you," Laura said absently, but after that Faith couldn't play in the sand because the sand stuck to her and made her itch; and she took to following her mother around the kitchen, clutching at her mother's skirt, and making whining noises.

This sort of thing had been going on all day.

Laura bore this nobly; she was three months pregnant, and she had told herself she must be careful not to hurt Faith's feelings now that Faith was going to be displaced. Faith was bewildered by this sudden laxity in the air and grew more and more distraught, and finally burst into tears in the middle of the kitchen. Laura despairingly offered her an orange popsicle to eat, even though she knew it would ruin the child's appetite for dinner.

At seven, Martin Andrews came up the front walk of their duplex garden apartment, and he knew the minute he entered the house that something was wrong. He was a well-knit and tall young man, with a firm and enterprising face, but suddenly he looked discouraged. Through the kitchen door he saw Laura crouched beside the kitchen table, holding the popsicle out to Faith, whose face was pink and streaked with tears. The vacuum cleaner was lying in the middle of the living-room floor. Cautiously, he put down his briefcase. "Hello, everybody," he said.

"Oh, hello, dear!" Laura cried, and rose to go to him and kiss him, but Martin was opening and closing the front door to see why it stuck sometimes and sometimes opened freely. "These modern houses are put together with chewing gum," he said. "I've had a foul day." He kept his eye on the door, closing it slowly, with great care, watching it alertly. "Aha!" he said. "I see where it sticks."

He looked hollow-cheeked and cowardly, bent over by the door.

"God," Laura said. "It's shocking, the way men are so full of self-pity."

After that, Martin refused to talk to her or to tell her what had gone wrong at the office. In persecuted silence, he went upstairs and changed his clothes and put on bathing trunks. Then he and Faith played with the hose in the back yard, squirting each other and running around on the grass with noisy laughter, while Laura resentfully cooked pork chops for supper, putting out of her mind the fact that she always said that pork was indigestible when the weather was hot.

Martin put on shorts and a sports shirt, and the family had their dinner almost in silence. Faith told her father she had gone to the store with her mommy. "We had a letter from Aunt Dorothy today," Laura said at one point. Martin raised his eyebrows and said pointedly, "You're in a poisonous mood, and I'm not going to pretend you're not." Pale and haughty, Laura went to work fiercely on her pork chop, hoping that if she cut the pieces small enough they wouldn't make her sick.

Immediately after dinner, she took Faith up to bed. Outside Faith's bedroom window was the sunset, all crimson and runny. Laura laid the child in her bed, turned on the air-conditioner, and tiptoed out of the room.

She was wearing a sun dress, and suddenly she couldn't bear the sight of her bare arms. She went to her bedroom closet and got down the box of her old maternity clothes. They were wrinkled and looked faded; after all, they were four years old, and her waist hadn't enlarged enough for her to wear maternity clothes yet. Besides, she was keeping her pregnancy a secret so that it wouldn't seem so long.

She leafed through the dresses in the box and finally pulled out what had been her favorite— her dress-up outfit, with a high white collar and long sleeves, and pleats. It hung loosely on her now, and it smelled of mothballs, but she didn't care. She descended the stairs, and, in full maternity regalia, sweating, she did the dishes.

Martin was sitting in the back yard in a lawn chair drinking a highball, solitary in the suburban dusk. Laura turned out all the lights in the apartment and went outside. Down the row of apartments, several of the yellow back-door lights were turned on, signifying that the occupants were secreted in their yards, leaving only that light to guide them if their phones should ring.

The evening was no cooler than the day had been. "It's so hot," she said. "I'm tired of its being so hot."

Martin drank from his highball glass. Laura watched the outline of his Adam's apple in the darkness, and then she clumsily climbed into the hammock and lay there in her maternity dress, an absurd figure, dabbing with a Kleenex at her forehead.

"I would love to hear the sound of a human voice," she said at last. "The hoofs of the rescue party, sort of."

Martin stirred in the lawn chair. "I'm sorry. I thought you liked the quiet."

Laura made a disrespectful noise, a snort. "You're angry with me and you know it."

Martin said nothing.

"A penny for your thoughts, you bastard," Laura said after a while.

Martin laughed abruptly, with obvious discomfort. "Why do you want to know? You'll only get mad at me because I wasn't thinking about you."

Laura was stabbed by that remark—by the fact that he hadn't been thinking about her. "No, I won't," she said. "Tell me."

"I was thinking about Ferguson." Ferguson was the head bookkeeper in the office.

"In August? When everyone's on vacation?" Laura said incredulously.

"Yes," Martin said, sighing, and picked up his highball glass and clinked the remnants of the ice cubes. The tinkle floated on the air, and Laura said, "Oh, do that again, Martin, please. It was so pretty."

Martin laughed and did it again. Then he lifted the glass and sucked the ice cubes into his mouth and crunched them up. The noise was strangely sharp and clear in the darkness. All the leaves were absolutely motionless.

She was still hurt because he had been thinking about his office. "You're a beast," she said, and began tearing off bits of her Kleenex and dropping them in the grass.

"Me!" Martin was startled. He had thought she was coming out of her mood and growing peaceful.

"You torture me," Laura said. "You play with my feelings. God, you must hate me!" She stretched out one arm in the darkness.

"Oh, Laura," Martin said plaintively.

"And the baby, the poor child I carry. I can feel what you're doing to it. It's all knotted up. If you only knew how unhappy it is."

"For God's sake," Martin said. "For God's sake.

Laura, do you realize your so-called baby is little more than a fish at this point."

"Oh, you're inhuman," Laura muttered. "You really are."

"And you're the dark woman of the sonnets," Martin said, plucking a handful of grass. He stood up, and, holding his glass in one hand, dropped the grass from his other onto Laura's hair. "Stop picking on me, honey," he said and went into the house. Laura lay in the hammock; the grass tickled her ear. Suddenly she was terribly frightened, and not at all sure that Martin would come back. He might get dressed and walk out of the house. He might find a woman somewhere. Laura wanted to cry, but the tears wouldn't come.

From the house, Martin called, "Laura! I can't get the ice tray unstuck!"

Laura slid off the hammock. She walked slowly, drowsily, into the house. Martin was bent over the icebox.

"I must have some disease," he said. "My fingers —Oh!" he said admiringly as Laura did something mysterious that loosened the tray in its bed.

Martin took out the tray and closed the icebox door. "I love the way you do things like that," he said. "It's really lovely to see—that flip of the wrist sort of thing. My."

"You think of me as a clown, don't you?" Laura sounded infinitely long-suffering and gentle. "I ought to wear floppy shoes and turn somersaults, I think. Would you be sorry if I never looked foolish again?"

"No, of course not," Martin said unconvincingly, as he ran hot water over the bottom of the ice tray.

"If only—" Laura folded her hands over her bosom—an absurd, perspiring figure in her balloonlike maternity dress, with the smell of mothballs emanating from her, and on her face a look of such matchless calm thoughtfulness that it was impossible to believe she was serious. "God knows, I try to be intelligent, Martin. You should respect the effort I make, if nothing else, and—" But she couldn't think of what to say next.

"Aunt Dorothy have anything to say in her letter?" Martin asked, sighting carefully as he dropped the ice cubes in his glass.

"They're going to be in town next week," Laura said wearily, turning away. "They'd like me to come in and bring Faith."

"Well, do it, then."

How sweet the silence of this hot evening was, Laura thought; it seemed to lie around the house like a great, dark cat.

"Yes, I suppose so," she murmured. "But it's so hot for a child. And she might catch something. Oh, I'm a terrible mother. I want to take her to see Aunt Dorothy, but I wouldn't take her in to

see most people. I wouldn't take her in to see
Cousin Eleanor, for instance. I use that child for
my own purposes."

"You don't like Cousin Eleanor," Martin pointed
out. He restored the ice tray to the icebox. "You
do like Aunt Dorothy. I don't think that's so awful."
He was careful to sound rational and friendly, but
not too sympathetic, because he was afraid of what
emotions sympathy might release.

"Yes, of course," Laura said, laying her hand
to her cheek. "I forgot that. Sometimes I get myself
all upset over nothing." She felt disappointment
washing back and forth in her chest, like waves.
"I think I won't take Faith, anyhow. All those
diseases . . ."

"Then don't take her," Martin said. He added
water to the Scotch he had already poured.

"But Aunt Dorothy will be so disappointed."
Laura wrung her hands, hoping that now she was
on the trail of her real unhappiness, that her
quarry wasn't far ahead.

"Laura," Martin said. "Aunt Dorothy can live
without Faith. So can practically everyone, except
us."

Laura interrupted. "You're jealous of her,"
Laura said. "Oh!" she added inanely and went out
the back door, across the lawn, toward the wonderful, comfortable hammock, suspended in the darkness. Martin walked behind her, and as Laura

started to climb into the hammock, she felt him holding it steady for her. She sank down on the cloth and lay with her eyes closed. When she opened them, she saw Martin looking down at her. "What's wrong, lovebug?" he asked.

"I don't know," Laura said. "That's it. I just don't know. Everything seems so awful, so sad—especially me. I—I've done something awful, I suppose. I suppose it's my subconscious or something getting back at me, but I don't know why. I don't know why at all. I don't understand one thing I do."

"But you must have some idea," Martin said. "Please tell me. I promise not to get angry. Please tell me, Laura dearest. Let me help. I can't stand it when you're like this."

"Oh, it's the most dreadful feeling . . . dreadful."

Somebody in the row of garden apartments was playing the radio loudly, and the music of a string quartet swam on the heated, motionless air. Someone else had hung a Japanese Lantern in another back yard, and it glowed like a frail moon among the dark leaves of the bushes and trees. And in the middle of this whole scene, Martin bent over the hammock, peering helplessly at the strange, distorted figure of his wife wrapped in that absurd maternity outfit.

"Martin, I'm no good," Laura said. "I'm a terrible person." She paused but she wasn't getting any nearer to what she felt. "I'm growing older," she whispered, "but I don't act older, and I'm ashamed." But that had nothing to do with anything, and in the darkness Laura sighed and folded her arms over her forehead, hiding her eyes. "Martin, I really don't know what's wrong. Isn't that silly."

Martin was bent over, his arms around the entire hammock, holding Laura to his chest. He looked very uncomfortable bent over like that, and Laura suddenly embraced his head, pressing it tight against her breast.

"You mustn't talk," Martin whispered. "If you say things, Laura, you'll start to believe them. I know you. Just don't say anything. Just lie here and relax. In the morning this feeling will go away, I promise. But I can't stand to hear you talk like this. It kills me, Laura. It really does. I think the heat's just got you down. God, I'm all distraught!" He moved his head out of her embrace and kissed her sticky cheeks. "If you knew what it does to me to hear you talk like this, you wouldn't do it."

Laura turned away; the last thing in the world she wanted was to talk about Martin.

"Listen," he said, "I have to go inside a minute. I'll be right back, and I don't want you to be upset while I'm gone."

"All right," Laura said. She smiled at him, but

it was a sickly smile, and she was grateful it was dark and he couldn't see her too clearly.

Lying in the hammock, she covered her eyes with her arm and listened to Martin's footsteps moving rapidly toward the house. Then the screen door slammed and the sound died slowly on the night air.

Oh, why can't I feel better? Laura thought. Why am I unconsoled?

And quickly her mind poured forth accusations, reminding her of her temper, her foolishnesses, her selfishness. She stifled a groan and stirred on the hammock. She was low, she was terrible, she would never be able to show Martin she really loved him and wanted to be good, because her wicked nature got in the way. And she was punished for this because when he tried to console her, she didn't feel consoled. "I'll never really know how much he loves me," she thought. "There's no way I'll know. I can only suspect it." At that her tears started to flow, and it seemed to her that she had found one of the secret springs of sadness that water the whole world. She wasn't a fool to feel sad at all.

She cried mostly for Martin's sake. "Poor Martin!" she thought. "Poor Faith!" She couldn't cry for herself because she disapproved of herself so severely. "They're saddled with the most awful woman, and we'll never know how much we love each other, never, never, never." And each time she thought this, her tears flowed faster.

Martin came out of the house. He saw that the hammock was swinging gently back and forth, and he smiled. He knew at once that Laura felt better, and he was serious and proud because he had consoled her. Not that he knew what he had done; in fact, as he walked across the grass, he felt small, and awed by the mysteries of what went on between a husband and wife.

"You all right?" he whispered.

"Yes," Laura whispered tearfully.

"You want to cry on my shoulder or do you want to cry alone?"

"Alone," said Laura. "But don't go too far away." Oh, the world was sad, she thought. Oh, the separateness of people. Oh, the clumsiness of being a woman.

Martin sat in the lawn chair and drank his highball. His heart was full. And, smiling peacefully in the darkness, Laura cried.

GLORIA MUNDI

BARTLETT ROBINSON was fifty years old and somewhat melancholy. He sat at his desk in his office at the small New York bank where he was a vice president and looked out of his window at the gray March day. It was on a day like this, not more than a year ago, that Bartlett Robinson had come in to work from his wife's funeral, his shallow blue New England eyes dry and harsh as always, his thin arched nose transparent and slightly red, his long thin hands shaking, not as always because he was usually calm, but from the exhaustion and the cold of the cemetery with its graves making a ruined checkerboard of the earth. He had sat at his desk and contemplated his wife's picture. He had not quite known what to do with it, whether he ought to put it away or leave it where it could be seen; he had no emotional leaning either way. He merely wondered which was proper.

Sometimes, in bad moments, such as saying good-by to his daughter at Grand Central Station when she had to return to college, in the great concourse, in the noise and confusion of the millions of separations, with the clock ticking, and his daughter's small serious face eluding him behind the lipstick and the little hat and the college grand manner, at moments like that Bartlett found himself taking refuge in propriety. Propriety, Bartlett Robinson thought, is the last refuge against the irrational. Also against the things one didn't want to believe in, and he sighed and straightened his tie by the faint reflection in the window behind which New York gleamed somberly under a gray sky.

At the funeral he had had to fight down a sickly feeling of unreality and it was only later back at his office where he had fled to escape his son (the boy's a fool, Bartlett Robinson thought and could not bring himself to remember his son's face with its pointed nose and drooping eyelids and its expression of grief which was merely a "there's a bad smell" grimace outlined on the pink skin) that he had been able to remember anything about his wife. He had let himself stare at the picture, slipping into the momentary fixation slow men so easily muster, and he had remembered, raspingly, the days when at twenty-eight he had seemed at last to escape his lonely childhood with glad feelings and a sturdy confidence. How pleased he had been with spring, with his sharply creased white ducks, with his fair hair that shone when combed and wet, with the girl whose eyes were mysterious with youth and gentle with inexperience. On green lawns, in white summer homes, at discreet balls he had sought her out. His mother had taken the girl's two hands in hers and looked up at her from beneath the wide-brimmed hat and kissed her welcome into the family.

Everyone had told him he was marrying well. In the middle of a glow of approval and envy and self-pride he had married the girl, taken her into his arms, his heart, his house—even his inmost hope and dream.

And then he had discovered that she would bring him no particular happiness.

When she had died he'd discovered that some dry and foolish part of himself had loved her, that there might have been an otherwise. At fifty, Bartlett Robinson was oppressed not only with the coming of age but with the presence of regret and sorrow.

The photograph had shown a woman in a loose sweater open over a blouse with full hair ruffled in a wind, squinting at the sun with an easy semblance of nobility. "I don't know why you keep that picture," she'd said, "when it doesn't look at all like . . ." The day of the funeral he had not turned on the light in the office; the world was gray like cheap flannel, gloomy and silent. Gently, his thin reddened hands trembling, Bartlett Robinson had taken the picture from his desk and put it in a drawer.

Bartlett Robinson glanced once more out of the window and then began slowly with his shrewd bony dignity to put the papers on his desk in order. His farsighted eyes looked down over the arched nose; his mouth grew thin; the lower lip pursed in thought.

He could not go in search of a cure. Submission was essential to pride. He strung his life on the gray

March days and the towers of New York and the bank that murmurously spun its webs behind its hundred doors. A long time ago he had discovered that there were rites and soothing rituals that propped up the mind's lostness. He had not as a child been able to rely on affection for that; affection had been rare and necessarily used for other things. He could not feel affection for his job but the routine was dear to him, the counterpart of sleep.

The self was no shelter. But it is possible to preserve the surface of existence and tack it up like a few shreds of bright wallpaper . . . his pencil quivered, made a mark. He was working. That was the best you could hope for.

Gloria Mundi, the smaller things: at four o'clock, grown restless with his papers, Bartlett Robinson looked up, pleased, and saw the bank president enter the room.

It seemed he would have to perform an unpleasant duty. One of the clients of the bank had recently died, a former immigrant, a Hyman Cohn, who had made a fortune of nearly two million dollars in various small enterprises. He had died suddenly, at sixty-two, and left behind the simplest will bequeathing everything to his wife. Just before he'd died, he had asked his wife to turn the money into a trust and let the bank handle it for her.

The president said, "I don't know this woman. I've heard she was the brains behind Cohn. I knew him. He was as sharp and unpleasant, as illiterate and suspicious, as coarse and incomprehensibly clever, as the most prejudiced person could desire. I don't envy you, Bartlett. But I think she'll admire your type and behave—and be more tractable than if we send anyone else. She doesn't have to put her money with us, you know. Why this man didn't choose a Jewish executor I'll never figure out."

Bartlett Robinson arrived in the lobby of an apartment house that overlooked the East River. He loved the river: its dark puritan factories, its dismal barges, its tugs that beetled back and forth reminding him of bent Irish servants running back and forth in the lower hallways of the house in Providence. He sighed and went up in the elevator to the twelfth floor. He really didn't like Jews; they seemed unnecessary.

A woman came to the door. She was tall, big-bodied, with a square handsome face and round shoulders and easy posture. Her hair was white, in a roll around her head, and her eyes were a slightly faded blue. Her mouth was small, not at all tense; her nose was small with a gently rounded tip. She looked Jewish.

"Are you Mrs. Cohn? I'm Bartlett Robinson from the bank."

"Yes, I'm Mrs. Cohn. Come in, please." She had a faint, unidentifiable accent. She was wearing a plain black dress with a square neck that showed the healthy flesh of her neck and upper chest. Her arms were large and pale. On one hand shone an amethyst in a large, synthetically antique setting.

She seated Bartlett Robinson in a big chair by the French windows that overlooked the river. She brought him coffee, over his protests, and a pack of cigarettes. They talked of trust funds and how they operated. Bartlett spread his papers over the coffee table. To his surprise he enjoyed talking business to her; she listened and responded without vagueness or restlessness or undue shrewdness, either; she listened and seemed to understand. Once he went too fast and she touched him on the hand: "Slower," she said. "I think business in Yiddish and I have to translate."

When he finished explaining the comfort and security of a trust fund and the stability and intelligence of his bank, he sat back and waited for her to speak.

"I don't know," she said from the depths of her chair. "I thought I might go into business." When she said "thought" it was almost "tought," but not quite. "I get bored just sitting." She smiled into Bartlett's blank façade. She said meekly, "I thought I might buy a little business."

Bartlett placed the fingertips of his two hands together. "Well," he said thoughtfully, "it is of course up to you, Mrs. Cohn, but I should think a woman—" He hesitated, then decided she would take it: "—your age would not enjoy the strain. I hope I am not being presumptuous."

"Oh, no," Fanny Cohn said. "You're here to advise me, aren't you? Go right ahead. Tell me what to do."

A sudden picture of some of the more embattled dowagers he had to face in his work came into Bartlett's mind and made him laugh. He shook his head to stop himself and quickly apologized.

"I've been laughed at before," Fanny Cohn said. "It bothered me once. But now—" She spread her arms and smiled. "—now I'm old and I don't care who laughs. It's their pleasure."

"Well," said Bartlett, ashamed of himself, "a business might prove too much of a strain. It might lose a great deal of money."

"I suppose you're right," Fanny Cohn said restlessly. She stood up and walked to the window. "What am I going to do with myself?"

"Your family perhaps," Bartlett suggested discreetly.

"I have a son," Fanny said. "He calls himself Cantwell. Which is a rough translation of Cohn, they tell me." She laughed, without malice. "He's a professor and he's got a fancy wife. I have nothing personal against the girl. But I embarrass her." Her voice grew very soft. "I know how the boy feels. He's different from me and his father. So . . ." Fanny Cohn sighed. "I should stick my money in the bank and spend my life writing checks? No, I got to find something to do. Hyman wanted me to be safe so I put half the money with you and I'm safe. Isn't that right? The other half I'll keep."

She turned around from the window and Bartlett noticed for the first time a sort of animal quality she had in her large frame. She was still well-shaped, still strong. He found it easy to picture her young with a square, bright-cheeked Russian face, blue eyes bright and full of life . . . no, the eyes probably always held some fear in them. Even now it was there under the faded eyelashes, beneath the fleshy lids, the look of repressed fright, like weariness. Bartlett wanted to be helpful.

"Wouldn't you like to travel?" he asked gently.

"Sleep in strange beds alone?" Fanny Cohn grimaced. "It's bad enough sleeping in my own bed alone." She looked at Bartlett sitting in her wing-backed chair listening with an air of neat propriety, and she smiled. "That's just my way of talking," she said to him.

Bartlett found himself smiling back.

"I might go to Mexico," Fanny Cohn said. "I went there with Hyman after he got heart trouble. They have skies like turquoise sometimes, imagine, and the children, oh, you should see the children. It hurt me though that they were so poor. And I can't speak the language." Fanny Cohn heaved a gigantic sigh. "It's better I should stay here. I got some charities I work for." She looked at Bartlett from the corner of her eyes to see if she was boring him; she was pleased to see that he was watching her. "I don't want to burden you with my *tzuros*," she said. "I got plenty to be thankful for. I have two grandsons, beautiful boys. You don't know how smart they are. They have a governess and the littlest one has a little English accent, imagine." Her small mouth curved maternally. "He's a doll, that one. Anyway I've took too much of your time, Mr. Robertson. You draw up your papers and bring them to me to be signed. For half the money like we said. I like you to come here because in those downtown banks I sometimes don't feel comfortable."

Bartlett stood up and smiled. "I understand." He had enjoyed this woman; he'd found her amusing and honest. He held his hat in one hand and stood in the doorway. "I'll do just that." He was pleased when she held out her hand to him that she did it so well, that her hand was so pretty. He felt rather that she was cute. Which was silly, he thought as he rode down in the elevator, since she was nearly as tall as he.

Nevertheless, he thought as he paused and looked at the East River, he'd enjoy watching over her money for her.

Three times in the next month Bartlett found it necessary to visit her. She did not like to speak over the telephone, and Bartlett did not like to send his secretary to her. It had occurred to him that the woman was proud, and his own pride responded delicately and surely; life, Bartlett thought, did its best to make pride impossible; only man, only men helping other men, made pride possible. And though much about the woman made him want to laugh, she was so honest in her way that he found her admirable. The condescension he felt didn't bother him, and he didn't think it would bother her. After all, she was an alien in a society that was his tradition.

It always amused him to catch sight of the two of them saying goodbye in the small hallway of her apartment. There was a large mirror across the living room in which he could see the scene quite clearly, the tall, bony, somewhat red, somewhat dry, white-haired man, the equally tall, fleshy, blue-eyed woman; he standing very straight so that the cords of his aging neck were visible, she erect but easily so in the manner of full-bodied women; his reddened hand with the waxy skin drawn taut and wrinkled over the knuckles lying in her fleshy, beringed hand; his formal smile made of thin lips and mannerism, her sturdy seriousness made of hospitality and concern over whether the hospitality had been proper or not; her perpetual black dress, his perpetual gray suit; and the perpetual finality of his back turning away as the door closed.

The third time he went to see her the papers were at last signed. It was after five, and he stayed and had a cocktail with her. She made an excellent martini.

"These are good," he told her.

Fanny Cohn shrugged. "I learned how because it was good business. Hyman could drink a lot and not get dizzy."

"Well, they're very good," Bartlett said and smiled at the shrewdness of the woman. Something in Fanny Cohn's manner mocked each thing she said as if she had learned always the shallowness of each endeavor, a life spent in doing things which were not deep enough for the soul to swim in. This pleased Bartlett Robinson and helped him to relax because he found it difficult to take the world very seriously. It was true that one cared but the caring was irrational and wearing. After all man was little more than an envelope of flesh filled with a dull scrawl of veins and nerves and no matter how fancily the envelope was stamped or how noble sounding the address, the destination was, the message was still the same and still incomprehensible. The ineffable pomposity of pretending one was important, of assuming semi-regal postures of belief, of playing prophet and seer about business and politics filled him with trembling weariness and a great boredom. But here in Fanny Cohn's overstuffed living room with the East River imitating eternity outside the French windows, the world was put in its place and all the meaning was somehow concerning the savor of the individual. Fanny Cohn's revelations, her monologues, her care in pleasing her alien visitor were all so personal, so warm that Bartlett relaxed. The body which he was slightly tired of bent into its chair and the martini which rushed through him like a fire drowned the noise of the physiological processes and left him a feeling of peace. He had not been feeling well for several weeks and the cocktail gave him a sense of great well-being. Then he began to feel giddy; his hand began to shake. He managed to put his drink down before he blacked out totally.

He came to feeling sick and with a tremendous ache in his head. Nothing felt right and he knew that he was disabled. He did not even try to rise. Breathing was a little difficult; to his intense disgust he found he had to make each breath whistle through his long nose.

He was in bed in an unfamiliar bedroom. He had enough wit to recognize that the frilly lampshades and the green color of the walls marked a guest room. He remembered he had been at Fanny Cohn's. Then the door opened and Fanny Cohn looked in.

"Hello," he said weakly. "Did I do something foolish?"

"You passed out," Fanny said. She walked over to the bed and put her hand on his forehead as if feeling for a temperature. This made Bartlett smile feebly; his mother had always done that even if he had a broken arm or a cut finger. "I called a doctor," Fanny Cohn said looking down at him. "He'll be here any minute. Have you done this before?"

"No," Bartlett said; he realized he was undressed and he unobtrusively pulled the covers up to his chin. Another thought struck him as he looked up into Fanny Cohn's solicitous face. "How did I get to bed?"

Fanny Cohn smiled and bit her lip slyly. "I carried you. You're skinny. How do you feel?"

"Not very good."

"I bet you feel like hell," Fanny Cohn said reassuringly and patted his hand. She turned to leave the room. Over her shoulder, with an obvious grin, she said, "You're very well shaped for a man your age."

Bartlett helplessly coughed up a laugh. In spite of his pain she made him feel like a rakehell.

The doctor was a short fat man with a florid face and the most sensitive hands Bartlett had ever seen. The doctor made little jokes as he fussed with his stethoscope over Bartlett's chest.

"I blacked out," Bartlett said.

"You should leave that to the movie theaters," the doctor said. "Ever have heart trouble before? And I don't mean with a blonde either . . . ha, ha."

"I have slightly high blood pressure," Bartlett said faintly. He was feeling worse.

He had had a heart attack, the doctor told him. The doctor would give him some pills; tomorrow he would call Bartlett's doctor. "Meanwhile you better spend the night right here."

"But this is Mrs. Cohn's apartment," Bartlett said weakly.

Fanny Cohn was standing worriedly in the doorway. "You think there'll be a scandal, at our age?" she asked. "You think I'm sexy or something? You stay right here."

The doctor pushed a pill in his mouth and helped him swallow some water. Bartlett felt himself going woozy. He saw Fanny Cohn and the doctor leave the room and then he fell asleep.

When he woke again the room was dark and silent. His watch said three o'clock. It no longer was such an effort to breathe and the ache in his head was much smaller, but correspondingly he felt quite lost and depressed. Actually he was surprised to be alive, perhaps even resentful. He wanted to clear his mind and lie peacefully but his mind swarmed with inchoate colors and impressions: some part of him was excited to be alive, was haranguing him from some internal pulpit. Startled, Bartlett Robinson discovered he was in pajamas, silk ones that fit; he had always rather enjoyed silk pajamas. Hyman Cohn had been a small man; Fanny Cohn must have sent out and bought these. Details were comforting. As long as he thought of details like this his mind stayed quiet. It occurred to him that Fanny Cohn had to put the pajamas on him . . . Bartlett Robinson essayed a smile in the dark. He wondered if he could make it to the bathroom. Just then his door opened and Fanny Cohn, looking warm and voluminous in a kimono, hurried in with a tiny flashlight in her hand. She shined the flashlight on his face.

"Oh, you're awake. Good. You have to take a pill. How do you feel?"

"Much better." For some reason the two of them were whispering. "Did the doctor say this was a bad attack?"

"Oh, no. Or they would have taken you to the hospital. This was a very little attack."

"That's good," Bartlett said. "I have a great deal of work at the bank."

"You'll have to rest a while, I think," Fanny Cohn said delicately. "You can't take chances with a heart."

"I don't think I'd like to live on a regime," Bartlett said slowly; to his surprise there was bitterness in his voice.

"When you think a little more about death," came Fanny Cohn's voice muted in the darkness, "you'll settle for a regime."

It was true; Bartlett hadn't thought about death; he had thought only of the gentleness of surrender, but death itself, the irreversible progression beyond this world . . . it made him suddenly cold. He was a child again, happy and hopeful, hugging the promise life made that when he should become a man the narrow red brick house would open up and let him roam free through all the meadows and compartments of the world. Death was a giant bird with black wings, chill wings, sleep's wicked sister that took one away, that tied one's eyelids. . . . Blond and dewy-skinned the child had been, and Bartlett knew his hair was white, his skin brittle and dry, that he was all paleness and water, but something in him grew rigid at the thought of death. Not now, not safe beneath the covers—he decided he would not go to the bathroom—not here in the presence of this large and comforting woman.

"Do you mind sitting down and talking to me?" Bartlett asked. "I feel confused. I want someone to

talk of life to me, to remind me . . . I'm very confused." He sounded proud, genteel until the last
word; then his voice caved in and he sounded lonely.

Fanny Cohn remained standing. She blinked her
flashlight off and on. "I felt like that once. When I
had my baby. I wanted to talk . . . but I didn't know
anyone. I felt like going up to all the women with ba-
bies and asking—I don't know—asking how they
did it. But I didn't speak English good then. Is that
how you feel?"

"Yes."

"When Hyman died it was the same thing, like
having a child. I knew how much it was going to
hurt, that I couldn't stand it—you want to stop the
whole thing but it's too late. You can't bring back
the dead; you can't plug up a baby. But it hurts."

She's trying to reassure me, just as I asked, Bartlett
thought. She's not just talking too freely as I might
think. She's telling little stories to show me life goes
on, to reassure me. . . . It sounds melancholy, the
melancholy Jews . . . but it's not.

"When my wife died . . . ," he said and slowly his
voice faded. He didn't want to talk; he wanted this
woman to tell him her stories, just as his mother had
once given him bright and shining at bedtime a wonderful world of fairies with true justice and a gently
yielding reality, so this woman would give him a world
of people warm and individual, caught up in sickness
and ambition and the simpler cycles, stripped of the
clouds of glory that most men attempted to trail be-

hind them, and that would comfort him. He made his voice gentle, worried that he might make her shy, and asked, "Did you love your husband?"

"You wouldn't think it to look at him."

"He wasn't handsome?"

"Hyman? Dear Gott, he was ugly. Even in Odessa people thought he was ugly. I was a very pretty girl. You might not think it to look at me now but when I was young I was considered very attractive. Big maybe, but attractive."

"But you loved him."

"Maybe not at first too much. But he worked hard. He brought me to the States. When the people would laugh at me for being so big and dressing so Russian he took me uptown and we waited until we saw Mrs. Vanderbilt come out of her house. She was a horse, that woman, bigger than me. And I worked with Hyman, we made money together. I got to love him. I don't know. Sometimes I tink a woman loves anyone who loves her."

Bartlett Robinson sighed. Fanny Cohn was a strong woman; she would not approve of what he had done. But he was anxious for her to like him; he would have to tell her. He said: "I loved my wife. I didn't know it while she lived."

"That's a terrible thing," Fanny Cohn said.

"It wouldn't have done any good to have spoken of it. We weren't the happy type." With what fierceness he could muster he said, "There really was no earthly reason for my loving her but I did."

"That's the way it goes," Fanny Cohn said with a sigh.

It was the woman's sigh of contentment, Bartlett thought; she was just enjoying the conversation. She was not judging at all. She was just talking to him. Oh how crude, how barbaric . . . how lovely and gentle. . . . Bartlett Robinson began to laugh helplessly. Fanny Cohn laughed, too. Bartlett knew she was just laughing to be polite, to share some of her matchless warmth with him. He coughed from the laughter; Fanny Cohn raised him and hit him on the back. He thought how laughter was a cry disguised. He cried, "How late it is. How late it always is."

Fanny Cohn, suddenly shy, stood away from him, blinking her little flashlight on and off. "It's almost four o'clock," she said. "Very late. You got to take your pills."

Bartlett felt very giddy, so complicated, so much a brittle male in front of this tough, soft woman. He pressed his fists against his temples; his eyes were watering with the pain. He felt old and needful. Fanny Cohn slipped the pill between his lips; she raised his head and held the glass of water for him. Her eyes were blissful with the joy of having someone to take care of.

Bartlett smiled feebly at her. "Thank you, dear Mrs. Cohn."

Fanny Cohn bent her head. "It's really nothing, but you're very welcome, Mr. Robertson."

She tiptoed out the door and closed it. The hall

light disappeared. Bartlett Robinson unaccountably felt two tears on his dry cheeks. She didn't even know his name. . . .

When next he woke he was in a hospital room. His doctor had been called the following morning, had given him an injection to keep him from awakening ("any strain we can avoid is that much to the good, Mrs. Cohn"), and had had him taken to the hospital. Bartlett soon felt much better. His daughter nursed him dutifully. She teased him about being found in bed in a woman's apartment. She seemed to take for granted that Mrs. Cohn was his mistress. The books this generation reads, he thought to himself. Finally he had to explain that he could afford a much younger woman if he wanted a mistress and then he noticed that both he and his daughter felt somewhat disappointed with the meager truth. His son appeared and managed to irritate him.

At last Fanny Cohn came. She only stayed twenty minutes. Bartlett had tried to greet her warmly but she had been clumsily involved in a huge fur coat she couldn't get off somehow. And then shyness had stolen over him, and distaste: the woman's skin was old and her eyes had that deep liquid fright, and what she had been was irretrievable, and what she was was so final, so complicated, so alien. If one tried one could remember that she was being natural, but the impulse was easier merely to accept her mannerisms as unlearned lessons, incompleteness: she'd be more cultural some day. Bartlett felt a certain warmth toward her but he was well and it was daytime. It was, Bartlett thought, a shame to have the stiffness to mar their little meeting. He was genuinely grateful to her for her kindness.

After she left he walked out and sat on the balcony of his hospital room and let his gaze rest on the jiggling complexity of the tenement street that ran below his room. People ran in and out of doors, busses and taxis held true to their dreary schedules, children embarked on their afternoons and sailed far away into games. The image of the Cohn woman refused to leave his mind. Her animal awkwardness in the smooth thick coils on coils of the fur coat; her tiny apologetic smile on her tiny sweet mouth; her strange little accent that turned th's into t's, but not quite; the grace of her hands; the softness of her voice; the strength in her face and the concealed fright in her eyes: and yet he knew she was shrewd and maybe even ruthless in her way, what did he know of her? She was an interesting and foreign and remarkable woman . . .

. . . And he was in love with her.

The tenement street receded; there was suddenly only sky and wind ruffling his white hair and a new lightness around his dry and tired heart. That it should happen to him before he died thrilled Bartlett Robinson; that he should share in the ripening of this severe and geometric flower, this long sought, long denied vegetative righteousness made him suddenly, alone on his balcony beneath the delft-blue sky and active wind, clasp his hands and smile and blink back two tears; then his dry aging Yankee's face could reassert its sway and close the curtain on his emotion.

He would have to plan, if he could. One could not, even in one's mature years, suddenly let one's past repressions crackle into strange blossomings like drunken twigs in early spring. One had to plan. His banker's mind fought and struggled, pointed conscience-stricken fingers dutifully, and then solemnly, to Bartlett Robinson's immense confusion, began to dance with strange persistence about the image of Fanny Cohn.

Oh my, Bartlett Robinson thought and he began to laugh. Gloria Mundi . . . late, so very late; but more than he deserved. Or at any rate, thought Bartlett in an access of new pride, more than I expected.

It began to seem impossible as soon as he left his hospital. His superior came to visit him, made a few rather clever jokes about passing out in a Jewess' apartment, and Bartlett felt his first twinge. Then there was his daughter's proud briskness, not designed for burdens or a parent's exotic attachment. And Fanny herself. When he called her and asked her to join him for dinner she grew flustered, even unpleasant, and flatly refused. But his needs clustered in his head like children confined on a rainy day and tormented him. Slowly, even grandly, he felt his reactions, himself, his desires turning off the superhighway, down around the cloverleaf with a cyclical grandeur, down onto a not-so-common road. Individuality was a glorious thing, or eccentricity, or call it what you will. The tides of mobilized social and corporate virtues with their streamlined fenders faded from his mind and he could see the trees. Very well, he would have to give up his job. It would, Bartlett thought without surprise, rather be a pleasure. He needed this woman. She was his rock of flesh in which he could find his shelter and his childhood.

He began paying discreet calls on Fanny Cohn. He found it easy to talk to her and she seemed to enjoy his presence almost fiercely, sitting, the great block of her, on the edge of her chair with her tiny smile turned toward him and her eyes shining with interest. They spoke a great deal of business. Fanny had bought a small store on Fifth Avenue; she was thinking of backing a Broadway play. On Bartlett's advice she had gone shopping for paintings and had bought a Braque, a large Modigliani, a Whistler girl, and a Renoir nude. It was the most incongruous collection Bartlett had ever seen and when Fanny hung them all in the same room he found himself wincing. He finally persuaded her to move the Whistler into the dining room. A day or two later Fanny told him that he had been right and that "the Whistler goes very well with food."

As his visits increased in frequency Fanny watched him more and more closely but she said nothing and Bartlett said nothing. Day by day their intimacy increased to Bartlett's intense delight. Familiarity cast an enchantment over all of Fanny's mannerisms, and Bartlett had to remind himself not to stare at her so constantly; he was sure he must look a little foolish, rather like a child watching some outrageous fantasy that he wanted true. And at the same time, he performed a sort of gentle tutelage, trying to ease the hurt in Fanny's eyes by showing her some of the richness of the world that she had been deprived of in her childhood. He felt immeasurably strong and secure. Only he wished Fanny would not take such eagle-eyed care of him. He was not an invalid, though he still suffered from sudden bouts of extreme exhaustion. He didn't mind them. When they occurred he would lean back and to the gentle accompaniment of Fanny's ministrations he would let his being relax. It seemed to him that parts of himself that had long lain unused were flowering. All his days were sunny, because now he had hope and love—both very nice things indeed.

His nights he spent planning his proposal. He knew Fanny feared him and his strangeness, and he knew she feared the world. He wanted to guide her to an acceptance of him, and for that he would have to be very tender. Yet, he did not want to lose his position in her eyes where she had to worry about what he felt; that was very soothing to his masculinity. It seemed to him that Fanny in spite of her size was a small and timorous bird, very strong and brave in its way, but with hurt implanted in its very form, and happiest in flight and privacy.

Eventually they began going out together, to dinner, to plays, and to concerts. Bartlett had planned, as best he could, for any difficulties that might arise. He was quite sure that he was immune, but he knew Fanny wasn't. Therefore, he planned to be dry, cool, cagey, and unembarrassed, because that would immediately put whoever was being difficult in the wrong and that would appeal to Fanny's pride. He knew he was sailing in uncharted waters, but he had the memory of Fanny standing in the darkness blinking her little flashlight on and off to guide him.

One night at the theater, after the third act, as they were leaving, they met Bartlett's superior and his wife. Bartlett immediately was dry, cool, cagey, and unembarrassed, but almost at once he found himself beset, and he had to draw on every particle of his gentleman's feeling of eminence to hold himself erect in that rococo theater lobby before the polite amazement and stiffness of his superior's slender, aging, and Connecticut wife. Fanny stood in immobile dignity inside her huge fur coat that proclaimed her economic right to be superior, and her face had been as impassive, as shallow as a second-rate terra-cotta Buddha; but whenever she spoke her voice had been low and controlled, and she made the superior's over-coiffed and dry-lipped wife seem frail and frantic. It was a very unpleasant scene.

But Bartlett as he moved away with Fanny on his

arm felt impelled to turn and wave out of his stubborn habitual gallantry. Then he felt Fanny grow rigid on his arm. As he helped her into the taxi she avoided his glance and she sank into her corner of the seat with a soft rich rustle of fur without looking at him. Bartlett wanted to apologize and explain and reassure. He leaned forward. "Fanny," he began.

"I tought it was a very good play," Fanny said quickly, defiantly, "didn't you?"

"Yes," Bartlett said, taken aback. "Very much," he added with relief and gratitude.

"I mean," said Fanny with a little smile, "the second act was a little poor but you can't have everything."

From then on when they were out Bartlett nodded pleasantly to those people whom he knew but he did not speak to them. In the course of his life he had learned to accept the cruelties and thwarts that life deals out as a matter of course; but now he was in love and he wanted to protect Fanny. Love said that life might be perfection, and then cruelty seems a sudden and savage thing.

There seemed no end to Bartlett's love. Whenever he saw Fanny, emotion welled up from deep within him, from some jumbled psychological strata formed in the volcanic throes of youth and it quite overwhelmed him. It was confusing but warm; and Bartlett found it infinitely more desirable than the cold and endless coherence of duty. He loved Fanny Cohn; he would build his life on that.

It was late at night, after several martinis, sitting

in the wingbacked chair in Fanny's apartment overlooking the East River, that Bartlett began his proposal. "Fanny, you must have guessed by now that my feeling for you is quite deep."

Fanny gently set her demitasse cup down on the table. "Don't talk about it," she said miserably. "Then it doesn't seem so serious."

"I want it to seem serious," Bartlett said gravely. "I love you."

"It's crazy," Fanny Cohn said. She jumped to her feet. "I'm a Jewish woman with an accent. You nuts or something?"

Bartlett laughed; he was protecting her. "We'd go away. Where no one knew us. We can tell people I'm Jewish, too."

Fanny uttered a short laugh. "All these years you been a underground agent. . . ." She turned serious. "You'd have to give up your work. What would you do with yourself? You're a young man yet. You're fifty. I'm fifty-five. I could be your mother."

"Hardly," Bartlett said dryly.

Fanny rebuked him with a glance. "I could be a mother to you; you come see me, just like this, it's very fine. You tell me all about your life. It's lovely to hear of your childhood with a governess, imagine. Let's go on like this," she pleaded.

"No, Fanny. I'm more or less determined. It's time now for us to—"

"You couldn't do without your friends and your job and your children. Be sensible."

"I want to give up my job. Some of my friends will remain my friends; that doesn't matter because I'll want to spend my time with you. I have money. We can go wherever we want. My children will like you. We'll be away; we'll be no problem to them. I don't like problems any more than you do. I want to be with you."

"You don't know the problems," Fanny cried. "You know what people will say? They'll say I was your mistress that you married when you got feeble in the head. That's what they'll say."

"Fanny," Bartlett said with some irritation, "must you exaggerate so? You're not a social outcast."

"Exaggerate!" Fanny shouted back. "You think after forty years' discrimination I can't *tell*?" She turned away and grew calmer. "I know I'm not a social outcast," she said quietly. "I'm a dumpy little woman with an accent."

Bartlett laughed shortly. "You're hardly a dumpy little woman."

"I must have got that from a play," Fanny said unashamed. "Oh, I always tought bankers were cool types. You strike me as being very fiery."

"Indeed," said Bartlett happily, "fiery"?

"But—" Fanny grimaced.

"What is it, Fanny?" Bartlett asked gently.

Fanny looked at him. "You want a martini?"

"No. What is it you started to say?"

"I can't explain to you if you don't know." Suddenly there were tears on her cheeks. "I can't. . . ."

"Fanny, don't you love me?" Bartlett cried desperately.

Fanny's arms fluttered toward him, then dropped. "That doesn't . . ." Her voice trailed off wretchedly. She looked up at him and spread her arms in a wide gesture. "I can't face it." Tears streamed down her face.

"We'll go away, Fanny, anywhere," Bartlett cried. "We'll live in the country—"

"But I like people," she said; then she broke down. Sobs racked her. All the way across the large living room, sobbing like a child, stumbling, blindly, she groped toward her bedroom door. She leaned against it for a moment, and then she turned around. "I can't marry you. Who's brazen?" And her sobs exploded again; she stepped through the door and then turned around again. "Thanks for asking," she said miserably. The door closed.

Bartlett sat numbly. He had not expected a rejection. Finally he rose and went to get his coat. He reached into the hall closet for it and put it on; carefully he wrapped his silk foulard around his neck. His skin was so dry that little except silk was comfortable. He picked up his hat from the hall table and caught sight of his reflection in the hall mirror; it was the same reddened, arch-nosed face he'd always had; the blank appraising New England eyes faced the world just as cautiously, as knowingly. Bartlett could hear Fanny's crying very faint and far away. He smiled ruefully. In the mirror the smile was cool and dry. It was more mockery than Bartlett could stand. He slammed the door behind him and rode down in the elevator frowning. Outside, he buttoned his coat; he paused for a moment and looked at the dark, tumbling mass of the East River. Jews, no—Bartlett corrected himself—women were middle-class and unadventurous. A sigh crawled from the depths of his chest and broke from his lips like the expiring gasp of an ebbing tide.

He turned and started up the street. He admired the shapes New York buildings took on crisp nights like this one when the lighted windows presupposed buildings one couldn't quite see. Man's incomprehensible urge to pile bricks. . . . He should have been more dominant, Bartlett thought. He should have asserted himself. He stood on the street corner and desultorily hailed a cab. His head was inside the cab when he changed his mind. He thrust a dollar in the cabby's hand and turned back.

You couldn't spend your life being hurt; you had to impose yourself on the shape of things, he thought as he rode upward on the elevator. Maybe it didn't work and you were the one responsible, but if you didn't try, you were a mere creature. That's why men piled bricks and made unlivable cities that they lived in. That was turning off the superhighway, that's what individuality meant. The elevator reached the twelfth floor. That's what individuality was, impracticable but divine.

The doorbell sounded dimly inside the apartment.

The door opened. Fanny stood there outlined in the light that streamed from the living room; she bulked large and strangely soft as if her breasts were clouds and her woman's being were soft rain. It was all a little absurd, Bartlett thought wistfully, but she couldn't be won any other way.

"I love you, Fanny Cohn," he said. "Let me in."

"It isn't right."

"I'm getting old, Fanny Cohn, and I don't much care what's right and wrong. I want my own way."

"You want a martini?" Fanny asked meekly and stepped aside.

"Yes." Bartlett took off his coat and rubbed his hands together. They were shaking. He thrust them into his pockets. "Fanny," he said, "of course I don't understand you. But that doesn't mean you have to say no and run off to the other room. Why can't we get married and just not live close to any of these people?"

Fanny's eyes were reddened from crying; they started to blink suspiciously. "Because I want to be close to people. Maybe I don't have too much soul, but I like to be with people."

"We can be with them, just not too often." Bartlett went to her and hesitantly put a hand on her shoulder. "We love each other, Fanny. It's strange that we do. Perhaps we ought to go on being friends and separate in a few years with brave little smiles. But I'm selfish and the world is not a certain place anymore." Bartlett took a deep breath and forced himself on; this was the longest speech he had made in his entire life. "Why shouldn't I have some happiness and some pleasure in my own way? Why shouldn't I be unreasonable?" Bartlett's voice had dropped from authority to pleading. "Why, Fanny? I've worked my life away and it's been dull. You bring me excitement. I have always wanted to be bold," he said.

Fanny was crying again but softly. "You can say that," Fanny mumbled. "I'm being practical. We should just get married to tend each other in our old age? We should make fuss and trouble and get everyone all upset? I can hire a nurse."

"There's more to it than that," Bartlett said. "Fanny, don't you have a single dream, a dream I can give you to make up for . . . for everything I can't give you?"

"I'm not used to thinking that way," Fanny said, restraining her tears. She wiped her eyes and put her head on Bartlett's shoulder. A soft radiance spread through Bartlett. "I just want a family and a home and to . . . to belong or something."

"I can't give you that, Fanny," Bartlett whispered. "Isn't there anything else?"

Fanny dried her eyes and looked up at him. "You'll laugh."

"No, I won't."

"Well," said Fanny, tilting her head sideways, "I always wanted to be a lady like I saw in the movies carrying baskets to the poor."

Bartlett smiled gently. "We could buy a house in England."

"No, not England. I couldn't fool anyone there."

"Where, Fanny?"

"I wanted it in Mexico."

"It wouldn't be easy. Mexicans distrust foreigners."

"But I'd be good to them," Fanny said. "I'd love them. They'd need me. They could just call me the sweet Jewish lady."

"Oh, Fanny, you'll never grow old, I'm afraid," Bartlett said. "Will you be Mrs. Bartlett Robinson?"

"Me, Mrs. Bartlett Robinson," Fanny said, "imagine. Sure. Sure, I will," her voice paused and then said sweetly, "Bartlett."

"Fanny."

"Yes."

"You've made me work so hard."

"It was good for you."

"I need you, Fanny, you know things."

Fanny was half laughing, half crying.

"You've never said you love me," Bartlett said stiffly.

Through her tears Fanny reached up and touched one infinitely gentle finger to his dry, reddened cheek. "I'm mad about you. I'm absolutely mad about you."

"Imagine," Bartlett said gaily and took her in his arms, "imagine that."

THE SOUND
OF MOORISH
LAUGHTER

ACROSS the street from my house was a Catholic church. It was really a parochial school, rather drab and old, built of dried-blood-color brick with white trim; but inside, it had a chapel, and every Sunday, cars filled our quiet suburban street, bells rang—small, almost shrill bells—and women dressed in stiff little hats and gloves stood and talked on the school steps. The school was sort of an eyesore in our neighborhood, which had been built, somewhat hopefully, in the closing years of the twenties and which consisted of a number of small one-family houses. My mother didn't like living so close to a parochial school and quondam church, because of the noise and traffic on Sundays and the lack of privacy. Also, our street, Courtney Avenue, had been designed to have a parkway running down its middle, like a boulevard, but the church had asked to have that space left for parking. My mother (my father was dead) had bought our house thinking there was going to be a parkway in front of it, and she was sullen about the church and the nuns and the brisk, athletic priest that ran it.

During the week when the church was a school, the noise was almost worse. Children played in the yard of the school (that yard was a shame, my mother always said; it had hardly any grass; and its seesaws and jungle-gym and swings were old and unsightly) and sometimes they chased their balls right up to our front steps and trampled my mother's flower borders. Sometimes, too, the nuns would raise their voices or a child would cry and the noise, disquieting and alien, would upset my mother and fill my grandmother with rage. My grandmother was seventy-eight years old; she was fierce and unreconciled; she despised most of her seven children and so far as I could tell liked only two of her fourteen grandchildren, both pretty girls. My grandmother didn't like me but she had the grace not to hide behind her age, and she fought me man to man with a kind of virulent hatred that was almost as good as affection. She used to pinch me and give me sandwiches for lunch that I didn't like—I hated baloney, for instance, but baloney I had four days out of five. But then on the other hand, when I called her names or talked back to her she never told on me. She merely shook one bony finger and warned me that I'd come to no good end and that she'd get even.

Anyway, grandmother hated the church. She had left Russia shortly after the 1888 pogrom in Odessa, and while she never spoke specifically of the horrors she had undergone, she sometimes would speak of how awful it had been, "with the priests leading the mob, flying their banners, and mocking at the poor dying Jews."

I didn't believe her. She was a dreadful liar.

The priest across the street was very young and athletic. Sometimes, coming home from school, I would see him with his gown tucked in, playing ball with some of the older boys of his school. The priest was dark-haired and rosy-lipped; after a few minutes of baseball, he would grow flushed and excited, and he would shout as loudly as any of the boys. Sometimes he would dance around the sidelines when his side got a hit or worked a man around into scoring position. Usually the opposing team was totally disheartened by all this; they seemed to feel they were playing against the blessed side. Sometimes, though, they'd set their faces, accept a league with the devil, and play with a kind of wild intensity—usually this was after considerable goading from the priest— and their air of defiance was enormous and moving.

At times, my mother would send me to the store and I would cut across the parochial school's playground to a Kroger's grocery store on the corner of Peabody and Corcoran. I would dawdle on the path watching the baseball game over one shoulder. There was something mysterious in the priest's relationship to the boys, something powerful and paternal and unquestioned. I wondered what it was in the priest that made the boys so docile. And often, I heard the boys call him Father.

One day, our neighborhood was in an uproar. My mother came home from her office early, and she and our neighbors and I stood on our front steps and watched workmen finish putting up a six-foot-high wire-mesh fence around the school's playground. Inside the mesh was a steam shovel.

"By God, they're going to put up a church," my mother said. "This is the end of the block."

Mr. Morgan, who lived on the corner, said he thought it might be a parking lot for the present chapel; perhaps the city had forced them to stop using the street. "Goodness knows," he said, "we've all complained often enough to the city manager."

My mother said she hoped Mr. Morgan was right but she would bet Mr. Morgan was wrong. My grandmother sitting by her window was stiff with rage when I went inside. "They'll be out burning our houses next," she said darkly.

"Don't be stupid, Grandma," I said, purposefully shoving her rocking chair a little. "There's a law against that."

"Who wants a cross hanging over their house all day long?" my grandmother said, but she was only talking, making noise because she was lonely; she had outlived everybody she cared about; and she was surprised still, after fifty years in this country, that things were so comparatively peaceful and uninteresting.

In the cold weather, I used to wear a bright red lumber jacket an older cousin had passed on to me.

It was made out of a Hudson Bay blanket or out of the same material, and since I was particularly subject to colds and it was the warmest coat I had ever had, I wore it every day. It was an object of envy and mockery to my classmates, but the little boys at the parochial school were absolutely fascinated. They used to crowd to their fence and watch me walk by.

Sometimes they created incidents. One afternoon, coming home from school, I was waylaid by five or six of the parochial school boys. They jumped out of the bushes at the end of the block and surrounded me. I raised my book—I was carrying a large geography book—over my head and began to curse them. My blasphemy so startled them, they gave way and I ran down the street and got safely home.

But these incidents didn't happen often. Once, on a cold, late-November evening, I sat idly on one of the swings in the parochial school's yard. The foundation for the church had been dug and covered over already for the winter. I was swinging with my eyes half-closed, trying to imagine the piles of dirt around the foundation were mountains. I had never seen mountains. Two boys from the school were playing desultorily at the other end of the yard, passing a football back and forth. The evening was drawing in and a cold wind nipped and twisted. The Father came out of the school and walked down to inspect the foundation; on the way back, my red jacket caught his eye—it was a very bright red—and he came over and asked me who I was. I told him, shyly, that I lived across the street; I asked him if he was building a big church. He was even handsomer up close than from a distance: he had a cleft in his chin and a perfect shave; he had sad dark eyes with thick lashes; his mouth had a curiously lonely expression as if he had never quite gotten used to his responsibilities or to the quality of life in our lonely suburb. He said, amiably enough, that it was going to be a medium-sized church. He felt my jacket and said, "That's quite a coat you have there."

"It's the warmest coat in the world," I burst out. The Father patted my head and went away.

That was how I came to fall in love with him.

I took to waiting on our front steps in the cold December afternoons and when the priest came out of his school, I'd smile and wave at him. Then I would go and hide in the basement. I wasn't capable of bearing two waves in one afternoon.

Later, I hid in the attic, away from my grandmother, and stared out the dusty window at the school. I kept my passion an absolute secret. But I could not resist asking my mother one evening what she would do if a Father talked to her; I had to be prepared.

"Be polite," she said. "Why? Has the priest across the street been after you?" She looked at me sharply.

"No, no," I cried. "But if he had, would it be wrong?"

"Well, he would try to convert you," my mother said. She was watching me very closely. "You must be careful. Don't trust him an inch."

When spring came, I built a tree house in the maple that hung over our driveway. I could sit in the tree house and watch the school across the street. Often the priest came out and inspected the work the men were doing on the church. He beamed at them—which was a good thing; but often, he gave orders—which was not such a good thing; but he never saw me which was the best thing of all.

Without having the Father to think about, that would have been a terrible year for me. My best friend, Harry Bucker, had moved to California, and I had no other close friends. The other boys who were left were a dull crew. Listlessly I played war games; I patiently sat through games of torture, even though Johnny Parsons had once tied me to a chair and burned my sweater with a heated soldering iron and my mother had blamed me. I was bored.

I was difficult to play with. I enjoyed marbles, but I liked to win; I only played with boys I could beat. Over the years I won more than three hundred marbles. I kept count. When I played cops and robbers, those of us who were shot had to lie down and wait to be buried before they could get up and join the game again.

"You can't leave bodies all over the lawn," I'd argue disgustedly; "it brings the plague."

In the middle of a conversation I might yank a toy plane out of my pocket and bomb my companion. If he didn't immediately fall shrieking to the ground, I wouldn't play with him again. I would fall to the ground, if I was bombed, and it was bad for my health.

That left the Father, and he was my delight for almost six months. I even used to hover by the wire-mesh fence when he was playing baseball with his boys. I would hang on the fence with one hand and sort of spin back and forth until someone looked at me and then I'd go away.

The church was rising by leaps and bounds. My mother thought it was hideous. I liked it. It was a big building of gray stone with a high tower on which there was going to be a concrete statue of Jesus. The façade of the church was covered with a scaffolding, and I used to play on that with some of the other boys in the neighborhood. We climbed, daring each other, all the way to the top of the tower. We ran up and down the ramps where the workmen wheeled barrows of mortar. We played tag on all fours on the half-finished roof.

One day when I was alone on the scaffolding—it was a Saturday, a warm sunny day, in June—the priest came to look at his building. He saw me perched up near the tower (as a matter of fact I was

looking at the statue of Jesus which lay in the blocks
on the roof) and called to me to come down. When
I climbed down, he proceeded to lecture me on
how dangerous that was and that I must never do it
again or he would tell my parents. I got tears in my
eyes. Then suddenly, he saw them, smiled, rather
embarrassedly, and asked me if I liked his church.
He wanted to console me for his bawling out. I said
it was beautiful. He asked me if I wanted to see the
inside. I said I did. He took my hand, while my heart
palpitated, and led me into the church.

It was actually the first church I had ever been in.
Shadows hung along the walls as thick as curtains.
The pews gleamed newly; I thought the confessional
booths were marvelous. I thought they were where
shy women sat so they wouldn't be seen.

The interior was mostly completed. There was a
small lobby and then doors and then a little
vestibule marked off from the main part of the
church by fluted concrete columns.

"We'll replace those with marble ones some day,"
the priest said briskly. He had a habit of striding forward, while I ran to keep up, then stopping suddenly, dropping his head to look at me, firing his
sentences, and then striding on. He reminded me a
good deal of my mother when she was being busi-
nesslike, except that he was holding my hand, and
his voice would occasionally slip into a booming
theatrical register that made me feel as if I were

hanging on in a high wind. With two more athletic strides—closer to leaps really—he had me next to the water basin.

"Holy water," he barked. "The basin's Italian marble, real Italian marble."

"I think that's wonderful," I whispered shyly.

"Acanthus leaves," he said pointing to a carved frieze that ran around the edge. "Grapes. Pitchers of milk and honey."

I sighed admiringly, as I had heard my mother do when seeing a friend's new house. "They look very expensive."

The priest's eyebrows went up; his eyes fastened on my face. "You like such things?" he asked tersely.

"Yes, sir." I could tell that he was very lonely. The look on his face was a mixture of hope, and of the wariness that had come from a number of rebuffs in the past.

He sat down in a pew and pulled me down next to him. He told me that I shouldn't call him sir, I should call him Father. This seemed nearly blasphemy to me, a terrible and wicked pleasure, that I ought to avoid. I told him I didn't believe in him; did calling him Father mean that I believed?

He explained to me the hierarchy of the church, dwelling with a kind of loving eagerness on the titles of monsignor and bishop, archbishop and cardinal. When he went on to try to explain what such titles meant, his face grew flushed, and his voice stumbled searching for terms of sufficient glory to describe them. He even stammered a little in his excitement.

Then we talked about me. He asked me, as he studied me with his extraordinarily young and vivacious eyes, how old I was and if I prayed at night and if I liked school. It seemed to me he was growing to like me and I became uneasy. I decided to warn him now, rather than have him learn it later when it would hurt me more. "I'm a difficult child," I blurted out.

The priest's eyes kindled. "Well, I guessed that," he murmured. "I can see you're a regular Tartar. But it's quite all right with me."

Originally, of course, the priest had only meant to be kind. He had started to bawl me out and I had nearly cried, and his gentleness had led him—his gentleness and his embarrassment—to show me the church, to distract me, and that, by showing me what he took such pride in. But I had seen the church and showed no signs of wanting to leave, and I was staring at him with widened eyes; it was adoration, almost, but he couldn't guess that. He thought perhaps it might be religion.

He asked me, "Do you believe in God?"

"Oh yes, sir—Father."

"Do you know who Jesus was?"

"Yes, Father."

"Who?"

"The man who preached and started the Catholics."

"He wasn't a man, child. He was the Son of God."

"Oh, I don't believe that," I cried.

The priest sat there, perplexed. He couldn't quite comprehend then what I wanted; but at last a light grew in his eyes. "It's architecture you're interested in?" he asked me joyfully.

I didn't know quite what he was talking about, but I said yes.

"Would you like to see my treasures?"

"Oh, yes, Father."

"I haven't shown them to many people," he said, taking my hand, and striding toward the back of the church. "I am said to have a problem with spiritual pride." He shook his head briskly. "But it simply isn't true. I believe that worship should be grand, don't you?" Then he recollected who I was and smiled at himself. "Of course, you don't even know what spiritual pride is," he cried exultantly. "And now just look at that stained glass window! French. It's French. Have you ever seen such a crimson? Or such a blue?" His voice dropped to a whisper. "It's St. Thomas. And that one," raising his voice, "is St. George slaying the dragon."

"They're grand, they're grand," I said eagerly.

"And now to the storeroom!" the Father cried, in the voice with which he shouted at baseball games. We flew down a short curving corridor, the Father's cassock whipping against my legs and tangling them hopelessly. The Father produced a key and unlocked a door, switched on an overhead light, and released my hand.

"There!" he cried. All around the room were objects of gold and silver, some half in boxes, others standing on boxes with shreds of excelsior hanging to them, sticking in their filigree. "These are for the church," the Father said briskly. "They were inordinately expensive. . . ." His breath escaped in a long sigh. "Mortgages, mortgages," he murmured. Around the walls were tacked blueprints, not ordinary blue and white blueprints, but ones of black lines on heavy white paper and under each sheet were small ink drawings of façades and altars and interiors, of doors and stained glass windows, even of pews and the water spout. I knew with sudden clairvoyance that the Father had drawn the pictures. I asked him and he nodded.

"However, I was not allowed to build that church!" he said with some bitterness. He led me to a table at one end of the room and among a pile of bills and receipts brought out an architect's drawing of a façade. It was high and narrow.

"I don't suppose it matters what kind of house you build to worship God in," the priest said with heavy sarcasm, his voice theatrical and pulsing, "but this suburb is ugly enough without planning on its turning into a slum fifty years from now."

A chill ran up my back, a sensation of a malevolent world watching me. Slum? In fifty years? My home? What would happen to me? The Father was saying,

"After all, I raised the money. . . ." He sat on one of the packing cases and put his head in his hands.

I realized that something had gone wrong. I said nothing. I blinked and then I walked around the room and saw a statue of a woman holding an infant. The statue was painted, and it was larger than I was. "Who's this?" I asked.

The Father raised his head but kept his hands in front of the lower part of his face; it was a curiously childlike gesture, though theatrical with his raised black eyebrows and piercing eyes staring over the tips of his fingers.

"The Virgin and the Infant Jesus." He kept his hands raised, as if he feared he was going to be laughed at. "Do you like it?"

"Yes," I said, enthusiastically.

"It's Italian." He rose and came over. "Genuine Italian work. Have you ever seen such a blue?" The Virgin had a blue cape. "Now, look closely. Do you see the tiny silver stars inlaid in the wood? Have you ever seen anything like that?" He was growing brighter by the minute. "It's going to stand in a little chapel under a blue window. Won't that be wonderful with those stars? And come look at this censer, it's true Spanish work, from Mexico. I have another one just like it, but it's not unpacked yet. In another hundred years, these will all be treasures. And come see the altar screen. It's gold-leafed. Here's the flight from Egypt: Israelites," he said, beaming at me, "just like you. And there's the Sermon on the Mount. Isn't that fish border marvelous?"

The fish spilled in golden profusion, sporting delicate, nearly transparent fins, out of a cornucopia that Jesus held above his head; on the cornucopia was engraved the word Charity. One fish twisted its head roguishly and bent adoring eyes on the figure of Jesus. I clapped my hands.

"Yes, the fish are heavenly. Now, look at this chasuble. The Bishop gave me this three years ago when I first came, to encourage me in getting a church built. You see, it's the garden of Eden." I saw the trees and a naked man and woman and a serpent.

"They're naked," I said.

"Sssh," the Father said, half-laughing, "you're not supposed to notice that at your age. And these are the cedar boards one of my parishioners gave me to make two closets in the rectory."

"Two," I cried, "whatever for?"

"They keep moths out," the Father said to me, "but it's the smell that's so glorious. Smell them."

He was right, the smell was glorious. I looked at him in delight. "Two!" I cried.

"Two!" he murmured with mild modesty.

Now, there was nothing left to look at. Silence descended. I stood with my head lowered, waiting patiently for the Father to begin the ritual grown-ups usually followed in getting rid of a child: he would ask me if it wasn't my dinnertime.

But the Father stood with his hands clasped behind his back. The excitement hadn't left his face. Slowly he opened his mouth. "Two thousand years of Christ," he said and slowly raised his head until his eyes were fixed on the ceiling, "and we are still building churches that look like gymnasiums. It maddens me, maddens me. . . . For the Lord who died for us we will not build a decent tabernacle—if this is spiritual pride, I will gladly take my penance. Gladly!" he roared and took a quick look at me, a little surprised, probably, at how small I was.

"I'm not a Catholic, sir," I said weakly.

"I know, child. But who would want to be and worship in a gray warehouse across the street? If you only knew how beautiful churches can be! I suppose you've never seen Milan. Milan," he sighed, "is nearly blasphemous. And Notre Dame? Notre Dame may be a little heavy and over-logical, but it has spirit, esprit, soul. . . . Chartres, I don't even mention. I won't discuss Chartres. Chartres is a miracle. This is not the age of miracles. What kind of Chartres could there be in St. Louis? No, I don't mention Chartres."

Idly I took three pieces of excelsior and tried to braid them.

"God is beautiful," the Father said. "His churches should be beautiful."

"Father, if you want a nicer church, why don't you build one? Who would stop you? Why do you let people boss you around?"

"Stop me? Let them?" He smiled; his eyebrows shot up; but then his face melted back, and he looked saddened and defeated. "Let my Bishop boss me . . . that's quite a novel thought, a charming thought . . ." His voice trailed off.

"Sir," I said in a low voice. "I'm very sorry if I said something wrong. . . ." The priest looked at me; our glances met on a sharp incline; and it was one of those moments, when an emotion stands clear, easily recognizable, even in a child, even between two strangers. The priest gave an audible gasp. He had not even imagined what my feelings were or thought to wonder why he talked so freely to me. But at that moment, he realized everything. He had responded to the presence of love. He had warmed himself in it, even though it came from a ten-year-old child. In a spasm of embarrassment, he began to cough; he covered his mouth and coughed for several minutes, while I stood there nervously.

"My father's dead," I said, at last; I felt I had to explain. The priest could not help smiling, not because of any pleasure he felt, but because it was the only gesture he could allow himself. The smile played about his lips as if it were a small bird. "I have to go home," I said, miserable with shyness, "it's my dinnertime."

"Ah," the priest murmured. He stood up in a sudden flutter of his cassock. "Well, you come back and visit me again. . . ."

"I—" I began; I was trembling a little. "I'd have . . . I'd have to sneak in. . . ." I was sorry now the priest had guessed my secret, that he had to consider what was possible and what was not. . . . It was humiliating, and I felt the dim stirring of anger.

"Perhaps," the priest murmured, "I might talk to your mother and explain—" But I was shaking my head violently, and he paused. His eyes glittered. I think the love I felt for him must have seemed attractive; in every man there must exist somewhere the urge to be a father, or to play at it for a little while. . . . He gazed at me, probably wondering at himself for having such feelings. "You have a high sense of loyalty," he said at last, a faint shade of rebuke in his voice, "to your mother, don't you?"

I nodded.

"I've enjoyed your visit very much," the priest said and held out his hand; he had lapsed into sheerly masculine dignity.

I thanked him for showing me the church. "I appreciate it very much. It was very kind of you."

"Kind?" he said; he raised his arms, perplexed. "I try to be, child . . . I try to be. . . ."

The whole episode, so much of it taking place in gesture, so embarrassing and odd, had lasted only a few minutes. When I left the priest, he was standing in the middle of the storeroom, pulling idly at his ear.

I was furious with myself for giving everything away. I ran out the back door and then turned and gave it a kick; then I ran around the block and down Courtney Avenue to my house.

The clear June day was ending with a tumultuous sunset. An extraordinary effulgence of light blistered gold streaks on the bottom of fat-bellied clouds, cast out tangled streamers of lavender and crimson. The dazzling light flowed down Courtney, gleamed along the docile fronts of the modest houses and set a pinkish flush on the gray stone of the uncompleted church. Now, the street was a river of light; now, the clouds began to plunge into the gap in the western sky. I wasn't old enough to have heard, faint in the distance, the sound of laughter from within the courtyards of Islam, among pierced walls and blossoming almond trees, where philosophers know there is no God but Allah.

That June day, as the sun set, I stood on the front steps of my house and gazed wonderingly at the parochial school. I heard my grandmother fling open her window (she hated fresh air) and stick her angry head out into the cool flush of evening: "What are you standing there for? You want to catch your death of cold? You want the Catholics to think

you're admiring their church? You come inside. . . ."
I made a face at her, hands to my ears, my tongue
out, nose wrinkled. I wonder if the Father saw me.
At any rate, my grandmother slammed the window
down and I ran inside to do battle with her.

A WELL-REGULATED
IMPULSE

WHENEVER anyone speaking to me uses the phrase, *what I really mean,* or the other, stronger one, *the truth is,* I grow rational and expectant. I think I'll know in a moment whether the man or woman I'm speaking to is seriously interested in what I think of as "reality" or "truth," or is so concerned with his own safety that he can see nothing, see no truth in anything except in that which makes up his own safety, as a pupa can see nothing but its own chrysalis. Those people who have broken out from time to time from the fibrous binding of self-involvement, and who do touch and feel something of the roughness of the real world, are usually marked around the eyes and the mouth and so one knows before they speak—one *guesses*—that they are not chrysalids; or rather, to be exact, occupiers of chrysalids. *Pupa.* The word comes from the Latin word meaning doll or puppet or girl.

The chrysalis dwellers are positive in their judgments of other people; they will say something like, "Herbert's a good man." An escapee from the chrysalis will say, "Herbert's a good man compared to what you usually find . . . his word is more or less reliable; he's fairly discreet; thoughts will cross his mind about your welfare when he's speaking to you; he has the grace to feel guilt that he's the perpetrator of his past and that his children cannot hope for more in the way of a father than what he is. . . ."

Perhaps no one talks that way except in my fantasies. But many people of sense will say, "Herbert's not bad, considering . . ." Considering what? Considering other people, of course.

The world is relative and it's best we keep judgments meek because the probability is we see only what we want to see. Draw deductions from your favorite truisms: Doesn't *look before you leap* mean the world is unsafe?

I shouldn't speak for the world; only statistics and a referendum can do that. All expressions of opinion should begin with, "I think . . ." Let us keep in mind that reality starts with two people; a solitary soul doesn't have to compromise; no one is there to say he is mistaken, to call him a liar. Your great men, thinkers like Freud, generals like Alexander, politicians like Lincoln, have the sense of the two-personed world to a great degree: from that comes their success. They see outside themselves and aren't happy. We have to imitate them if we want to get somewhere in this world.

Marie de Médicis built the Luxembourg as a boast, but she was forced later to live there as a humiliation. Its gardens are pretty. Across the street from it is a café. It was spring, two years ago, and I was more confused than I am now. I was out of love with a girl named Toot-ums, or Toot-o, she was sometimes called, tall, pretty Toot-o, a junior from Smith on her year abroad, blonde, long-waisted, and with high, happiness-inducing breasts. I had announced that I was tired of fooling myself that she loved me, that I thought our love affair was pretty much over, and it was only intelligent to admit it. "As I see it, I'm stupid at this point," I said, "but I don't have to remain stupid. I can learn. The first thing is to clear up the—uh—dishonest situations in which I find myself."

Toot-ums said, "You expect too much out of life. You're a perfectionist." She said with a sigh, "You'll look and look and look and never find what you want." She did not yet believe I meant what I said; she wasn't willing yet to agree that our love affair was moribund. "I don't see why you aren't grateful for what we have," she said impatiently. Aided by her bright, young unself-consciousness and considerable vitality, she was chiding, cross, patient, put upon, and contemptuous—all at the same time. I was nervous. I was afraid of her. I was exasperated, tired and anxious, and I broke into a nervous fit of jubilant laughter, miserably and childishly pleased to the point of silly laughter because Toot-o was not eager to let me go, and because here I was having a serious conversation about love with a girl I was having an affair with (I have never gotten over the childhood fear that sentimental novels were accurate and no one went to bed very often). It was self-satisfaction and nerves and shock at what she'd said that made me laugh. Shock and exasperation.

And I choked as I laughed. It was the desire to hit her that kept me pretending to laugh a moment longer when the choking closed off the real laugh. I thought: *She has no courage. She'll settle for anything.* Of the excruciatingly tiny number of women who have loved me, not a one had had courage. Look who was talking about gratitude! When had she been grateful for what we had? She'd gone out with other men and away on trips without me. She hadn't been bold—take it or leave it, either. She'd lied. About her other dates I mean. She'd protested, and added tears to the protestations as proof, that she didn't want to go to Greece with her aunt and leave me. But she'd gone; the postcards had arrived from Corfu, Delphi, Mykonos—you knew the routine. When she came back, I was suspicious of her; perhaps I'd walled myself off to protect myself against panic. And that—according to Toot-o— made me selfish, frightening, a man not to be trusted. She berated me because I did not love her enough to make her—in the new language of love—"secure," so that she could love me without terror; so her strictures ran. But it seemed to me Toot-o's security ought to rest on the event, on the proof of her character and ability to please that would spring from her contriving a year for us to love each other in, as in a large warm bed. But perhaps she had a greater than normal need for reassurance. She couldn't bear to have me complain; it made her feel an amateur—an amateur at love. Whenever I did complain, she'd turn hurt, weak, need a cigarette, be too jumpy to touch me or be touched by me. One complained, or one had pleasure. It was either/or with her. One lied and flattered, one loved totally, or one was out in the cold. Happiness, days—or nights—signalized by her blonde, slightly pinkened face ripe with crying and laughing—relief, release, peace, elation brought tears sometimes—came and went as Toot-o willed. I had an impression of Toot-o whisking our happiness away when it suited her as if in a political kidnaping. I would suddenly become a detective, a secret agent, and lie on my lumpy bed in my room on the Rue de Vaugirard, with my fingers pressed together and my mind active and play the detective. That is, I must ask *cui bono?* as good detectives ask in English thrillers *to whose good, for whose good,* was this crime committed? I also had to ask what were the chances of recovering the victim unharmed, whether to punish the villain or pay the ransom and let the kidnaper succeed. Whatever I decided, someone would have to pay—in one currency or another. Someone always has to pay. It's one of the hazards of life on this island. What island? John Donne's island which he said was part of the Continent.

And the character of the criminals must be studied. Is it vanity or carelessness that drives them? Unwillingness, or an afterthought, to love? A desire to hurt? Here is Toot-o about to depart for Prague: "I don't want to go. . . . I'll miss you terribly. . . . I'll cry every night, I know it. . . ." But how can she *not* go to Prague? How can she let a chance like that escape her? Her lover when she returns says, "Toot-o, I missed you. Don't go away again." To which Toot-o replies with a laugh of pleasure, a quick agreement; and then in a day or two, tired of love perhaps, she begins a sporadic and disjunct discussion of male jealousy and selfishness, and of the rights of women. Women do have rights. I had been selfish: I admitted it; I saw my error—I was, after all, mad about her. But on the subsequent occasion of her jaunt to Istanbul, I was not so agreeable. I pointed out to her that affection could not survive the strain she was putting on ours. "Let's be friends and not lovers. We can still sleep together," I suggested. Toot-o cried and said she would change, she could not bear to lose me, but she did not change. Our arguments, our lovers' quarrels, then began to be noticeably grotesque. They hinged on the question whether Toot-ums had changed or not. But what had Toot-ums been before? What was she now? How to measure change? It was a long time before I saw I could not measure change, that there would be no change: in one corner of my mind was a picture of Toot-ums as I'd observed her, and in another was a picture as Toot-o had told me she was and which was propaganda; and all I did was see now one picture and now the other and think Toot-o was changing.

Toot-o introduced legend into our affair: we were Tristan and Isolde; we were Hero and Leander; we were lovers separated by circumstances, never by our own faultiness. Did she try to confuse me as part of a plan? I think she improvised; she constructed moments; the moments became part of us like frescoes of *trompe l'oeil* on the wall of a room—a real fresco, a real illusion, an illusive reality. Did she know she was obscuring issues between us so that we could solve nothing? It's hard to say. The possibility of Toot-o's not knowing anything was very great, she was so young. It might be that she knew and was innocent *and* greedy and simply wanted as much of everything as she could get. But that is not convincing, because if one *loves,* how much else does one want? Or perhaps she believed on Mondays in a legendarily kind and just and fair Toot-o, and in the perfectability of man, and in the notion that gloom goes only with ill-health, and on Tuesdays did not so believe, and despaired, and hid it from me. I lived for months on the sweetness of the Toot-o I imagined hiding her bitterness and shyness and despair from me, giving me only her best self.

But what was her purpose? If we are alive, we have purposes. All our casual acts are pieces of strategy. Was Toot-o's purpose to destroy herself? See Toot-o come upon a Memling at the Louvre and go, "Ahh," or enter the Place des Vosges and sigh or catch sight of some woman in a particularly chic garb and grow round-eyed (sable always made her gape with pleasure). Or watch her eat, or watch her blush at sudden whispered compliments or requests. Watch Toot-o rise to her knees in bed (beside me) on a late Sunday afternoon and stare toward the shuttered window and say, "Let's go out and be with the people." Watch her argue the principles of existential Marxism: her arguments advocated the destruction of almost everybody but herself. She believed she had the truth, but it was *her* truth, nothing imposed on her, that constricted her. In front of the Petit Trianon we stood, hand in hand, on a chilly but sunny day in February, and Toot-o said, "That would be a perfect place for us. To have a weekend. Of course, we can be happy in a hut. Still in a People's State . . ."

"In a People's State what?"

"We'd be given a weekend in the Trianon."

"Why?"

"For merit."

Then Toot-o blushed. She had meant sexual merit—orgasms for the good of the state. We both begin to giggle, but for different reasons. I realize I cannot prove she did not want to destroy herself. I can only say I don't believe that was her chief purpose.

After the happiness of the first months when I had felt Toot-ums and her girlish, unformed, mildly animal, expectant enthusiasm, her intelligence and her emotions, more or less her entire being, suspended from me like a merry-go-round from a breathless, agog, and unmoving—quite still, quite sturdy—center, and the lesser (and less oppressive) happiness of the following months when I shared her bed (it was my bed we used, however), her body, her afternoons, her affections (with the cat she fed, with France, with her friends, with her Illinois family), it was difficult not to make excuses for her, not to find a hundred reasons for what she did, rather than think she didn't care for me. That, in one way or another, she didn't care. Because in some ways she did. I didn't want to admit or even suspect that she was a girl (a junior woman) who would never tell me in words what her actions already expressed: that the price she put on my love, she, Toot-o, the blonde, the young, the sexy, was low. I accepted any other explanation or theory my mind or feelings came up with, for a while. But then I asked myself the obvious question: in practical terms, romance and legend aside, why should Toot-o love me, give her life to me? I'm not rich, I'm not handsome. I'm moody. I'm demanding and uncertain—an unpleasant combination. I haven't made the decisions yet about what I believe is true that would give me a definite shape and make my behavior predictable. I'm highly unpredictable, as what man of my kind isn't, awash on the sea, perhaps the sea of indulgence, perhaps the sea of self-discovery. One day I'm afire with rage at the world; and the next, I'm ironic and resigned. And so forth. I veer. It isn't unmanageably hard to conjecture that a woman might fall in love with me and then change her mind. *Oh, oh, I didn't know what I was getting into. . . . He's sweet. I'll change him. I'll work it out.* Of that painfully small corps mentioned earlier, of women who have found me necessary to their happiness for even a brief period, most have had their reservations. Why not Toot-o? She had reservations but wasn't certain she wanted to let me go. We'd had— we had—our pleasures. So, she tergiversated. She was temporarily a quasi-Marxist; Marxists are ardent materialists, wrapped up in thoughts about money and social position—they wouldn't trouble to expend so much effort to reform something they did not think of major importance. And perhaps Toot-o dreamed practically. Without doubt, Toot-o could have a wide choice when it came to men. The daydreams of the men around us nibbled at her as she sat at the café table with me. Why should she settle for me or be servilely grateful for what we had? She had resources.

But it was blind and arrogant of her not to grant that I, too, might have resources and need not be grateful. I've been lucky the last few years with women. I have my expectations. I don't think she knew how unjust she sounded. I think she meant only to protect herself from the thought that she had failed to hold me: that is, her lie was not mean but came because she despised reality when it seemed reality might hurt her. Freud somewhere remarks that women anyway are more concerned with envy than with justice.

But what was I to do or say to someone who lied so strenuously? Where was our common language? The air smelled faintly of wax and of cordials and coffee; it smelled sour and sweet and bitter and sugary beneath the awning of the café, where we sat across from the Gardens of the Luxembourg. In French, one exaggerates and says *all the world* or *all France* or *all Paris is walking by* when one means only that the sidewalks are crowded. All the world was passing by that afternoon. Across the street, beside the gate to Les Jardins du Luxembourg, balloon and toy and soda and ice-cream vendors hawked small pleasures. I said, "Toot-o, you're not being honest. Admit it."

Toot-ums had blushed when I'd laughed; now, her eyelids violently raced up and down—Toot-ums' most noticeable nervous mannerism—and she turned her face up and fixed her eyes on the striped underside of the awning. "You mean like about the way you like to hurt people?" she asked angrily.

"And the way you've been spoiled by women? The truth is you can't bear to settle down!" She was breathing rapidly, exalted by her truth-telling. "You're very, very immature!" She shivered. She leaned on her elbows and cupped her hands around her own shoulders and said, "I wish I were a bitch." She sighed; turned to her glass of Pernod; drank from it; and then looked at me. She looked martyred. She'd put me in my place, spoken a truth she'd long withheld—out of affection for me and because she was a lady and did not believe in nagging—and it had pained her.

The first time she told the "truth" about me to me—to put a name to what she said and her manner of saying it—was three months after we met; it was at Fontainebleau. Her accusations then were much the same as the ones she made—seven months later—in the café and roughly every six weeks between the two occasions.

That afternoon at Fontainebleau, we'd ridden out on a motorcycle I borrowed from a French friend. When we reached the woods, we necked for a few minutes and then I told her that by accident I'd seen her in the Place de l'Opéra the night before when she'd told me she had to study (she was taking courses in French literature and history at the Sorbonne) with a tall, prosperous, moustached, older man. "I wasn't spying," I said. "I didn't know you'd be going to the Opéra." From my remark on, we followed the shortest line psychologically from her wrongdoing to mine. We started with my rather weary, *Toot-o, I'm tired of your childishness* confession of having seen her. Point Two was her explanation that the man was a business acquaintance of her father's and someone she had had to see but had been afraid to tell me about because of the way I might react. She was terribly afraid of me, she said. Then came her accusations. Point Three-and-a-half was my eager acceptance of her accusations. I was so relieved with her explanation that I agreed my failings had caused her to lie. I apologized and was happy I would not have to be sensible and discard her. Point Four, the Foreign Aid section of the program, was our reconciliation, begun in the woods and brought to a conclusion between gray sheets on a hotel bed in Fontainebleau.

There, in the bed, Toot-o tearfully told me she loved me and always refrained from saying anything that would upset me. "Love is so hard," she said, weeping as we undressed each other. Weeping and contrite, pink-skinned, dark-nippled, Toot-o comforted me with her body for the elusiveness of her mind.

Toot-o often claimed that she never nagged or bitched at me. But she had, frequently in words, and in pantomime. She played Cleopatra, and I was Antony, but instead of the kingdoms of the East, I brought her small alterations in myself. I flattered and courted her and did not wear the black knit ties she disliked with my plaid wool shirts. I was always free when she wanted to see me and gave up using a toothpick at the table like the French. But I did not grovel or give her her head. On matters of intellect, we came to no accommodation. We felt each other out, lion tamer and lion, eye to eye, the roles interchangeable as befitted two badly educated philosophers, and we settled for irresolution.

At Fontainebleau, that afternoon, we lazed after the first bout of lovemaking. Then we woke up, groggy, like our distorted reflections in the shiny brass columns of the footboard. The window was shuttered, but a great cloud of gray light filled the room, and Toot-o and I, side by side, my leg atop hers, were warm where our skin touched each other, warm, slightly moist even, although the air in the room was chilly and damp. I was sleepily mesmerized by the contrast, which seemed to me very meaningful and the essence of love, between the large bones and reddish coloring of my hand and the considerably frailer, yellow-white, fine-boned delicacy of her ribs on which my hand rested. I began to talk in the hushed, queer, tiptilted intimate voice that one uses when the ear of the person one is talking to is so close to one's lips. After love sometimes, it is as if you are in the dark, in a closet hiding, or in an air raid: it is a special time, a rule-less place. I said I wanted to confess something. I had no self-respect, unless she gave it to me: so I was demanding and vicious because I could be bought with bits and pieces of affection, of triumph. "I try to be honorable but I am self-forgiving—you know the way people are. I always think I'm doing the right thing." I asked her if she really believed, as she'd said, that I was immature and a sadist, because if she did, wasn't she afraid of what she was? Shouldn't she, if she believed that I took pleasure in cruelty, want not to be with me, oughtn't she be afraid of the pain I'd caused her? And she said she never said what she meant but spoke as the French did, according to a social rhythm, and metaphorically—"You're supposed to understand what I mean from what I don't say," she said. I said, "I think that's a stupid use of language." Toot-o said she knew what she meant even if it did not always look as if she did. I didn't know if she was boasting or telling the truth. I asked her, "If you know what you're doing, do you love me in spite of myself? In spite of yourself? Do you?" She said, oh no, what made me think that, why was I so unconfident? Then she apologized for what she said earlier—"I was temperamental," she said.

"You mean what you said was untrue?" I asked; she turned and our faces confronted each other on the pillow. I could feel her breath on my lips. Toot-o said, well no, she wouldn't say she told me untruths, but some things were better left unsaid.

"Then you are upset because you hurt me so much?" I asked.

She grew solemn, which somehow created, out of the air, the stuff of sex. She said, "No. You're tough. If I could hurt you, it would be nice. . . ."

"But you did hurt me," I said, beginning to be excited again, and, to be frank, appalled at what a myth about the difficulty of hurting me could lead to. But then I was distracted by a tremble that ran through her when I touched her.

"You—weren't," she said in a low, crushed voice. "You weren't hurt. . . . You were just—startled—to see that I—don't slavishly—adore you. . . ." Now she was kissing my nose and cheek and was lying twisted like a wood shaving, yellow-white (but blue-veined, breathing, alive), sweet-smelling. "I was, I am," I said, idiotically. She said, "You don't look hurt." Of course I didn't. I looked dim-witted and thick with lust. Foolishly, stupidly, I laughed. She laughed. We laughed. Sexuality made us laugh. We were silly enough to tickle each other because our sexual hilarity made us uneasy and belatedly we wanted an excuse. We were embarrassed by our animal expansiveness. We wanted an up and down, a right and left. We wanted to escape knowing how out of control we were, the two of us naked and laughing on the bed, in that hotel room, so we poked at each other and pretended our tickling each other was what was making us laugh. But it wasn't. It was animal delight. Certain men can argue that drugs increase one's pleasure, but the drugs I've tried haven't sharpened the edge of pleasure or increased the clarity and urgency of my body past what it feels when it is tightened and enlivened by exercise and fresh air as much as just being proud of how pretty the girl I have in bed is.

Then Toot-o and I stopped laughing. I touched Toot-o's stomach and said that it was white and reminded me of a drum, too. "Well, then, let's be drummers," I said.

Afterward, Toot-o cried. She more often than not, with me, cried at climax. I was shaken the first time she cried and almost cried myself to keep her company. After that, when she cried, I played Poppa and held her on my shoulder and stroked her back while she talked, in little incoherent bursts, about her happiness or mine, how lucky we were, how much life had to offer, or how awful it must have been for her mother and grandmother who had not been sexually emancipated. One day when she'd been especially passionate, I threw *my* head on *her* shoulder and said, "Oh God, oh God," and uttered my own incoherent paean to pleasure. She began—just as if I were silent—her usual speech, and it occurred to me I was somewhat less than real to her, that it was pleasure she loved and not me. Finally, I asked her to shut up and stroke my hair and listen to me tell her how beautiful she was. She shut up, but a lot of things were difficult after that.

Sometimes, I feel very strong and forgiving and simplified and sturdy. But sometimes I feel cruelly complacent, dominant: like a pimp. This is something I don't usually mention, this side of myself; I am hypocritical and reason that I may be exaggerating what may be a small and unimportant character trait. But I have that trait.

What if it were what my unconscious unconsciously seeks, to be spoiled and indulged by women, to rule them, to despise them, to break them and have them meek and docile? What if this is my secret plan that guides my action so that even without knowing it, when I am being polite or wistful or amiably lecherous, I am being an enemy.

Then love is a delirious, and delicious, journey into mutual cruelty, and it would be sentimental to say if we loved each other, we would be kind.

Yet, the fact remains: Toot-o was often kind, and so was I. I do not believe Toot-o was devoured by a demon who drove her to demolish the confidence and dreams of men. I do not think evil tenderly rearranges my actions to have perverse and marvelous effects on women. I do not believe that this is an age of individual villainy.

That afternoon in the hotel in Fontainebleau I said to Toot-o I was perhaps an odd kind of Don Juan who had to be victimized by his victim or he couldn't free his conscience. I said that perhaps the deepest pleasure of sex had to do with struggle (perhaps a struggle against the aridity of the universe);

as evidence for this was the fact that during it and after, I so often feel triumphant. I told Toot-o these things partly to give her a certain *frisson*. My friends and I held, at that time, the view that a woman giving herself to a man she knows to be irresponsible is the most freeing and passionate of all sexual acts for her. "She throws herself into his arms as into a furnace," said a bearded French friend. "She does not understand why. She thinks waifs and strays, tramps, and pimps are more sexual than other men. Ha. What it is with such a man is that a woman does not have to try to *win* anything by her lovemaking, and she relaxes and *feels*."

And I know of myself that in that moment after lovemaking when I secretly and shamefacedly feel like a pimp, or in those moments when I am stirring up Toot-o's *frissons* in an agony of lust and ambition for a more intense embrace, that I am being *given* these privileges by the girl. It is at those moments that I realize a girl is in love with me, she is permitting me these pleasures, and when I do not have them, it means the girl does not love me.

In short, we are so entangled with each other that it is impossible to tell whose wish precedes which act or whose applause rewards what performance. I led Toot-o to act as she did, but who guided me, if not Toot-o?

The friend from whom I borrowed the motorcycle is French. He prefers to love boys, "younger than I," he said, "younger than you." He said,

"Young boys have feverish imaginations. I find my-self playing very amusing roles. . . . It is a comic Venus I serve."

He said to me once, "You are always testing your power, bargaining, to see if you are well enough loved. You are very feminine."

He said, "You, if your love affairs do not go well, you babble, frustrated and crazy like a rat tor-mented by a scientist. But a man can only feel him-self loved a little while before his nerves go numb. So, he increases his demands. Or he goes off, goes elsewhere to reawake the magical pulse. It is insane to mix sex with sentiment," he said. He said, "Senti-ment is for mothers."

He is an intelligent man, but he is a pederast, and I do not believe a fraction of what he says. Still, his opinion, being more definite than my own, was use-ful to me in trying to calculate my shape and weight in relation to Toot-o in a feat of psychological trigonometry. He said (but he is not to be believed) that I was immature, sadistic, fantasy-ridden, a Don Juan with, I must not forget, the face of a victim. My victim's face deceived everyone into tenderness; it recruited love.

But I repeat: he was a pederast and had his own aims to serve. I *am* a victim, I am sinned against, I am the creature my childhood made me. I am some-times gentle and kind, and sometimes I struggle as a defense to be tougher, colder, more wicked, and

more calculating than I am, and sometimes I am calculating more than necessary. What is interesting is
that this is the description I would give of at least
half the men I know in Paris. Either men *are* much
alike, or else, when I look around, I see only myself.

I am a peculiar Don Juan if I am one at all. I beg
each girl to be honest, to be interested in reality, to
see me for what I am. I told Toot-o I'd been described as a Don Juan. I, no doubt, hoped to pique
her interest; but I did give her warning. Toot-o said
(perhaps deceived by novelty as I was when I assured
her she wasn't selfish), "You're much too sweet to be
a Don Juan."

I said, "I like sometimes to think I am. You know
how it is. Everyone wants to feel he is important, he
is someone. So, we play at being a Symbol: a Husband, a Rich Boy, a Homosexual, an Addict, Genius,
a Don Juan. . . . It is very flattering to be a symbol.
Who wants to say, 'I haven't hit on the right girl yet'?
It's much more impressive to announce, 'I'm Don
Juan.'"

Now Toot-o ascribed truth, at least in part, to that
charge. *The truth is,* she'd said. Blind child.

I don't know if I blushed or not. I leaned back in
my chair and said, "I see. The truth is I can't settle
down. The truth isn't that we don't—don't get
along, or for that matter, that we don't love each
other anymore, if we ever did. It is clear you love me
and I love you. We enjoy perfect love. Only a fool

could possibly doubt it. Only someone neurotically unstable. A Don Juan. Right? But think what you like. Who am I to analyze any situation?" I subsided into gloom, reached for my pack of Gauloises, and buried my confusion and uneasiness (perhaps I'd sounded stupid) beneath a debris of little acts.

I licked my upper lip, which was sticky from Pernod, put a cigarette between my lips, searched out the box of matches. And then I looked at Toot-o.

Her eyes were bright. Her blonde hair was pulled back like a wing and imprisoned by a clip; her face, in turn, was held, as in a clip, between the wings of her blonde hair. When I first met her, it had been her principles as much as her prettiness which had drawn me. I'd thought her a girl who went at things directly and did not flinch at anything. But now I saw that her character was as confused and indirect as anyone else's.

She said—obtuse, stubborn, "I'm sorry, but I think we do love each other. And please don't say it's merely a selfish illusion of mine. I may not put words together as well as you do, but I know what is happening. You make things too complicated. It's your defense."

"Good God, Toot-o," I cried, "don't you know you're saying you know what reality is and I don't? Do you think I *make* things complicated? Do you think things are *simple*? Do I only have to let them

alone and then they'll be simple? Do you really believe you know what *I* feel when no human being
can even be certain he's hearing what anyone else
says and not misinterpreting it? The world is relative; and the mind is funny, Toot-o. Funny. Laugh
and be modest, Toot-o."

Toot-o said, "It's very sweet of you to try—the
charm is incredible, your big face all twisted and unhappy—just to convince me that breaking up is
really my idea. But you don't have to let me down
easily. You don't have to persuade me this is all my
unconscious wish. Please. Don't be—don't be caddish. . . ."

"Hell," I said and put out my Gauloise and
reached for my pipe. "I don't want to be caddish," I
said with a collegiate irony that was unfortunately
apologetic as well. It disconcerted me that Toot-o
was bitter. It depressed me. I said, "Toot-o, I admire
your grip on reality. I think your instinct about what
is truth is very great and that you ought to give yourself to philosophy. I think your instincts have a certain I.B.M. accuracy and must be respected. If your
instincts say something's caddish, that something's
caddish. They say you love me and that I love you—
they must be right. A man would be a fool to deny
anything your instincts announced. . . ."

Toot-o suddenly blushed; perhaps she saw she'd
been matronly and opinionated. She wanted to be
intellectual, or at least intelligent, and she usually

took pride in her conversation, and perhaps she was embarrassed for herself. After all, why were we sitting at that table if not to talk reasonably instead of going off to be alone with our separate and differing despairs? She said, "Of course, I don't know everything—oh, it's too much! You are ruthless. I have to admit *I'm* in the wrong!"

Tears appeared in her eyes. Regret? Fear? Bruised love? Shame? Almost immediately tears appeared in mine, to keep hers company, caused probably by the same emotions. I have a great need for other people's emotions; I'm not always happy with my own. I said, "Toot-o, I swear you don't love me. It's just that women don't like giving up men who have loved them. That's what's griping you. I swear you won't feel so badly tomorrow."

"You don't know what I'll feel!" Toot-o cried desperately. "Really, it's too much—to lose you, to have a debate, to have you insist I lose that, too!" She brushed her hand over her face as if to clear away a flight of nagging midges, and I suddenly felt clumsy and ashamed.

"Sorry," I said stiffly. "I never know when to stop."

Then Toot-o suddenly turned into a corporation executive (I like decisive women because I am usually indecisive) and said, "Oh, let's get out of *here*. I'm tired of talking *here*." Then she added, "This is no place to talk." She glanced around disapprovingly.

I paid off the waiter and joined Toot-o who stood, her arms hugging herself, in the sunlight by the curb.

"Where do you want to go?" I asked her.

"I don't know. Someplace quiet."

"Les Jardins . . . ," I said, indicating the Luxembourg across the street.

"All right. Oh, damn it, yes!" she exclaimed with a sudden burst of emotion and reached into her purse for a handkerchief. I held her arm across the street, and we walked into the gardens.

Under the trees, she said, "I've never thought I was crazy before."

"Why should you have?" I said. "You're not crazy." Hand in hand we walked on the gravel path. "But you ought to consider how many things preoccupy the mind. It has the entire past, the real past, not the simplified one we remember, to deal with. It uses it like dressmaker's dummies to make dresses, decisions. Meanwhile, the senses are busy, the present is roaring like an earthquake splitting open a factory—*boom, boom, barrabata, boom.* The Sensual Present is *the* Great Noise. *Boom!* . . . Meanwhile, self-respect whines away, the earthquake rumbles, and the brain is handling its daily Armageddon— you know, the *last* battle between Good and Evil. It always seems like the last battle, but it isn't. In the mess—the whole melee—the brain is cheating to make sure Good will win—whatever wins it calls Good—unless the brain is French or very intellectual, and then Evil wins because Good is *bourgeois* and Evil is saintly. It probably is." I spoke with bitterness. "But—but the brain has to keep the flag flying, the desire to live flapping away smartly, as smartly as possible, enough to persuade us to find our way through the night and wake up again sans psychosomatic cancer or paranoia or—or any of the final situations. And the whole time the brain's doing all this, it's being hectored by Heredity! Environment! The Racial Unconscious! And the Zeitgeist! Also, perhaps the lust for God, and God knows what all else. I've just thought of a pun: hectored by a heckuva—a Hecuba-lot of woes, but who am I to Hecuba? Never mind. Here's the point. The mind cannot *think*. It's too *busy*. It's a highly specialized machine. It's nervous. It gets eccentric. It lies. . . . I ache from trying to think. . . . But my mind can't think. If mine can't, then why should I think yours can? And vice versa. Which means you'd better distrust my theories. Only there are—there are facts. But they're hard to come by. Toot-o, I—never mind. . . . I think I should have been a minister. I'm tired."

"Sometimes I think you really are more intelligent than I am," Toot-o said.

"But you soon squelch that notion, right? You soon realize you're probably deceiving yourself."

"You watch me all the time, don't you?" Toot-o said. "Yes, I'd 'squelch the notion,'" she said with distaste. She ran her hand over her arm. "After all, you're confused. I think I have more sense about the world than you do."

"Of course," I said.

"You do nothing but nag. You're terribly feminine!" Toot-o exclaimed.

"You mean it's a woman's right to pull the rug out from under a man's pomposity, but certainly not the other way around!" I said angrily.

"Why are you being so hateful?" Toot-o asked.

"I don't know. Maybe something you said upset me."

"I could make a fool out of you for the way you talk, but I won't. You sound quite, quite phony, and quite rehearsed. You use a lot of perfectly meaningless, pretty words—"

"But meaningless."

"The way you talk is nerve-racking sometimes."

"I apologize," I said. "I really do. Really. Really. Really. My vaudeville numbers are a little phony. They're about my beliefs and they make sense and they must sound peculiar in conversation."

We stopped by an ice-cream vendor's cart. "Do you want an ice cream?" I asked.

"No," she said.

I paid for my ice cream and unwrapped it and smiled at the vendor who smiled back. The French are not rude; they're intelligent and unsycophantic. Toot-o stared at my ice cream.

I said, "Would you like a taste?"

She nodded, and when I held it out to her, she guided my hand and took a large bite.

I was staring at her, and Toot-o raised her eyebrows questioningly. "I was thinking what a difficult and prickly person I was," I said politely. She blinked and nodded, agreeing; she still didn't really believe we were breaking up, that I thought she ought to approve of me.

"Oh, that's good. May I have another bite?" she said.

"Of course," I said. "I bought it for you."

She smiled, pleased.

I wondered irritably why she wasn't concerned not to irritate me. Had I, or had the world, made her too sure of herself? Then she said, catching my mood, or perhaps reading my mind, or perhaps merely being restored to self-confidence by the ice cream, "I really don't see why you're unhappy." She meant with her. "Am I such a terrible person?" she asked proudly. "Am I worse than any other woman?"

I sighed heavily; I did not want to talk about Toot-o any more. "I'm not necessarily *unhappy*," I said. "I may be *restless*. Or I may be the prisoner of some dreadful psychological pattern."

"I've really tried to make you happy," Toot-o said emotionally.

I thought a moment and then I said, "If you lose your identity and live, that's fine. But people go on being the same while they say they've lived or died for love. . . . You and I, we've done what it suited us to do. I mean, we have no right to complain about love. What sacrifices did *we* make? Did we lay down

our lives for each other? No, we laid each other. . . .
We got what we deserved. We didn't make it, that's
all. But we gave each other a lot, didn't we? What we
could spare."

Toot-o said, "Oh stop." She added nervously,
"You're in no mood to be reasonable," and took my
arm with both of hers, hugging it as if to comfort it.
"It's a pretty afternoon," she observed accurately. A
golden afternoon. Children shouted *Sur les Jardins
du Luxembourg.*

Toot-o turned her face up into the sun. "Why do
people bother with dreary postmortems?" she said
in an unhappy voice.

I thought she meant to ask a question; I didn't
think she was being rhetorical. It was as if she had
made, not necessarily peace, but a truce. Look you,
as my bearded French friend says when he tries to
speak English, the essence of two people together
can be described as being like that of a team of
spies. Will they betray each other? Will they succeed
in their half-noble, half-degraded, and entirely dishonest occupation? In asking a question, if she was
asking, then it meant, I thought, that she wanted to
learn. I said, "Because they want to stop being stupid; stupidity is hell." She made a face. "Don't you
feel that way?" I said to her snidely, feeling I'd been
taken in. She winced. She looked hurt and I realized
suddenly that I was not *repelled* by her. My desires
could still occasionally attach themselves to that
body, to that face.

She seemed very frail and vulnerable.

I said, "We can do without a postmortem if you like. No one's dead—yet." I paused and added, "I didn't say we should stop seeing each other. I've said we shouldn't count on each other. I'd like to go on seeing you." I meant, I suppose, to be polite; yet, what I really meant was that she was not to assume I loved her, but we could still sleep together. Somewhat shyly and uncertainly I put my hand on her shoulder, on the thick, blue sweater she was wearing; she shivered.

Her mind still hovered over the postmortem idea. She wanted to know why I'd fallen out of love with her. She said, "I always did everything you asked."

"*C'est le temps de cruauté dans les Jardins du Luxembourg,*" I sang, mimicking God knows who, French art songs, sorrow, and the conviction one has been wronged. "Always—you *always* did what I asked. *Always!* And I am cruel, cruel, cruel," I declaimed. I said, "Ahh, the nobility of sacrifice. Ahhhh, the beauty of the soul. Toot-o," I cried, "Toot-o, we are human beings. Let's keep our assertions in scale."

She blushed. "I did do everything for you!" cried the blonde leftist in her eighty-dollar sweater.

"And I died for you!" I shouted. "An entirely new soul has come to dwell in me." I sank to one knee on the graveled path, in the trembling sunlight. A child stared gravely at me.

Toot-o said, "I'm sick of your abstractions. Give me one *fact,* one specific thing I did that was unloving!" Clearly, she intended to argue that I was mistaken about her. She was going to argue me into loving her. I said, "I well remember how you moved into my room, and cooked and cleaned for me, and how you always spent the night when we made love, and never lied, and never left me, and never talked about your novel—"

"Ooof," she said, as if insulted by my pettiness. Her eyelids batted violently up and down. She said passionately, "That's all very important—I can see that."

She hadn't moved into my room or spent the night because she hadn't wanted to push her family (i.e., her father) too far. She'd wanted to preserve appearances, to keep our affair down to a manageable intensity. She had insisted, too, on spending some of our afternoons writing her novel in my room. The novel was about the hypocrisy of the American middle class and was purportedly feminist; but the men were drawn more flatteringly than the women were, except for the young heroine, of course, who was a marvel of poise and sensible goodheartedness. Of the heroes, the chief was an elderly Mephistophelian banker, infinitely rich, infinitely powerful, infinitely knowledgeable—an extraordinarily *real* character to be found in every novel written by women (except by women like Jane Austen, say). The book's sarcasm altered into admiration whenever the banker and the young girl appeared; those two were demigodish, mythical, and absolutely entrancing to Toot-o. Her sentences were sprawling, Joycean, and then, in spates, ladylike (ladylike sentences are grammatical, limp emotionally, and stiff with opinion: *Some men have no ear for love as others have no ear for music;* everything Sean said was off-key and grated on Marianna's nerve endings). Her novel struck me even when I was in love with her as being the work of a young lady-bitch who felt sorry for herself. But I lied to her and told her I liked it and we spent three-quarters of our time discussing it. For a long time, I did not think Toot-o was connected to her novel, any more than I was to my scuffed-up loafers which I planned to throw away as soon as I had enough money to replace them.

She wouldn't cook; and she said her French wasn't good enough for her to shop for us. But at times when bed, as Toot-o said, was particularly sweet—like a tree house; did you ever climb into a tree house with your friends when you were a child?—and we'd lie in there in each other's arms and talk and make love and talk, then borrow my friend's motorcycle and putt-putt back and make love and talk—at those times, Toot-o shopped, cooked, gave up her novel, and said she wanted desperately to spend an entire night. And then something, me perhaps, or the situation, or fear or boredom, would drive her away. She'd become ob-

tuse, difficult. Each time, so it felt, was a cut direct.
A cicatrix formed. A girl is on a swing, and the swing
strikes me on the jaw. Stand back farther. Take precautions. My melodramatic reactions, my adolescent
pains, tired and bored me. I grew sick of myself loving her, then of loving her, then of her. In that order.

"Those things interfere with love?" she asked
scornfully. "My God, I don't know if I can stand it.
You don't know how you hurt me. You trust people
and then they turn on you, it isn't worth it to . . .
One gets slapped in the face *all* the time."

. . . *All* the time. . . .

My mind skimmed as if my eyes had thrown it like
a skipping disc over pebbles of the walk, parti-
colored like spaniels, over the figures of children
grouped around the pond, children with thin
necks, whose hands held poles; on the slate-gray
pond moved sailboats, white sails with wind.

"Life is a sad poem," I said.

"Shut up, shut up," Toot-o said. "You're revenged.
You've struck back. You've gotten even."

"Pride and perversity," I said, touching my finger
to her ear. "I'm carving the mark of Don Juan on
you."

"What does it matter?" Toot-o said bleakly all of a
sudden. She was beginning to believe I did not love
her.

She leaned against me. I put my arm around her;
a man sitting on a nearby bench flicked the page of
his book. It occurred to me then that it would be

exciting to take Toot-o to bed without having to go through the confusing rigmarole of saying I loved her. If I didn't have to pretend I loved her, I could desire her ardently, I discovered at that moment. It was her meekness that aroused me. I said, "Toot-o— oh Jesus—I'd like to degrade you. . . ."

She grimaced. "I wish I thought you cared that much," she said wanly.

"Shall I prove to you I care that much?" I put my hands on Toot-o's shoulders. "Shall I?"

"I hate myself," Toot-o said. "I'm a bitch through and through. I hurt everyone I touch."

"Tell me, Toot-o," I said, "would you like—" I bit my tongue. Perhaps we'd get to bed faster if I waited. Toot-o wanted to talk. She talked about herself, her childhood, her father. I could afford to listen. A woman makes love like a spider silk. These miracles in nature have to be appreciated; a man has to pay a woman what he can. He has to be silent at the seance where the wavering, now here it is, now there it's gone, half-ghostly sweetness of love is raised.

I listened. Toot-o was bitter that she had caused herself this woe, had caused me woe. "I wish I could change myself!" she cried.

I thought, ah, that was what she had wanted from me all the time, for me to be the agent of her change to—to excellence. I had wanted her to be real. She was in debt to me.

In the shadow of the gray palace, I was at first exhilarated—it is inexpressibly rewarding to come to even the most tentative understanding of anything—and then I was overwhelmingly depressed. Love was use. Love was function. Love was a flattering mirror, a period of inflation when emotions that had lain idle pounded away and filled memory and saddled us with new debts: a Boom, a great Prosperity: *C'est l'amour.* I felt cheated and I clenched my fists and looked up at the sky; the sky was very clear, very pale; it trembled and was bottomless overhead.

In my apartment, when we made love half an hour later, it was as if we had been changed into different people. I was harsh, condescending, cruel, and dominant. Toot-o was meek and performed all the acts she'd learned gave me pleasure. We were supplying excuses for each other just as we'd tickled each other to explain our laughter at Fontainebleau. It was clear the pleasures we doled out were not wrenched from us by love. It is highly sexual, sex without sentiment. We were agonized. Politeness, sexuality, abasement, surprise, cruelty, astonishment came and went as the light faded and twilight came on. But it wasn't as it had been once in the days when we had invented each other, and were exultant, solemn, and startled as inventors should be. Nothing caught fire. As the twilight darkened, we worked on and on.

In the park, Toot-o looked at me and exclaimed, "Oh, what's wrong?" I said that suddenly I was without hope. Later, Toot-o said, "It was hideous, you were so sad. I couldn't get over how much I'd failed you." Another time, she said, "Once, at the end when you were sad in the park, I really loved you."

In my apartment, as we made love, I said to Toot-o, "I can't live without you. . . . You are an incredible woman." She cried, "I love you," and "I really love you," and she screamed but once, "I belong to you." It was a polite lie, but it was sufficient.

When it was dark in my room, we lay side by side and held hands. Through the window came the street noises as obtrusive as the knowledge we now had of each other. We were not lovers anymore; we were merely intimate.

In the park when Toot-o's arms rose to clasp me, I gasped and moved closer to her and pressed my head against hers. "I don't think we have any choice, I don't think we can help ourselves," I said unhappily. One half of my field of vision was filled with trees, blackened and gilded by the light, with nurse-maids and children and old women on the graveled walks, with people and trees tucked into the silver-gray box the air and perspective made. And the other half of my vision was occupied by the close-grained, yellow-white skin at Toot-o's temple and the pinkish skin of her scalp, where fine, loose, nearly white, tiny hairs curled underneath the long yellow strands of hair that were pulled back over her head. I whispered, "Toot-o, come to bed with me." Toot-o said, "If you want me to."

Afterward, in my apartment, after the sex, I lit a cigarette and admired my arm and thought how painful it was to admit that Toot-o and I didn't love each other anymore, that we hadn't known how to love. But it occurred to me I shouldn't judge all love by that, that I'd been wrong to think in the park I knew what love was. I'd been immodest and forgotten that nothing was clear. I reminded myself I ought never to say anything was clear, only *I think*, or *it seems to me. . . .*

Toot-o broke the silence. "We love each other," she said. "We may not be able to work it out, but it's true. We have loved. We do love."

In the park, I embraced her, hurriedly, and then we hurried through the golden afternoon toward my apartment, toward our fools' rendezvous.

BIBLIOGRAPHICAL NOTE

These stories in this collection originally appeared in the following publications:

"Trio for Three Gentle Voices"   *Mademoiselle*
"Gloria Mundi"   *Discovery*
"The Sound of Moorish Laughter"   *Harper's*
"A Well-Regulated Impulse"   *Esquire*

"The State of Grace," "First Love and Other Sorrows," "The Quarrel," "Sentimental Education," "Laurie Dressing," "Laura," "Piping Down the Valleys Wild," and "The Dark Woman of the Sonnets" originally appeared in *The New Yorker.*